Four stories by four authors…one fateful New Year's Eve
Four kisses at midnight…
Three different sisters…
Two old flames…
One bet that drives it all!

The Devine sisters return to their hometown for New Year's Eve each year to attend the annual ball. Part of the tradition is their decade-old bet: whoever has no date at midnight has to kiss their nerdy neighbor Lewis Kampmueller.

Tess—burned by love, the glamorous Broadway star isn't interested in a repeat performance…until she encounters an old flame.

Grace—the tough FBI agent has an easy time being one of guys, but is she woman enough to keep a man?

Annabelle—when the local etiquette expert gets caught breaking the law, her heart might have to pay the price.

Lewis—the shy nerd has made millions over the years…but is he smart enough to catch the woman of his dreams?

Who will lose the bet but win out in love? Four charming stories written by four different authors about one fateful New Year's Eve.

The champagne is poured. The clock is ticking.
Join the countdown!

COUNTDOWN TO A *KISS*

A New Year's Eve Anthology

COLLEEN GLEASON
HOLLI BERTRAM
MARA JACOBS
LIZ KELLY

Countdown to a Kiss: A New Year's Eve Anthology

"What Are You Doing New Year's Eve" © 2012 Colleen Gleason
"The Keeper of the Debutantes" © 2012 Liz Kelly
"Kiss of a Lifetime" © 2012 Holli Bertram
"The Perfect Kiss" © 2012 Mara Jacobs

ISBN: 978-1-929613-97-7

The use of the name Henderson honors the happy memories of one of the authors. So, to the citizens of Henderson, NC, we apologize for the gross inaccuracies and hope you enjoy this completely fictionalized version of a town bearing the same name.

Tess

For S.H.

What Are You Doing New Year's Eve?

Chapter One

Henderson, North Carolina
New Year's Eve

"I AM NOT going to kiss Lewis Kampmueller at midnight."

Tess Devine glared at herself in the rearview mirror of her BMW, practicing for the firm refusal she was going to give her sisters tonight. Then she realized the traffic light had turned green and she returned her attention to the road, accelerating smoothly out of the parking lot of Henderson Community Hospital.

She waved to Mrs. Linkline, giving a little toot of the horn, as she cruised toward downtown Henderson, which was all decked out in cheery holiday decor. Mrs. L, her old Algebra and Geometry teacher, waved back and made motions that clearly said *See you tonight!*

Right. See you tonight.

No way am I going stag to the party. And no way am I going to kiss Lewis.

For the last decade, Tess and her younger sisters had lied, cheated, dodged and otherwise manipulated each other, determined not to be the one in their family to kiss Lewis at midnight.

And if the confident, flamboyant, never-without-a-date, semi-famous Tess Devine actually had to finally kiss the geekiest guy in town, Grace and Annabelle would never let her hear the end of it. Hell, it would probably end up as a sidebar on Page Six or on one of the gossip sites: *Broadway Star goes Stag to Own Family's New Year's Eve Bash/Forced to Kiss Sisters' Reject.*

Someone would probably even post a picture on Facebook.

Her sisters would especially love it, for in the decade since they'd first made the bet, Tess made sure she never had to kiss Lewis. It was usually poor Grace who'd had to kiss him…not that he minded at all. Anyone with a pair of eyes in their head knew he'd been in love with the middle Devine sister since he was sixteen. And Tess figured it was her job as matchmaker and older sister to help facilitate True Love.

Tess grinned at her reflection, remembering how nearly every year, Lewis—sometimes with her help or Annabelle's—made sure poor Gracie would be left high and dry without a date at midnight. No matter how hard the middle sister tried, her escort never lasted until the witching hour—if he even made it to the party in the first place.

Poor Lewis. If he didn't close the deal this year, he was just going to have to give up. What the hell was wrong with the guy?

Just then she heard the perky tones of *Bibbidi-Bobbidi-Boo* coming from the depths of her purse. Speak of the devil.

She pushed her Bluetooth earpiece and answered the call. "Hey Grace." Her sister—an FBI Special Agent—would never know she'd picked such a fluffy song for her special ringtone. If Grace ever found out, she'd probably do one of her FBI moves on Tess and break her neck. (Although Grace always denied having any lethal moves, Tess didn't believe her.)

"Are you almost here? I can't wait to see you!"

"About fifteen more minutes. Had to stop at Birdie's and then the hospital to visit some of the children," Tess replied. "And I know why you want to see me so badly—because you haven't picked out anything to wear yet, have you?"

"Nooo," moaned Grace. "Belly's going to have my head. Can't you get here any sooner? I have to have something before she gets here. She sent me links four months ago. And then another month later. And she tried to set me up with a damned personal shopper. What the hell am I going to do with a personal fucking shopper? Have you heard from her?"

Tess was laughing. Poor Grace. If she had her way, she'd throw on a black t-shirt and a pair of dress slacks for the party, not caring that everyone else would be in tuxes and evening gowns. "No—but she's supposed to be en route from Raleigh."

"I've been trying to catch her on her cell for the last hour, and all I get is voicemail."

"You know her—she's probably dictating seating charts or picking out a dress...for next year's party. I wonder who she'll bring this year for her date," Tess said hopefully. If Annabelle didn't have a date either, their agreement dictated they would both have to kiss Lewis.

"I don't know—but you can bet she'll bring someone. She swore to me she wasn't going to be stuck with Lewis this year."

"How about you? Who's going to be on your arm?"

"A big bad wolf, as a matter of fact," Grace said mysteriously. "What about you, big sister dear? Now that you're single again...."

Tess laughed, hardly even feeling the pang of pain and shame thanks to her pending divorce. "I'm not telling. You'll have to wait and see." After all, there was still hope. Maybe the bartender would be cute. "Well, I've got to run. I'll see you in a few."

As she ended the call, Tess braked in front of Clavell's Pharmacy to let a woman and her two children cross, then stuck her head out the window when she recognized her. "Hey, Deanne! You're coming tonight, right?"

The woman waved and brought her children over to the car, ignoring the light but steady traffic going through the quaint downtown. "Hi Tess! You know I wouldn't miss it for the world. Joey and I look forward to it every year—well, at least I do. Joey would rather not be stuffed into a tux, but he knows he'll have fun anyway."

"I can't wait to see your dress," Tess said. "You always wear something fabulous. Did you get great shoes?"

"Oh yes—Annabelle sent me a link to a great online shoe place and I found the perfect pair. Wait till you see them!"

"Make sure you get there early," Tess told her. "And park in the side lot—it's easier to get in that way. The band is going to be great, so don't forget to bring your socks so you can take off your shoes!"

One of Deanne's children, Dusty, tugged on her mom's hand. Deanne bent to her and said, "Say hi to Miss Tess. Do you remember her? She was Belle when we went to see *Beauty and the Beast*. Remember, when we visited Auntie Susan in New York?"

Tess smiled at Dusty and her younger brother Joe Junior. "I remember you—you came to visit me backstage after the show. I showed you the glass with the rose inside it, remember?" The little girl was cute as a button, with just the right amount of freckles on her pug nose. Tess tightened her insides against an envious pang.

"You don't look like Belle," Dusty said, shielding her eyes from the noon December sun. "She had hair…." She moved her hand in a gesture that clearly indicated Tess's long honey blonde hair was not the same as Belle's brown, elegant updo.

"That's because I wore a wig. See?" Tess snatched up the Belle wig, which she'd tossed on the seat next to her, and was now muddled up with the familiar yellow dress. She still wore that costume to visit children in the hospital, for they never tired of Belle.

A gentle toot behind them made Deanne and Tess look around. "Guess we'd better move," Dee said. "See you tonight!" And she hurried off with her two munchkins.

Dee's parting words brought her thoughts back to the problem at hand. Because…really. Tess Devine could *not* go to the biggest shindig in Henderson without a date. Hmm. Maybe she could just pretend she was still married…. No. She didn't want to be attached to Barry any longer.

Whatever. I'm not going to kiss Lewis, no matter how hard Grace and Belly try. I'm almost twenty-nine years old. I've been nominated for a Tony. *I've been on the cover of* Fashion. *I've been on a date with Matthew Morrison.*

If I can handle a drunk co-star feeling me up live onstage, I can handle my sisters.

Especially since the drunken co-star had been a woman.

Lewis wasn't that bad—not anymore, anyway. Sure, he'd been a four-eyed gweeb with his face always in a computer back in high school, but the biggest problem with him hadn't been that as much as Mom and Dad. They'd had some medieval fantasy about joining the Devine and Kampmueller families for twenty years, and all three of the Devine sisters had rebelled against the idea of a forced marriage, so to speak. Poor Lewis wasn't so much a nerd as he was The Guy Your Mom Wanted You To Marry, So of Course You Didn't.

"Hell, maybe I should just give it up and kiss Lewis this year," Tess said aloud as she drove by the massive Christmas tree at the center of town. It always reminded her of the one in *How the Grinch Stole Christmas*. "Then I'll have had my turn and we can put this stupid game to rest. Ten years is enough."

I wonder if Johnny Wilder's in town….

A hot little shiver caught her by surprise when she thought of seeing Wilder. They used to be friends and had usually ended up hanging out in some form or another on New Year's Eve. Then things had changed.

It had been four years since that awkward night. They'd both had too much to drink and it was late and the things that had been said…well, she doubted he even remembered them. *Surely* he didn't remember them.

Besides. She was no fool. He'd just been trying to get in her pants, just like he did with every other female he encountered. Johnny Wilder was a Player—definitely with a capital P—and that was the last thing she needed in her life right now. She was turning over a new leaf, starting a new phase…and she didn't need a guy like him to screw it up.

What she needed was someone safe and easy.

Which meant she needed to work on Plan B…and quickly. Because she was pulling in the driveway now. After she parked, she pulled out her phone and, grinning, sent a text to Lewis Kampmueller: *Find me a date or you're kissing me tonight, hot stuff.*

That ought to light a fire under his butt.

Chapter Two
—

JOHNNY WILDER found it damn near impossible not to think about Tess Devine on New Year's Eve.

He supposed it was to be expected. After all, she'd pretty much fubarred every one of the last ten of them for him. Even the ones when they hadn't been on the same continent.

He hadn't seen her in four years—three of which had been spent nearly getting his ass blown up in Iraq. And the fourth he'd been safely down at NASA. Not hiding so much as...avoiding.

So here he sat, nursing an IPA in a tall, brown bottle and watching whatever was on ESPN, trying to forget it was New Year's Eve. Trying to forget the Curse of Tess Devine. He was determined that his date Laney would break the tradition tonight, because his track record was pathetic.

And the pisser of it was every damn time he heard "What Are You Doing New Year's Eve?"—which seemed to be the frigging favorite song of every female he'd ever known, not to mention on the soundtrack at every damned store or restaurant he stepped foot in—all he could think of was Tess. Because, whether he'd intended it or not, she was *his* New Year's Eve tradition.

The sharp click of heels caught his attention as his mom walked in from the garage via the kitchen.

"Back already?" he asked, craning to look behind him as she came into the living room.

"It's so cold out there," Mom said, taking off a thick scarf and gloves. "I can't remember the last time it was this cold in Henderson. They're even calling for snow tonight—which I don't believe for a minute."

"So how's Rhapsody today? Did she spit up? Fart? Fill her diaper?" He grinned up at her as she stopped and gave his too-long hair an affectionate yank.

"My only grandchild is a brilliant baby. She does everything right even though she's only three weeks old."

At twenty-seven, he was a commercial pilot, had completed two tours in Iraq—and seen things he needed to forget—plus knew how to navigate a space shuttle...yet his mom's affectionate touch made him feel all of ten again. Warm and comfortable. Come to think of it, it was probably the same for her. She hadn't seen enough of her only son for four years—a fact which she constantly reminded him.

"Not sure how so much brilliance can happen with a name like *Rhapsody*." Wilder laughed when his mom winced. He still couldn't believe Karen and Mark had named their daughter after a defunct online music service, and he had a feeling his mom felt the same way—though she'd sure as hell never admit it.

She knuckled down on his head, mussing harder, then plopped on the couch next to him. "Are you sure you don't want to get this mop cut before the soirée tonight? I'm sure Birdie could still fit you in. In fact, I'll make sure of it." She pulled out her cell phone.

"I had it buzzed for four years. I like it longer. All the better for some hot chick to run her fingers through," he teased, lifting his beer to take a drink.

She rolled her eyes and filched the beer from his fingers. "Laney Boudreau better behave with my only son tonight," she warned, then took a sip.

"Rick Stanick better behave with my only mom tonight," he retorted.

His parents had divorced five years ago—just before he joined the Air Force. And then he had to go and get shipped to

Iraq a year later and give his mom something else to stress about. Great job, Wilder.

Which was the only reason he was spending the holidays back here in Henderson—to make up for that.

"Oh, you'll never guess who I ran into at Birdie's today," she said, handing him back the beer. "By the way, ugh." She nodded at the bottle. "Too bitter for me."

"I'm sure Rick will bring you a nice bottle of cabernet tonight," he teased.

"He does have excellent taste in wine. And women. Speaking of which, John—you didn't even say anything about my hair. What do you think?"

"Huh? Oh, it looks *great*, Mom." She'd left four hours ago, and as far as he could tell, nothing had changed. "The color's really nice," he said, picking one of the two options he knew was available—color or length. He figured he had a fifty/fifty chance.

"You did notice," she said with a surprised smile. "I guess they taught you something in the service. Well, enjoy your—whatever you're watching. I've got to start getting ready. Takes me nearly ten minutes just to squeeze into my Spanx, plus all the other stuff we women have to do."

He had no idea what spanks was—but it sounded like something he didn't want to know. The idea of his mom dating (and presumably having sex) was still a little awkward, and spanks sounded vaguely dirty. Definitely something he didn't want to know about. "Okay."

She started to leave then stopped. "Oh yes, I didn't tell you who I ran into at the salon. Tess Devine. Apparently she's in town after all. All the ladies at Birdie's were a-twitter—ha!" —she poked him— "because she came in to show them some wigs and hairpieces they're using in *Wicked*. Did you know they have over a hundred and fifty of them in all?"

But he wasn't listening anymore. He'd stopped after *she's in town after all.*

No frigging *way.*

How the hell did that happen?

"Rick should be here in about two hours. Remember your Southern manners, Johnny-boy," she said, and laid a loud kiss on his cheek. "And if you leave before I see you, make sure you save a dance for me tonight."

"I will," he said weakly, wondering how much of a chance he'd have of sweet-talking Laney into staying home in the hot tub instead of going to the Devine-Kampmueller shindig. It'd be a lot more fun trying to peel her out of a red dress than making small talk with Tess Devine and her asshat of a husband.

Probably a snowball's chance in hell. The soirée, as his mom called it, was the biggest to-do in Henderson, and everyone who was in town attended. It was a damned tradition. Which was why he'd made certain Tess Devine was still doing her stint in *Wicked* on Broadway before deciding to come home.

Or so he thought.

He lifted the beer and drank. What the hell was wrong with him? She was a girl he'd hung out with in high school. But he'd never even officially gone out with her, let alone slept with her.

He'd only kissed her once. And that was under duress. Why the hell was he letting her fubar his holiday—*still*—after a decade?

Christ. Wilder scrubbed a hand over his face, disgusted with himself and the whole situation.

He'd been in a damned war zone for four years and hadn't been this...whatever. Riled up. Freaked out. Unsettled.

But Tess Devine could do that to a guy, with her bossy attitude and deep chocolate eyes that just seemed to suck you down in. They could go from flashing anger to teasing to sultry in ten seconds flat. A guy didn't have a frigging chance when he took that into account along with the way she looked—all the right curves and thick honey blonde hair—plus that damned freckle on the sweet spot next to the hollow of her throat.

He might have made it home from Iraq in one piece—or mostly—but he sure as shit had a bad luck streak when it came to New Year's Eve.

Sonofabitch.

Chapter Three

COMING HOME was always one of Tess's favorite things, but coming home at the holidays was even better. It was home, it was family, it was familiar…it was comfort.

Part of the reason was that the house, a grand Southern-style estate, was always dressed to the nines in holiday trimmings. Each year, Mom had a theme to her decor and this year, apparently, it was The Holly & The Ivy, Plus Angels. Glittering red and green holly swagged the front entrance, gold ivy curved around the banisters. Ivy topiaries trimmed with tiny red ribbons and lit by tiny white and green lights sat on the foyer table. A huge glittering tapestry of angels hung on the two-story wall above the table. And she could see a trio of elegant silver celestial beings on the fireplace mantel in the living room.

"Honey, I'm home!" Tess called gaily, dropping her Balenciaga bag on the floor and poking her head into Dad's study.

"Hi, sweet pea," he said, rising quickly from his desk chair. "*Welcome home.*" He said the words reverently, as if she'd been gone for years. So he knew. She hadn't told him much, but somehow he *knew*.

They met halfway across the room, and he looked into her eyes as if to take measure of her well-being. Then he pulled her into a tight embrace, stroking her hair like he'd done when she was little. He smelled like her daddy and she inhaled the comfort and familiarity. "Do you want to talk about it?"

Tess had managed to keep it all under control the whole day—while she was at the hospital being Belle, at Birdie's showing off fancy headpieces, talking to Deanne downtown...but now that she was home, there was no need. To her horror, she felt her eyes begin to sting and she hugged her father tighter. "Thanks, Dad," she murmured. "I needed that."

"I have a feeling you need this too, honey."

Tess turned to find her mom coming into the room, holding a big glass of red wine. She took the glass then flowed into another embrace, this time with her petite, familiar-scented mother. "Thanks, Mom," she said, taking care not to slop what was surely a zinfandel on her mother's crisp white slacks.

"You okay?" Mom asked, lifting Tess's chin even though she was five inches shorter than her daughter. Her gaze delved into hers just as Dad's had, then she nodded. "You will be." She gave her a gentle kiss on the cheek.

"I will. I'm so glad to be home for the party tonight. I thought.... " Her voice wobbled, but she held it together. "I thought this would be the first year I'd miss it. Ever." *Silly. Stop being such a wuss!* Last year was the worst, when she realized she was going to have to divorce Barry.

But it had taken her almost six more months to make that decision.

"Sit, Tess. You've got about five minutes before Annabelle the whirlwind shows up—and, oh, wait till you hear about that," Mom said. Her sea-green eyes danced merrily. "She was blazing into town as usual in that little hot rod—and, well...your baby sister's streak's been broken."

"Really?" Tess asked, a smile tugging her lips. "Annabelle met her match, huh? It's about time." She sipped, then hummed with delight at the rich woodsy, berry flavor. "Ah. Thanks. I really did need that. What about Gracie—where is she? Off to Target, shopping for a dress?" Her smile turned into an affectionate laug"She's upstairs trying to figure out what to wear," Dad replied with a sad shake of his head, sipping a rock glass filled with Scotch.

Of the entire Devine family, including their patriarch, Grace was the only one who was clueless when it came to fashion and style. If she could, she'd wear jeans and a white t-shirt every day, just for the simplicity of it.

"She called me, wanting to know when I was going to get here so I could protect her from Belly." They all laughed together and Tess felt another pang: this one of emptiness and yet comfort, all rolled into one.

Her parents had been married for forty years, and were still as much in love as they had been when they wed. They were a united front who understood each other, adored their daughters, and yet expected the best from each of their very different offspring. They had each other.

"Tell us about it, sweet pea," Dad said, patting Tess's knee.

She drew in a deep breath and looked at them both. "Well, it's been a little rough. The divorce. I mean, for me. Barry's been his normal self." She smiled grimly. "But I'm fine. It hasn't really hit the big press yet—only a few small outlets have picked it up. So some people know, but a lot of others don't. It probably won't go big, either, so that makes it a little easier."

No one had ever said anything overtly negative about the man she married two New Year's Eves ago during the party, but she'd sensed the distance between him and her family. And in retrospect, she understood why. They'd seen what she'd been blind to: his condescension, his attempt to control and change her, and, worst of all, his propensity for "mentoring" young actresses. On the couch.

"The divorce should be final by the end of March, but you know as far as I'm concerned, things have been over for a year. And…I left the show. I'm leaving the theater."

There. I said it.

Mom's eyes widened. She took Dad's rock glass from his hand and gulped a big swallow. When she brought the glass away she said, "You're leaving the theater?"

"Well, I'm leaving the *stage*. I'm just not…happy anymore. I know I should be grateful for the opportunity I've had, the little bit of success I've gleaned—"

"And your date with Matthew Morrison," Mom threw in. "He *was* a gentleman, wasn't he?"

Tess gave a short chuckle. "That was pretty awesome. And yes he was—unfortunately. That man is *ripped*. But there are thousands of young women who'd give anything to take my place onstage. And they probably already have," she added ruefully. "But—I'm almost twenty-nine, and thirty's just around the corner. Not old, but—I want a family. A normal life. I thought I was going to be able to do that with Barry, but…yeah. That didn't work out."

"What are you going to do?" asked Dad, just watching her.

She drew in another breath and smiled. "I'm going to do some producing, actually. Maybe being married to a director gave me the idea; I don't know. I've got some options with a couple smaller shows…in New York, but also in Chicago or Atlanta. You know I'll be good at that—bossy as I am. And that will give me more time to work with EverFun."

"You do enjoy that, don't you?" Mom said. She didn't look quite as shocked anymore. "You just light up whenever you talk about all the things you've done with that foundation—visiting the children in the hospitals, doing the fundraisers, the media interviews—everything."

"You'll be able to give your name to the Foundation, and that's good visibility for them," Dad said. "I think it's wonderful, sweet pea."

"Exactly. So—wait, is that Belly?" Tess stood, looking out Dad's study window. Sure enough, the bright red sports car was rumbling up the long drive toward the circle. She grinned, suddenly feeling lighter than she had in a long while. "Let's go hear about the cop who broke her streak!"

Chapter Four

New Year's Eve
Ten Years Ago

"MOM'S BEEN bugging me to dance with Lewis Kampmueller," Tess hissed to Grace, peering around one of the well-lit pillars. Fortunately, the dork was nowhere in sight.

Grace laughed, tucking her light brown hair behind one ear. "Better you than me!" She smoothed her simple black dress—the one that Tess had tried to talk her out of wearing.

"You always wear black, Gracie—why don't you put on something more exciting—like red or blue or even green?" Conscious of her own emerald green gown, Tess looked around and saw her friend, David Grathwold, standing with a group of guys from school. She and David had just finished starring in their high school's production of *Annie Get Your Gun*.

"Black is simple and easy," Grace told her firmly. "I don't have time to worry about what goes with what, and whether my makeup matches, and if I have the right shoes like you do." Then she gave Tess a shrewd look. "All right, 'fess up. Are you going to kiss David at midnight or what?" Geez. She'd be a great cop.

"No, I am not going to kiss David. For Pete's sake, Grace, I kissed him enough during the show, and believe me, it didn't do a thing for me. It was like kissing a brother—if we had one. Besides,

he's your age—too young for me. I'm more into college guys."
Her attention wafted back to where the man in question stood
with his friends. "Johnny Wilder's looking hot, though. He looks
just like a young George Harrison, with those heavy brows and all
that dark hair. Too bad he's too young too. And he's got a date."

"Too bad you dumped Brian last week—'cause if you hadn't,
you wouldn't have to dance with Lewis," Grace pointed out.

"You're right. I should have kept him around for another
week just so he could be my date. *Right.*" Tess shook her head.
"He was such a jerk during the show, always so jealous of David,
if you can believe it. I was tired of it. And think of it this way:
if I had a date, you'd be next on Mom's list—so you should be
grateful for my datelessness." She smiled. "I guess I'll just have to
find someone here tonight."

Grace scoffed. "Yeah, right. Like any guy you choose is going
to just jump to attention when you walk by."

Tess just raised her brows and looked at her.

"Well, all right. You've got a point," her sister conceded.
"They do tend to notice you. But that doesn't mean they'd *kiss*
you."

"I'll bet you I can find someone to kiss at midnight. And if
I do" —Tess's grin turned mischievous— "you not only have to
dance with Lewis, you have to *kiss* him."

Grace paled, but considered for a moment. "All right. But,
you can't count kissing Dad or any relative. And it can't just be
a peck on the cheek—it's got to be on the lips. And, if you don't
find someone, you have to kiss Lewis, and I'm going to tell him
you have a crush on him. You only have thirty minutes, so you'd
better get to work."

Tess shuddered at the idea of Lewis thinking she liked him.
But the thought of her sister—tomboy Grace who only thought
about studying and sports—kissing the bean pole nerd with a
huge Adam's apple made her want to giggle. "Deal."

Grace insisted on bringing Annabelle into the fold as witness
and the three sisters shook on it. Little did they know a New Year's

Eve tradition had been born.

"Hey, guys," Tess said brightly as she wandered up to the group where David stood with his friends.

"Yo, Tess," David replied. "What's going on? Hey, do you think your dad or Mr. K will care if we get a beer from the bar?"

"If you aren't driving, I don't think one beer would be a problem. It's New Year's Eve, after all. Just don't be obvious about it—and *don't* let my Aunt Helen see you drinking it." She looked over the group of guys, searching for a potential midnight kissee.

Dang. Johnny Wilder *was* looking pretty hot tonight. She noticed his steel grey eyes and relaxed stance where he leaned against the wall. He was tall and broad-shouldered, with toned biceps that showed through the clinging shirt he wore. Didn't he know he was supposed to be wearing a suit jacket? At sixteen, he already looked more manly than the rest of them...which was probably why he had a pretty blond date who was shooting eye-daggers at Tess.

"I think we're already past one beer," Wilder drawled in his low voice. "But I wouldn't mind another one."

"All right," Tess replied, her voice automatically sliding into a matching mellow purr. Too bad he was so young. No way would senior Tess Devine lower herself to kiss a sophomore. "Anyone else want me to snag them a beer?"

In all, she promised to bring back three. She walked away from the group, trying to figure out how she was going to carry three glasses while finding someone to kiss. She'd taken a few steps toward the bar when a long steel pole shot out in front of her.

"And just what are you up to, girl?" asked a peremptory voice.

"Aunt Helen!" Tess tried to avoid the cane wielded by her great-aunt from Maine, but the old lady was too quick for her. She had to grab a table to keep from losing her balance and had barely righted herself by the time the woman placed herself in her path.

"You're going to catch your death of cold in that dress," Aunt Helen scolded, and, to Tess's acute embarrassment, reached with a claw-like hand to yank the bodice higher. "In my day and age—and it wasn't all that long ago, young lady, do you hear me?—nice young ladies wouldn't be caught dead in a dress without a bit of lace there at the throat. Here, let me see. You hold this, Teresa, now, while I find it…." She thrust her shiny cane (a new addition to her aunt's persona) at her great-niece, and upended her gauche satin pink evening bag onto a table.

Lipstick, tissues, a plastic coin case, and a little net bag filled with birdseed clunked onto an empty plate. Helen scrabbled through the debris with her curled fingers while Tess tried to think of a way to extricate herself.

"Aunt Helen, I really appreciate your help, but I need—"

"Stay right there, young lady. Don't you be walking off with that cane! I might be an old lady—not that old, mind you, but old enough to get away with whatever I wish, I'll have you know—and it's not that I need that blasted thing to get around with—'cause I don't—but it makes me look old and frail and I have found several other uses for the thing. Ah-ha!" She held up a bit of frilly lace, mussed and crumpled, and most likely smelling of moth balls.

"Aunt Helen," Tess said again, more earnestly this time. *Ten minutes to midnight.* "I need to get back to my—"

"Here we are," said her aunt. And before Tess could blink, the old lady was jamming the bit of froth right down the front of her dress.

"Aunt Helen!"

"Did you need some help, ma'am?" drawled a voice behind them.

Tess jerked away and came face to face with Johnny Wilder. Heat swarmed up from her chest, warming her face, as she met his amused gaze with her own. Great. *Caught with my great-aunt's hand down the front of my dress. Perfect.*

Helen jerked her chin up, and Tess noticed the way the termagant scoped him out. "I have everything under control, here, young man. But you can be certain that if I am in need of assistance, I'll be calling on you." Her thin lips curved in something resembling a smile.

Good grief! Was Aunt Helen flirting with Johnny Wilder?

Tess looked at the clock. *Nine minutes.* The opportunity to win her bet with Grace was slipping further away.

"You bet, Mrs. Galliday," Wilder drawled. "In the meantime, I came to see if I could help you carry those glasses, Tess. We need a fourth one."

"I would appreciate that very much." She glanced at the clock adorning the wall above the deejay, and grimaced at the time. *Eight minutes.* How was she going to swing this?

Tess slowed so Wilder walked next to her. Hm. Maybe he *could* be a candidate. She had nothing to lose (except the bet)... plus she was bold, direct, and used to getting her own way. He was only a young kid—he probably wasn't all that experienced. He'd probably jump at the chance to kiss Tess Devine.

She slanted a glance at him. If only he were a couple years older.

His arm bumped against hers, and Tess took charge. She slipped her hand around his bicep as they walked, leaning slightly into him.

Wilder glanced down at her, but he didn't draw away as they walked toward the bar. She noticed the clock hanging on the wall behind the bar. *Five minutes. Crap.* Grace and Annabelle watched from across the room. Tess looked at them and saw the matching smirks on her sisters' faces. That was it. Time was up.

"Hey Johnny," she said, gently steering him away from the bar.

He looked down again. "What's up, Tess? Aren't we going to get a beer?"

"I need a favor."

"What's that?" That drawl again—so casual and uninterested.

She pulled him toward a corner decorated by a ficus adorned with lights. They wouldn't be so noticeable here ...but Grace and Annabelle could see them. Tess released his arm and looked up to catch him giving a little wave across the room. To his date. Ugh. She glanced at the big clock. *Three minutes!*

No time to lose. "See, I have a bet with my sister that I would kiss someone at midnight. So can you just kiss me real quick and then you can go back to what's-her-name?"

Surprise flared across his face and Wilder stared down at her in blatant disbelief. Tess felt her mouth dry. *Crap.* What if he refused?

"You want me to kiss you. In front of my date. In front of everyone. So you can win a bet?"

A flood of heat rushed over her face. Well, when you put it that way…. But she wasn't Tess Devine for nothing. "Yes. Come on, Johnny—it's just a bet. I'll explain everything to your date. It'll be fine." She flapped her hand.

Wilder stared at her. She could read the emotions on his face: incredulity and suspicion. "And you think that'll be okay with Jilly, as long as you explain? You want to ruin the rest of my night? I have *plans*." His slow smile indicated just what he had in mind for after the party.

She rolled her eyes. "Come on, Johnny. It's just a damned kiss. For one second."

Suddenly, the atmosphere in the room shifted. The hum of voices rose, and Tess turned just as someone shouted, "It's time! Get your champagne for the midnight toast!"

She looked back at Wilder. His gray eyes were cool, and skepticism still showed on his face.

"Ten…nine…eight…." Her dad had started the countdown.

Tess glanced across the room and saw Grace grinning like an idiot. As their eyes met, Grace used her two index fingers to point excitedly toward Lewis Kampmueller, who stood only yards away. She made smooching motions with her lips and then pointed at Lewis again.

"…Five…four…three…. "

Tess swiveled back toward Wilder, who was still looking at her like she'd grown another head. She grabbed his shoulders and yanked him toward her just as the room erupted in shouts, claps, and cheers.

She missed his mouth by two inches, yet as their faces collided in the midst of the revelry, Tess felt her body shut down… then *whoosh* alive. He turned toward her and their lips clashed awkwardly…and then suddenly Johnny Wilder was kissing her… really kissing her.

Chapter Five

_____

Present Day

EVERY TIME Wilder walked into the Club, he couldn't help but remember the first Devine-Kampmueller New Year's Eve party he'd attended—ten years ago. That was the night Tess kissed him in order to win some sort of bet. Little did he know that was the beginning of The Curse of Tess Devine.

All his plans for Jilly Henson in the rear seat of his roomy F-10 (or on the couch in her parents' basement, or even in the hot tub room at the Club—he wasn't particular) had gone to hell the minute Tess leaned into him. Not only had that kiss left him feeling as if he'd been punched in the gut, but despite his subsequent explanations, Jilly had eventually left the party with Vance Evans—and ended up showing _him_ her parents' couch in the basement.

In reality, the kiss meant nothing to either Tess or Wilder—hell, he'd kissed _a lot_ of girls; he wasn't shy—but it changed things anyway.

Until that night, he knew the upperclassman Tess only as David Grathwold's co-star in the school play and the daughter of one of the most prominent families in town. Plus Grace was in his class. But since he and Grat (a junior) were tight, and Tess and Grat had become close doing the show, the three of them began to hang out together during the rest of her senior year. Sometimes

Tess had a boyfriend with her, other times Wilder had a date, and usually Cara was there because everyone knew she and Grat were destined to get married as soon as they graduated. (They had.)

Heck, he and Grat used to ask Tess for dating advice. He could remember sitting at a late-night coffee session at Denny's, talking through his next move or how to ask out a girl he was hot for.

In fact, Tess had bought him and Grat their first box of condoms. He and David had been arguing about who was going to walk into Clavell's and buy them.

Tess had rolled her eyes, held out her hand for their money, and walked bold as brass into Clavell's. Moments later, she'd come waltzing out with a bag much too large for a single box of condoms. But it wasn't until they'd returned to David's house that she'd dumped the contents onto the table in front of them.

She'd bought condoms all right…ribbed ones and lambskin ones, gold coins, glow in the dark ones, lubricated with and without spermicide, and even a box of extra-large. "I wasn't sure what size you guys wore," she'd teased.

And she'd purchased samples of other contraceptive methods—foams and inserts and a tube of K-Y Jelly.

"I thought I was going to shit my pants when she said she told Mr. Clavell it was for us!" Grat told him after she left.

Now, ten years later as he escorted Laney into the Club's crowded ballroom, Wilder couldn't help but glance over at the corner where he and Tess had kissed—that one and only time. What would've happened if he'd given up trying to explain his actions to Jilly and instead hung out with Tess the rest of the night?

Maybe things would have been different. But probably not. It wasn't as if he and Tess hadn't had ample opportunity to hook up over the next few years.

It was just that the circumstances had never been right.

And now she was married. To a major ass.

"What can I get you to drink?" he asked Laney, admiring the

deep vee of her neckline instead of scanning the room for Tess. The dress wasn't red, but he found he didn't mind at all—black lace worked just as well when it was showcasing a generous rack like hers. Christina Hendricks didn't have a thing on his date.

"Chardonnay," she told him, her fingers curled around his arm. "Oh, look. There's Tess Devine! I haven't seen her in ages. She looks amazing. And she's *famous.*"

Famous, talented, bossy—and surrounded by rich and powerful men. She could have her pick. And she'd picked Barry Markham.

"I'll go get our drinks," he said as soon as he caught a glimpse of her heading their way. As he walked off, he heard Laney greeting Tess. *Coward.*

I'm just getting us a drink, he argued with himself.

Yeah, you beat it faster than a horny teen after his first make out session. Pussy.

I'm not hiding from her.

His inner self snickered and rolled its eyes.

Thank God there were empty stools at the bar. Wilder took a seat with his back to the ballroom, which was just across the way. With luck, he could hang out here for a few minutes until the women were done talking.

"Jameson, neat," he said to the dark-haired bartender. *Harry* was on his name tag, and although it took him a surprisingly long time to find the bottle of whiskey, he finally pushed a short glass over to him. Filled to the brim.

"Nice pour," Wilder said. *Jesus. Do I look like I need it that bad?* "A chardonnay, too."

"Right," said Harry, who turned to stare at the array of wine bottles behind him. He didn't seem to know what to do next.

"No hurry. Seriously."

"So who's the hot blonde?" Harry asked, pulling a glass down and setting it on the bar.

"Tess Devine," Wilder replied into his glass. Then he looked up, realizing he'd answered wayyy too quickly. "I mean, which one? There's a lot of hot blondes here tonight."

"Right. But only one as far as you're concerned."

Wilder frowned and looked around. What the hell? How did this guy know anything? And weren't there any other customers the guy could be serving? This side of the bar was tucked away and empty. Great. He took another sip, deciding he was in a hurry for the chardonnay after allBut then he glanced around and saw Laney and Tess deep in conversation. They seemed to be comparing shoes. Maybe not so much in a hurry then.

"So what's the deal? You're here with the stacked brunette, but you wish you were with the blonde. Story of my life," Harry sighed. He'd poured a glass of wine all right, but it was red. Wilder was about to correct him when the bartender lifted the glass and drank from it. "Mm. Very nice." He held onto it as he leaned forward companionably. "So...old flame, ex-girlfriend, or what?"

Wilder shot him an irritated look. "Isn't that the same thing?" When Harry just raised his brows, he capitulated. "None of the above. So what's the weather saying?" He gestured to the screen above the bartender's head.

"They're calling for ice and snow later tonight. Around midnight."

"In Henderson? Are they on crack?" But when he looked at the screen, he saw the weather advisories running along the bottom of the monitor.

Harry shrugged. "I've been watching the radar. It doesn't look like they're on crack. Looks like we're going to have a white New Year's Eve."

Great. Suddenly, Johnny felt more optimistic. *Excellent excuse for leaving early. Like, asap.* "How about that chardonnay?"

"Right. They're still talking you know. And another lady joined them. You probably want to sit here a little longer." Harry grinned, then, mercifully, went to serve another customer who'd slid onto a stool nearby.

Wilder swirled the whiskey around in his glass and watched it funnel down. Ten years of Tess Devine. The first year—that hot kiss—had surprised him. The second year, he'd simply hung out with her and a group of friends, and admired from afar. But it was the next year that changed everything.

Chapter Six

New Year's Eve
Eight Years Ago

WILDER HAD his hand down Kaylie Schwartz's dress and his mouth on her neck when a bright light broke into the darkness.

"Shit," he muttered, disengaging from her hot, sweaty skin to look up from the depths of the backseat of her car. Kaylie was beneath him, still fully clothed (but he was working on changing that), and she had her hand on his ass. He was hoping she'd move it elsewhere—like, front and center—but who the hell was out there, poking around with a light? He sure hoped it wasn't a cop. Or Mr. Devine.

He and Kaylie had been parked in the Club parking lot since one-thirty. Hadn't everyone left the party by now? He hadn't really been noticing all the cars leaving, but he'd heard the voices. And it had been quiet for a long time. Of course, he'd been a little distracted....

"Hold on," he said, aware that his voice was tight and gritty. Well, what did you expect? He'd been looking forward to getting Kaylie into the backseat for hours.

The light was coming from a car near theirs—the only other one left in the parking lot, he realized with a shock. And it was still shining because whoever it was was digging around in the trunk—whose lights were facing the car Wilder was in.

"Johnny," Kaylie said, shifting her hips suggestively against his. "I have to get home soon."

"Right," he said, and was just about to dive back in when he saw a flash of the newcomer's face. What the hell was Tess doing out here...by herself? "Uh, hold on," he said again, and eased away. "That's Tess Devine. I'd better see what's going on."

"Tess?" Kaylie whined. "Who cares?" She moved her hand around and grabbed the front of his belt, yanking him closer. "Come on, Johnny.... "

But Wilder's mom had raised his ass to be a gentleman, and a gentleman—while he might try and get lucky in the back of a girl's car whenever possible—wouldn't leave a stranded woman alone in the dark.

"I'm sorry. I better check and see what's going on. She looks like she might be in trouble." Knowing he was going to regret this, he eased away from Kaylie and slipped out of the car.

Tess turned from burrowing in her trunk (it was definitely her car because of the NYU sticker) when she heard the sound of the car door slam. "Oh crap, you scared me," she said. Then frowned. "What are you still doing here? I thought you left hours ago."

Well, she didn't seem distressed. But what the hell was she doing out here, wearing a dark suit coat over her evening gown?

"I'm er—" He shrugged and gave her a cheesy grin. "Kaylie and I were just talking."

She glanced at the Accord with its steamed-up windows and laughed. "Talking. Right. Just make sure you're not going bareback, cowboy." She turned back to her trunk, where she seemed to be replacing a variety of things she'd taken out.

"What are you doing?" he asked, walking closer.

"I was getting my boots—my snow boots because *we* actually get snow up in New York in December."

"But we don't have it here.... " He looked around, spreading his hands in question. He was still wincing over the bareback comment. Damn.

She laughed again and closed the trunk. She had a pair of snow boots in her hand. "I know. There's a problem inside and I was going to see if I could help."

"What sort of problem? And why are you still here? Didn't everyone leave, like, hours ago?"

"I was helping the band break down. They're friends of mine, you know, and I got them the gig. And I...well, they let me sing a few songs so I thought I'd help them pack up."

He remembered that. She'd gone up there and belted out "Don't Know Why" almost as well as Norah Jones herself. And then she made the keyboard player accompany her on "What Are You Doing New Year's Eve" just before midnight. And then she'd kissed a preppy-looking guy who was her date for the evening. Come to think of it, where was *he*?

"And where are they now?" He gestured to the empty parking lot. "And what about the guy you were with?"

"Aaron? Oh, he has an early flight tomorrow so he left already. The band's gone, but a couple of the catering staff and the club supervisor are still here—they're parked in the back. I was just getting ready to head home when I heard them shouting. Something happened in the spa with the hot tub and now there's a huge flood in the locker rooms, and it's going into the lounges." She shrugged. "They're trying to clean it up—there's no one to call at this time of night on a holiday—and the manager left early. I figured I'd give them a hand." She rolled her eyes. "They were totally clueless until I got them organized. But I didn't want to ruin my shoes any more than they already were, hence the boots. There's about three inches of water in there and we can't just leave it."

"Right."

As he watched, she slipped out of two flimsy looking silver shoes and shoved her feet into the boots. "So, off I go," she said, starting back toward the Club. "Remember what I said—suit up, space boy."

Wilder watched her tromp across the parking lot. She looked like a vagabond with her big clunky boots, sparkling evening gown, and black suit coat. An aggravated toot-toot of the car horn snagged his attention and he turned back to see Kaylie gesturing from the window. She didn't look happy.

He never understood what propelled him to walk over to the driver's side door and wait for Kaylie to roll down the window. If he'd just climbed in the damn car, he'd have broken the Tess Devine Curse just like that.

But, no. Thanks to his mom, he wasn't the kind of guy who could just leave. Especially since...well, Tess was here. Alone. With a bunch of people she didn't know...who knew who they were? What if they were a bunch of guys who'd been drinking while they cleaned up? Not a good idea.

"Hey, Kaylie, I'm sorry...I'm *really* sorry...but I think I better stay. There's a problem inside and Tess is helping them, and I think they could use a hand."

"Seriously?" she demanded, looking up at him with big pouty lips. One of her tits was nearly hanging out of her loosened dress.

His resolve wavered, but he held firm. "And I...uh...well, I don't have any protection with me. It's probably a good thing we were interrupted, because you were getting me pretty worked up."

Lie, lie, lie. He could practically feel the condom burning through the leather of his wallet into his ass. As if he'd come to the biggest party night of the year without a plan. To cover up the falsehood, he leaned in and gave Kaylie a kiss that nearly had him climbing back in through the window...flood or no flood.

"All right. Call me tomorrow?" she said, gunning the engine.

"For sure."

When Wilder walked back into the Club, he didn't have to search for the activity. There was a splashing, wave-like sound coming from the back of the place, and he could hear Tess barking out orders.

"No, no, we have to push the water this way, toward the lower part of the floor where it can collect. Then we can suck it up with the wet-vac—did you find it, Pete? Here, use a push-broom like I told you, Suzy. Those mops don't do a damn thing. Now you all push it this way, and I'll—Wilder? What are you doing here?"

"Another set of hands," he said, looking around. It was a disaster. She was a disaster too, with her hair in a loose ponytail and the edge of her expensive gown dragging in the water even though she'd put some sort of belt on to hold it up. She'd tossed the suit coat somewhere and her shoulders and cleavage were a very pretty thing to look at. "What can I do?"

She didn't blink, but launched into another round of orders. Find some fans, get the air conditioning turned on, empty the heavy wet-vac tank.... Apparently she'd been through this before, either from a hurricane or some other flooding experience.

They all worked side by side—Wilder, Tess, two college girls from the catering staff, and Pete, the Club supervisor—for hours, trying to funnel the water out.

It was Tess who suggested they open one of the bottles of leftover champagne—"After all, Daddy and Mr. K. paid for it!"— and they all had a toast. Or two. In fact, they ended up drinking three bottles of leftover champagne, which was just enough to give everyone a nice, healthy buzz. They also raided the leftover food, which had been packed up but now became fair game as they worked.

At one point, Tess started singing "Jingle Bell Rock" as she slung her push-broom, swishing water energetically across the floor in her bright red strapless gown...and the next thing he knew, everyone joined in. They went through a slew of songs, most of which he only knew because his mom played Harry Connick, Jr. and Frank Sinatra's Christmas albums every day from December 15 through January 1.

It was the most surreal New Year's Eve he'd ever experienced in his almost-eighteen years, and weirdly enough, despite the fact that he hadn't gotten laid after all, he was having a blast. Aside from that, he couldn't believe Tess was still going. It was nearly four o'clock in the morning. After burning up the dance floor with her sisters and visiting with everyone in town all night, trying to catch up on things since she'd left for college, she should be exhausted. Even the catering staff hadn't worked as hard as she did, because he knew she'd been here with her sisters doing the decorating early in the day.

"I think we can call it a night," she finally said, surveying the area. Pretty much every drop of water had been sucked up. The two catering staff were collapsed on a sofa in the lounge, having clearly been ready to quit long ago, and Pete went to put away the wet-vac. "Or day. Or year," she added, giggling a little. "After all, it's next year now, isn't it?"

Someone was punchy. Wilder grinned. She might be bossy but she was totally hot, and really cute when she was overtired. He could see exhaustion around the edges of her eyes.

"Let's go," he said. "Mind giving me a ride home? Kaylie drove, and I don't have a car." For some reason, the thought of riding home with Tess Devine made his insides flip.

"Aww, I'm sorry things didn't work out for you tonight, Wilder," she said, slipping her arm around his shoulders in a companionable hug. She was warm and soft. Her skin glowed from the hard work, and parts of her hair fell in her face and brushed against his chin. Made it look like she'd just woken up. "Maybe next time."

"Let's go," he said, suddenly very aware of her hip bumping against him and the tantalizing view down her strapless gown... and the way she smelled. Which was amazing. His mouth dried up and as he edged slightly away, he looked up. Pete, a thirty-ish guy with a neat goatee, was looking at him with a knowing expression.

He ignored the lascivious wink and led her from the Club. This was Tess, he reminded himself. His buddy. His dating consultant. Who had no interest in him other than a kiss to win a bet because she was dating handsome, rich, twenty-something college guys like Aaron. He remembered the suit coat Tess had been wearing as they walked out to the car. Aaron didn't need his coat. So he didn't mention it.

"Want me to drive?" he asked as they approached her little Volvo wagon. "You look tired. I can drop you off then bring your car back tomorrow."

"That'd be great," she said, swaying a little. "All of a sudden, I'm whipped. And man, am I going to have blisters…and be sore…tomorrow." She sighed and settled into the passenger seat.

Even though she was exhausted, as she claimed, she still told him how to drive. When to shift. How to get to her house. To watch for deer.

"Thanks, Wilder," she said when he pulled up to her parents' house. It was dark except for an exterior light and one glowing through the front door. A motion detector light came on as he stopped in the circular drive.

He turned to say goodnight, and there she was. Right there, close as hell in the front seat. Looking all mussed and glowy and sexy as hell. Her strapless dress showed off her shoulders and the curve of her neck, and even though the light was dim, he knew there was an interesting little freckle right next to that little hollow of her throat. His mouth watered. He really wanted to kiss that mark. To lick it, suck gently on it…then move to the side of her long, elegant neck.

Their eyes met and he felt his world swim…his knees weaken…and something inside him go *ka-blam*. Like his gut just dropped. His lungs felt tight.

"You didn't have to stay, and I really appreciate it. We couldn't have done it without you," she was saying. "Thank you so much, Johnny."

"Yeah," was all he could say. *Kiss her. Kiss her!*

She's got a boyfriend.

Who gives a shit? He left early. He missed out.

She's not interested in you, Wilder.

She kissed you back two years ago.

Yeah. She sure did—

Then all at once she was climbing out of the car. "Good

night, Johnny. Don't forget to wear a rain coat."

Her giddy, giggly laugh was the last thing he heard as she slammed the door and tottered inside.

Chapter Seven

Present Day

TESS COULDN'T find Lewis. He wasn't answering her texts either. Typical man. Typical *Lewis*. He was probably sitting in a corner somewhere, inventing a new smartphone app. That was how he'd made his millions, which, if Gracie played it right, could also be *her* millions.

Although, as she'd come to learn, money did not a happy marriage make.

But Tess needed to talk to Lewis. Not because she needed a date (at this point, she realized she didn't flipping *care*—she'd be just as happy popping a bottle of champagne on her own), but because Grace had actually had not one but *two* guys show up to be her date (nothing like overcompensating!). And neither of them looked like they were going to be easily bought off like all the other flunkies over the years had been.

Had Tess ever felt guilty about being part of the game, working with Lewis to make sure Grace was the one he got to kiss at midnight every single year? Not really. She figured if the guys Gracie brought were as easily bought off as they had been, they didn't *deserve* her smart, funny, kickass sister—and it was a good way for her to find out.

As for Lewis...since he'd been in love with Grace forever,

Tess thought the poor guy deserved a shot. A real shot. But for God's sake, he'd better make it happen this year, because she was done with the whole game.

"So where's your husband, Tess?" asked Laney Boudreau. They'd been chatting for a few minutes while Laney's date went to get her a drink. "Isn't he a director? I heard he was here last year."

"He didn't come—" she started, but Laney leapt on her words before she could explain.

"Did you bring someone else then—someone famous?" Her voice dropped to a whisper and she looked around as if expecting to see George Clooney step out of the shadows.

I wish.

Tess could have been irritated by the celebrity stalking, but she wasn't. After all, one year she'd brought the lead singer of Grammy winner Ferrie's Wake, and another time she'd brought Senator Goldstein's son.

She'd gotten used to this sort of reaction from the members of her hometown, and realized they were simply curious. And a little intimidated. They read gossip magazines and Page Six and entertainment blogs and just wanted to know what it was really like to have Matthew Broderick and Sarah Jessica Parker know you by name, and run into Jon Stewart at the Rockefeller Center and actually have a conversation, and know where Beyonce and Jay-Z's apartment was because you'd been there.

So she replied with the patience and grace she'd cultivated when dealing with these situations. "I'm actually here without a date tonight. It's a little strange, but I'm getting divorced, and, well, I just wanted to have a relaxed time tonight. Especially since it's technically my second anniversary. But," she added with a purposeful twinkle in her eye (she wasn't an actress for nothing), "if you see any hot, single guys, send 'em my way."

"Oh, I'm really sorry you're getting divorced," Laney replied. She seemed sincere. "I hadn't heard anything—I mean, in the gossip columns. Well," she looked a little mortified at having to admit it, "I do read Page Six. It's kind of neat when someone you sort of know shows up in it."

"I read Page Six too," Tess confessed with a smile, casting a subtle glance around for Lewis. Where was he? It was after ten. "And the divorce hasn't really made the news—we're definitely not a big celeb couple like Brangelina or whatever they're calling Ryan Reynolds and Blake Lively. Which is fine with me."

"So does that mean *you'll* have to kiss Lewis Kampmueller tonight instead of Grace?" Laney said with a broad smile.

Tess chuckled. Pretty much everyone knew about the arrangement (after all, it had been going on for a decade), and most people knew about the behind-the-scenes manipulation Lewis always did to make sure he kissed the right Devine girl. Except for Grace. "Well, it's definitely looking that way. I hope Gracie doesn't get jealous."

They were laughing together when Tess noticed her mother gesturing to her from across the room. "Excuse me, Laney," she said, turning back to her companion. "Looks like my mother needs to talk to me—probably about whether the band's been paid yet. You have a great time the rest of the night!"

It took her longer than it should have to make her way across the room—but it was to be expected. Everyone wanted to know how she was doing, where her date was (apparently news of her divorce was just beginning to filter around), when her next Broadway appearance was going to be (she didn't say), and whether she was actually going to have to kiss Lewis this year.

She finally extricated herself from Mr. and Mrs. Turniter and, ready to make a beeline toward Belly, turned abruptly. And came face to face with Johnny Wilder.

"Oh," she said in an embarrassingly gaspy sort of way. "Wilder." *Crap.* That still came out sounding like Marilyn Monroe. "Hi. I didn't know you were in town." *Oh my God, could you sound more idiotic?*

"Same here," he drawled. He had that way of speaking so low and carelessly…it felt like a little caress down her spine. "Didn't expect to see you."

Well, that's about as blunt as you can get, isn't it? "Last minute change of plans," she said, trying to smile casually.

Tess could not figure out why her heart was literally slamming in her chest. Johnny Wilder was just an old friend…well, yeah, who'd said some things during an opportunistic moment—but, Lord, one look at him and he was pushing *all* her buttons tonight. He was like a tall, cool drink on a summer day: mouthwatering. His hair needed a cut, but it looked good—a rich bronzy brown brushing the collar of his tux and in thick waves curling back from his temples. The last time she'd seen him, it was cut military short for the Air Force. His mouth was fixed in a familiar half-smirk but his eyes wouldn't quite meet hers. Tess had seen hundreds of sexy men in tuxes, but there was something about the way he wore his—with careless attitude—that really made her hormones buzz. He looked so cool and sharp: the crisp white shirt under the sleek black coat encasing broad shoulders, military straight and a stance filled with confidence. He wore a neat, understated black bow tie and sharp onyx cufflinks. It was a delicious package and her insides were all a-flutter.

"So…it's been a while," she said after an awkward moment. "A few years. I heard you were in Iraq. I'm glad you made it back safely…. " Her voice trailed off. Surely war had changed him. Maybe that was why he carried himself so differently…with an attitude, and strength, and something else. A subtle show of… not bravado but…wisdom? Experience. And not the kind with women, though he had that in spades too. "I'm sure you look at things differently now."

His eyes widened a little as if he wasn't expecting such a personal and intuitive comment and he seemed to relax slightly. "I do. It was…dark. And difficult. But there were moments of satisfaction and victory. I was proud to be there. Glad I went."

"Thank you," she replied. Meaning it.

Then, "Hey," she said, trying to jolt herself out of this very strange discomfort. She tested a little flirtatious smile. "I don't have a date tonight, and since I'm really not interested in kissing

Lewis Kampmueller, maybe you could help me out again? You know, for old times' sake?" She forced herself to sound light and funny and teasing, just the way she'd always been with Wilder. Pretending she didn't remember anything that had happened four years ago.

His gray eyes swept over her, suddenly turning Arctic cold. "I don't think your asshat of a husband would appreciate that. Nor would my very sexy date. Good to see you again, Tess." And he walked away.

Her cheeks flared hot and her whole body quivered with anger even as it flushed with shame.

Four years ago, he'd been playing the "I'm off to war, honey, send me off with a bang," card....

Damn good thing she hadn't believed him.

Chapter Eight

New Year's Eve
Four years ago

"THIS WAS A great idea, Tess," said Grat. "I've been wanting to see *Iron Man*, but with two kids it's a little hard to get out of the house."

"My pleasure," she replied, gesturing them into the home theater in her parents' basement. "Get comfortable. We've got all the leftover beer and wine—no champagne though—and some food. Wilder, you open a few bottles. Cara, can you get the plates? They're in the cupboard over there. And napkins too. Grat, some of us—like me—will want blankets. They're in the trunk by the wall. Gracie, here's the DVD. Brooks, can you light the fire? It's real wood, so you might have to use your Boy Scout skills instead of flipping a switch."

The annual Devine-Kampmueller bash had ended unusually early due to a widespread case of the flu throughout Henderson. The few people who'd actually made it to the party had cleared out shortly after midnight, either because their children were home sick, they were getting sick or had just gotten over being sick, or because it simply wound down early. Even Belly wasn't feeling well and had slipped off to bed right away.

So Tess had invited a group of friends over to watch *Iron*

Man and whatever other movies they could get to.

"Too bad Barry had to miss the party," Grace said when she handed her the DVD. "But at least you got to show off your new rock tonight."

Tess lifted her hand, loving the way the low lights in the room caught at the sparkles of the three-carat diamond. "Poor guy. He was so sick he couldn't even make his flight. If I'd known, I would have just stayed instead of flying down here so early. Go put that disk in, and let's get started. You know how much I love Robert Downey, Jr."

They drank beer and wine and watched *Iron Man*, then someone put in *Love, Actually* (over which the guys groaned and the gals sighed) and by then, it was past four. And everyone had had more than enough to drink.

"We'd better hit the road," Grat said, helping Cara to her feet. "Even though our babysitter is staying the night, I'm done. I haven't been up this late since college. You okay to drive, honey, because I'm sure not."

Grace yawned. "I'm off to bed too. I'll help clean up in the morning, Tess."

"See you all tomorrow. You'll be over to watch the game, right?" said Brooks.

"You mean later today," Tess replied, realizing the room was wavering a little. "Yes, we wouldn't miss game day at the Bennetts'!" *Whew. That last glass of wine really did me in.* But the warmth of a perfect buzz filtered through her and she was still wide awake—thanks to her nocturnal schedule back home.

Grace tromped up the stairs to say goodbye to Brooks and the Grathwolds, and Tess turned to put a few things away.

"Hey Wilder. Don't tell me you want me to put in another chick flick. I've got a bunch of them," she teased. "We could do *The Sound of Music* or *Pride & Prejudice*. Or how about *The Ugly Truth*. That'd be perfect for you."

"No thanks." He was gathering up plates and cups and setting them on the counter. "But I don't think I'd better drive tonight. Can I crash here?"

"Definitely." Tess wandered over and poured herself another glass of wine. "I'm not ready to go to bed yet myself, but I'm not interested in another movie. Want something?"

There was a pregnant pause that had her glancing up at him when he didn't immediately reply, then he said, "A beer. Thanks."

By the time she got the beer opened, he'd settled on the floor in front of the fire, leaning back against a heavy coffee table, his feet flat on the ground. The plush cream-colored rug was inviting, and Tess sank down next to him as she handed over the beer.

"I miss having a real fire," he commented. "Mom's got a gas fireplace, but there's nothing like the smell of real wood burning."

"Feels a little weird to have one when it's so warm out, but a fire says the holidays to me," Tess replied. "And it's a little chilly down here."

She stretched out her legs with a soft groan, pointing her bare feet toward the fire. Because it was her house, she'd had the luxury of changing into yoga pants and a t-shirt, but Wilder was still in his tux. He'd taken off his coat and tie and rolled up his sleeves. The top two buttons of his shirt were undone too, showing a hint of the silver chain from his dog tags in a teasing vee of dark hair.

Tess looked away from that tantalizing sight and sipped her wine. "So basic training is done and now you're being sent to Arizona. Any chance you might end up...overseas?"

"A very good chance," he replied in that rumbly drawl. It always snaked up her spine like a delicious little stroke. "Because I've been in the National Guard since high school, I'm more likely to be deployed to a...less friendly place."

"Be safe, Johnny Wilder," she said, nudging him companionably with her elbow. She felt mellow, warm, soft... and the room was like a nice little cocoon, pressing down on her.

"I intend to." He rose and she watched him walk a little unsteadily across the room.

His hair was short, buzzed in military style, and he held himself differently too. The severe cut made him look so very serious and mature, especially with his dark brows and very square jaw. Tess drew in a shaky breath. She'd stopped thinking of Johnny Wilder as a too-young boy years ago.

Her insides fluttered a little when she remembered the one kiss they'd shared, and the subsequent years of subtle awareness between them. Or at least, the subtle awareness she had for him. Definite animal attraction on her part. But she knew better than to let herself get interested in Wilder. He got around quite a bit (which was why she always ragged on him about wearing a condom), and she had a good idea how his mind worked when it came to women. After all, they'd been discussing his so-called love life for years. The nicest term for him when it came to women was "opportunist."

And there'd been the New Year's Eve two years back when they'd both been at the annual shindig with different people. She and Wilder had somehow ended up texting each other harmless, naughty little notes from across the room. She didn't even remember how it started….

Oh, right. It was after she got up and sang "Santa Baby" with the band, vamping it up with her very best Marilyn Monroe/Madonna impression. She was in a sassy, fuchsia gown and Tess knew she had the attention of pretty much every guy in the room—except for Wilder. He had an arm slung around his date's shoulders, whispering in her ear, making her giggle. Even from the stage, she could see his fingers playing with the ends of her hair and it was kind of sexy. Okay, really sexy.

Which was why, when she returned to Bill, her date, she was surprised to find a text message on her phone. From Wilder.

Thought Billy-Bob was gonna have a heart attack when u looked @ him like that. During song. Guy's whipped.

I do my best, she wrote back, grinning at her phone. *Maybe u and Betsy should get a room.*

Been there, done that.

Hope u weren't bareback, cowboy. Gotta take care of urself. Don't be stupid. World isn't ready for ur offspring!

Never stupid. U and Billy-Joe look bored. U should get a room.
Ha. Third date. U know I don't do it on the third date.
No wonder he looks like that. Guy's messed up.

Then, a while later after she'd danced crazily with her sisters, sang another song ("I'll Be Home for Christmas") and had more champagne, she received this message:

Why don't you blow off Jim-Bob and come with me to get some more beer...or something.
What about Betsy?
What about Betsy? he replied. *Non-issue. Let's blow this place. U and me.*
Ha! You'd be so lucky!!
Just think of what we could do with ur body. And my tongue.

Even now, Tess remembered the shock of heat and vivid imagery that rushed through her when she saw that response. *Whoa.* How much had he had to drink? She wasn't sure how to respond, so she sent back a quick *LOL* after a few minutes. She didn't see Wilder after that—come to think of it, she wasn't even sure he was still at the party when he sent that last message.

But the following year—which was last year—she remembered that provocative message. Well, to be honest, she'd thought about it many times over the year. Maybe she should pursue it. She'd always found him sexy as hell. So she texted him the day after Christmas and said, *What're u doing New Year's Eve? ;-) Want to go to party w me?*

His response...the next day...was: *Sorry. Got plans.*

So that was that. A whole year of wondering, hoping, waiting...fantasizing. And he didn't come to the big party that night either. So apparently, it really had just been talk.

Now, sitting in her parents' basement in front of the fire, Tess knew any chance she might have had to test out her attraction to Johnny Wilder was gone. She was engaged to be married, and his flirtations had always been just that: spur of the moment titillation. Beer (or wine) goggles.

Which was why when he turned off the lights, her pulse

didn't even spike. She agreed with his implicit opinion: it was too late for bright lights, and the fire was beautiful.

Wilder settled back on the floor next to her. "Much better," he murmured. The firelight played over his face and warmed her toes and Tess felt soft and mellow.

"So you're doing really well on Broadway," he said, glancing at her. "That's amazing, Tess. But not really. You've always had it all: looks, talent, drive. I admire that—that you went after what you wanted."

"Thanks," she said, staring into her glass. "It's pretty wonderful. I get to do something I love to do for a living. There aren't many people who do."

"No."

"But there are times when...well, it feels...oh, I don't know...." Tess sipped, tasting the full-bodied wine thoughtfully. "I don't know." She glanced at him and saw his profile, for he stared straight into the dancing flames. A strong nose and square jaw and full, sensual lips. A small wave of regret washed over her. *I'll never kiss him again. I'll never find out...what if?* Her heart was racing.

"It feels...what?" he asked, low and gritty, still staring at the fire.

"It's going to sound silly. Or...too esoteric or pompous or something." She gave a little chuckle and bumped his foot with hers. "I've had too much wine and I'm not making any sense." She slumped down lower against the coffee table. Maybe she'd just go to sleep right here.

"You can tell me. I'd like to know what's going on in your mind, Tess Devine."

She laughed again and elbowed him this time. "Don't tease me. But, fine. Since you insist. I haven't told anyone else this because...it'll sound—oh, I don't know—ungrateful is the word."

"Can you get to the point?" Gentle exasperation filled his voice. "Just say it."

"Well, being onstage is wonderful. A dream come true. But

theater is so…superficial. And fake. Everyone's always playacting—onstage and elsewhere. And it's…cutthroat. Sometimes. At least, it feels to me. Like there's no real *purpose* for it. No benefit to mankind, no altruistic aspect. Not like—you know—joining the service. Serving your country. All I do is stand up there and help people waste a couple hours of their time."

Tess looked at him, realizing sharply that he could leave…be shipped out…and she might never see him again. He could be sent off to the Middle East, and the worst could happen.

"Nothing wrong with a little entertainment," he murmured. "Everyone needs a laugh, or a way to get their mind off maybe something bad happening in their lives. You give people an escape. That's important too."

"I told you it would sound stupid," she sighed. "And ungrateful."

"So you're getting married," he said after a short silence. His voice was so low she could hardly hear it over the snapping of the fire.

"Yes. A year from now. Maybe two, depending how quickly we can get things together. We thought it would be neat to get married on New Year's Eve. Oh, but you've met him. I forgot. At your sister's wedding last summer."

"Yep. I met him. Barry." There was a tone to his voice. "I don't think you should marry him, Tess."

"Why not? You think I'm too young?" Her short chuckle was sort of choked off because of the way she was slumped down. "I'm twenty-six. Great age to get married."

"Yeah. That's it. You're too young." He gave a short, gritty laugh and drank from his beer.

"I'm in love with you."

Tess blinked. Her whole body went still…inside and out. She dared not breathe. Had she just heard what she thought she heard? Or was it the wine and the lateness of the night and the fact that his voice was so low she could hardly discern what he was saying? She really didn't know. Her mind was swimming, her body was alive and filled with odd, rocketing sensations and she tried, *tried*, to re-imagine the moment...the words he'd muttered.

"What did you say?" she breathed after a moment.

"Hm?" He was staring into the fire.

Her heart was pounding. *Stop it. You didn't hear him right. Wishful thinking, maybe? No, Tess, every man doesn't have to fall for you. Even one you've wanted for a long time.*

And you're engaged to Barry, whom you love. Don't be stupid.

"I...nothing." She finished the last of her wine. It was time for bed. She was hearing things—things she didn't want to hear.

"Do you have any idea how intimidating you are?"

"Wh-what?" Again she rolled her head along the edge of the coffee table to look at him. She was so confused.

"Makes it hard for a guy to.... " His laugh was short and self-deprecating. "I've been trying to catch you between boyfriends for years. Every single New Year's Eve. And now you're getting married. We could have had a really good time, Tess. You and me. It would have been...*amazing.*"

Suddenly she was rigid all over. Very nearly holding her breath. Because she knew if he touched her...reached for her— maybe even looked at her—she'd be done. That'd be it. She'd be breaking her vows before she even took them. Yet she fairly quivered with anticipation and attraction.

Johnny, why didn't you tell me this before? she wanted to say. *Why did you wait till I found someone? It's too late.*

She couldn't think of any response that wouldn't sound desperate or suggestive or sharp. He was drunk. She was well past tipsy. The chemistry between them blazed.

Anything she said could lead to something she'd regret in the morning.

They sat in silence for a long time, staring at the fire. And sometime later, she fell asleep.

Chapter Nine

Present Day

WELL, THAT *went well.* Better than he'd expected.

Wilder walked away from Tess with easy strides, feeling, for the first time fully confident of himself around her. He was no longer the fumbling, intimidated young man who adored the bright and shining, unattainable star.

Christ—he snorted at himself—*did I actually think those words? Bright and shining star? Unattainable?*

"Oh there you are, John. I've been looking all over for you." His mother's voice penetrated his thoughts and pulled him right out of the depths.

"Hi Mom. Hey Rick," he added, glancing at his mother's date, then back at her. "You look great," he remembered to say, then realized it was true. His mom looked hot. Really hot. He caught Rick's eye and gave him a cool warning look. *Spanks. Christ.* Now he felt vaguely ill.

Rick grinned and affectionately jostled his date. "Your son's giving me the hairy eyeball."

"He does that sometimes," she replied, looking totally pleased with herself. "But now he's going to dance with his mother, because it's after ten already."

Wilder didn't see how he had any choice, so he handed

Laney's chardonnay to Rick and asked him to deliver it to her. Then he set his own drink down and led his mother out to the dance floor. Thank God it wasn't a fast dance; he just couldn't imagine swiveling hips in front of his mom, or, worse, watching *her* swivel hips in front of him.

"What's wrong?" she asked as soon as they embraced then moved into an easy swaying motion, his hand on her waist, hers on his shoulder.

"Nothing's wrong," he said. Then he realized that only three couples away, Tess was dancing with Brooks Bennett. Which put her directly in his line of sight. She was facing toward him at the moment, giving him an unwanted view of herself.

Usually she wore her hair down, long and full and morning-after sexy. But tonight, someone had spent a lot of time doing it up in a loose, messy style. He'd been close enough to see a myriad of tiny braids and curls and sparkling clips, all pulled together in a disordered mess of honey-bronze-platinum. Her dress tonight was the color of a rich, full-bodied red wine with a high, modest neckline that cut away to bare her shoulders like an athletic swimsuit—and, thank God, hid that sexy freckle by her throat. Her only jewelry was a wide glittering bracelet. Probably real diamonds from her dickwad husband.

"Don't lie to your mother," said his mother. "I can tell when something's wrong. You were talking to Tess Devine…. " Her voice trailed off knowingly. "Tell me what's wrong."

"Mom, there's nothing to tell." He'd shifted them around so he didn't have to look at Tess, and he actually believed those words. Over and done with. Time to move on from the Curse of Tess Devine.

"She's getting divorced, you know," his mother announced. "I just heard."

He very nearly stopped in his tracks, but suddenly aware of how closely she was scrutinizing him, he managed to hide his shock. "Oh?" *Oh shit.* Wilder suddenly felt as if the floor was falling away beneath his feet. What had he said…something about her *asshat husband*? Who was an asshat, no doubt, but still….

Maybe he wasn't as good at hiding his reaction as he thought—or maybe it was just because it was his mother, but she squeezed his shoulder. "You've had a thing for her for a long time, haven't you?"

No. Yes. How the hell did you know? "What?" seemed like the safest response.

"Well, at least you aren't denying it," she said, looking up at him shrewdly. "Maybe we're making progress."

"What are you talking about?" They'd shifted around again, and he was once more facing his New Year's Eve Curse…but this time he had a view of her long, elegant, *naked* back. On which Brooks had settled one large hand…right above her ass.

Whoa. Suddenly he could hardly swallow. It looked so damn modest from the front…until you saw it from the rear. He swore he could make out the beginning of her bottom…those two sweet indentations right above the nice sassy curve. And her hair was up, so he could see where the wide halter buttoned with three glittering garnet fasteners at the nape of her neck.

He peeled his eyes away and realized he hadn't given a damned thought to Laney since he caught a glimpse of Tess. *Frigging idiot, Wilder. How many more New Year's Eves are you going to let her fubar?*

"Oh, look—there's Harry Devine. I've been wanting to dance with him. Hi Harry," said his mom in a very loud voice as the song came to an end…and because the band was killer, they knew better than to give their audience a chance to slip from the dance floor, so they went right from "Unforgettable" into "Lady in Red" with hardly a change of chord.

"Do you mind if I claim this next dance with your father, Tess? You can dance with him any time," Mom was saying as she intercepted Mr. Devine, who was just relieving Brooks from his dance with Tess.

The next thing Wilder knew, he was facing Tess in the middle of the dance floor. *Right* in the middle, so there was no easy escape.

Her face was stony, which, could he blame her?

"Guess we're dancing," he said, trying out his signature grin, and reached for her. "And, hey, it's your song—'Lady in Red.'" He gestured to her sparkling cabernet gown.

"I wouldn't want to upset your *very sexy* date," she hissed. But her cheeks had high patches of red on them that he was pretty sure wasn't makeup.

"I'm sorry," he said. "My comment was uncalled-for."

"It certainly was," she snapped. They weren't dancing, but more like facing off in the middle of a crowd of people. Strobe lights flickered around and over them and the music was loud enough that he could hardly hear her, let alone anyone else. "My ex-husband might be an asshat, but that's beside the point. I hope you have better luck getting into your *very sexy* date's pants than you did to mine. She might fall for your lines, but I sure didn't."

With that, she turned and flounced away.

Chapter Ten

AFTER THEIR little tete-a-tete on the dance floor, Tess hadn't seen Wilder again for well over an hour…which was just fine with her. He was probably shoving his hand down his *sexy date's* dress in some dark corner. That made her doubly glad she'd never fallen for his moves.

And…. She sighed. It was almost midnight, and she hadn't found Lewis anywhere. Texts to him had gone unanswered. She guessed it would be pretty darn hard to kiss the guy if he wasn't even present, so she figured the bet was off…even though she'd pretty much decided she was going to kiss him this year. Why not?

Annabelle seemed to be missing, and Grace was in what looked like some heavy conversation with her two dates. Or maybe they weren't dates at all. For all she knew, Grace could be in the middle of some FBI stakeout and the two hotties were her team.

So neither of her sisters would notice if she kissed Lewis or not. She was off the hook. They were all off the hook.

"Where are you going, young lady?" From nowhere, a clawlike hand grabbed Tess's arm. "It's nearly midnight."

"Aunt Helen." Tess tried to keep her lack of enthusiasm from being too obvious. "I was just…going to check the coat room over here to see—"

"Don't you have a handsome young man to kiss? What

about the one you were just dancing with? *He* looks like he'd be able to take out that pansy you married, and with one blasted hand behind his back." She spoke with relish, her silvery beaded handbag dancing violently from the handle of her cane.

"Vance? Oh, he's not exactly my type. Besides, I think he and Brooks and the other cops are going to get called into work. That supposed ice storm is really happening," Tess replied, and at that moment noticed a glint on the floor near the coat room. She bent and picked up a breathtakingly lovely evening shoe. It looked almost like a glass slipper—but it was even more gorgeous than any Cinderella had ever worn. "A Louboutin," she breathed. "What on earth is this doing here? And where's the other one?"

"What's that?" Aunt Helen screeched. "A lobo-what?" She stamped her cane on the ground. "Don't know how anyone could walk in those durned things. Heel must be six inches tall!"

"Oh, but it's worth it," Tess said, slipping her foot in just to try it out. Gorgeous. And expensive. Whoever lost it would definitely be wanting it back.

But she didn't want to leave it where it might be seen—or stolen. So she slipped it behind the coat room entrance, tucking it around the corner on the floor, and turned to attend to her great-aunt who was still babbling on about something.

"What about that Wilder boy?" Aunt Helen was demanding. At the top of her lungs. Thank goodness they weren't in the ballroom, but instead were at the coat room. "You've always had a thing for him since you were serving him beer when you all were too durned young to be drinking it!"

"What?" Tess couldn't believe the old bat could remember that far back, and in such detail.

"Oh, don't think I didn't notice that, Tessy girl. I've helped solve murders, you know. I see things even Adrian Monk wouldn't notice." Aunt Helen stomped with her cane again, and her evening bag slid to the floor.

Like the well-trained niece she was, Tess stooped to pick it up and noticed it bore a marked resemblance to her own handbag…

which reminded her she'd left it on the table behind the band. "We've been friends for a long time," she said. "But it's never been anything more than that."

"Hmph." Aunt Helen clearly did not believe her, even though Tess was speaking the truth. "Seems to me, missy, you'd be better off with a man who's been in love with you for ten years than that philandering sneak you married."

Tess gaped at her. She wasn't certain which part of her comment she found more objectionable—and she certainly didn't have any idea how to respond that wouldn't get her in trouble with Mom. Just went to show that even eagle-eyed Aunt Helen was wrong sometimes.

"I'm not gonna tell you I had a chance to be married, Teresa—b'cause I didn't. I never found a man could keep up with me, or one I respected enough. Back in my day, we was told to be quiet and let the *man* make the durned decisions. Take the lead. Have the career. Pah! I wasn't ever going to let *that* happen. But a pretty girl like you shouldn't have the same trouble I did—men're different now." She wagged a crooked finger in her face, her dark eyes gleaming furiously.

"Right," Tess said, nodding, trying to keep her expression bland. *Back away slowly.* "It's almost midnight, Aunt Helen. And it looks like something's going on in there—look, Grace is up onstage. With Dad." *Oh boy.*

Tess's heart squeezed. Even with *two* dates her sister couldn't make it happen? *Poor Grace.*

"What? Where's her date? Didn't she have *two* men here with her? Can't you durned Devine girls do *anything* right?" Aunt Helen stomped off as fast as she could go with her handbag thumping against her cane.

Tess heaved a sigh of relief and turned…just in time to see Lewis Kampmueller rush through the door of the Club. He looked wild and a little mussed.

"You're…here," she said, looking at him curiously. He looked…different.

"Yeah." He seemed to be slightly addled—but that wasn't unusual for Lewis. If he wasn't coding an app in his head, he was trying to remember something he wasn't supposed to have forgotten. "Uh...."

"Just in time for midnight. I should have known you wouldn't miss it," she said grimly. She glanced around the corner and saw Grace, still onstage next to Dad. Alone.

And she looked at Lewis. "It's less than two minutes till midnight. I think you should kiss me tonight."

He looked at her, looked around, and glanced toward the ballroom, where everyone was gathered. It was noisy—boos, shouts, catcalls, and the sound of clinking glasses as the waiters distributed champagne flutes. "Uh...."

"One minute!" someone called from the next room.

"I—" Lewis began, and Tess took matters into her own hands.

This is for Grace. She stepped toward him, grabbing his upper arms—noticing they were surprisingly firm and muscular—and said, "Let's just kiss each other and be done—"

"Why break your streak now, Tess?" A drawling voice from behind had her whirling from Lewis. "After all, it's been ten years. You've never lost the bet yet."

From the next room: *Ten!*

"Oh, hi Johnny," Lewis said as casually as if they'd just run into him at the store.

Nine!

But Wilder was looking at Tess. His eyes were iron gray. Determined and cool. But his voice was still low and even. "It's time to end this curse. And the best way to end it is...the way it began."

Eight!

"Nicely," Wilder said, advancing toward her, "and neatly."

Her heart was thumping wildly and she was hardly aware when Lewis ducked away, out of sight. The only thing she was aware of was Wilder. Tall, dark, broad-shouldered, and very cool.

In control. Her knees wobbled.

Seven!

"But what about your sexy d—"

The rest of her words were cut off as he curled his hand behind her head and pulled her to him, almost lazily…almost as if he knew she wouldn't resist. Then he covered her lips hungrily, just roughly enough to let her know he was in charge.

The kiss—deep and long and slick—was enough to make her toes curl, her knees buckle, her world contract into that moment of hot, sensual onslaught. Because it wasn't gentle or tender…it was an arrogant kiss, a demanding one. A thorough one.

She opened her eyes when he pulled away and Tess realized she'd grasped Wilder by the front of his shirt and was holding on for dear life. She was breathing heavily and her lips throbbed. Her whole body was hot and shivery and alive.

"Wow," she breathed—and was amazed she even managed that.

"For the last time: Happy New Year, Tess." He brushed her cheek with a gentle finger, then turned and walked away…just as the next room erupted with the sound of "Auld Lang Syne."

"Happy New Year!"

She stared after him. *Holy crap.* What have I done?

Chapter Eleven

One o'clock in the morning.

"YOU'RE KIDDING me, right, Mom? I just navigated home in the worst ice storm Henderson's ever had and you want me to go *back* there?" Wilder was incredulous. "For a damned mink stole? What happened to worrying about me all the time? Wouldn't it worry you to send me back out in this mess?"

"You were in the Air Force in Iraq for three years," she replied mildly. "And as you've reminded me countless times, you can pilot fighter jets and navigate space shuttles. I think you can manage to drive four miles in an ice storm in an SUV."

Wilder just gaped at her. She was dressed in a fluffy pink bathrobe, holding a glass of wine. And Rick was standing behind her, in sweats and a sweatshirt. He looked very comfortable—as opposed to Wilder, who was still in his tux, sans his very sexy date, and once again alone on New Year's Eve. And he'd just driven home on a sheet of ice.

"It's a mink stole, Mom. How could you forget a *mink stole?* It'll still be there tomorrow. I'll go back first thing in the morning."

But she gave him a mutinous look. "Someone might take it. Do you know how much those things cost? And Rick gave it to me for Christmas…I've only had it for a week! I forgot it because they were rushing us out the door because the roads were getting bad."

He still couldn't believe her insistence. Why the hell didn't she send *Rick* to get it? Then he looked at the older man and realized exactly why she wanted him out of the house. And all of a sudden, he was fine with *not* being in the same building while his mom and her boyfriend were…doing whatever. *Spanks.* He shuddered. "Fine. I'll go. But if I end up in the ditch, *you're* coming to dig me out," he told her. "And don't expect me back soon. It'll take at least fifteen minutes to get there. *If* I don't go off the damned road."

He slammed out the door, leaving Rick and his mother watching in his wake.

"What if there's no one there to let him in?" Rick asked, rubbing a hand down her spine. He had that look in his eyes, and Sandra Wilder knew what that meant.

"Oh, there's someone there," she replied, smiling up at him.

He lifted an eyebrow. "Apparently there's something you're not telling me. Well, at any rate, we might want to get busy… before he returns."

She shook her head and linked her arm through his. "We have all the time in the world. He won't be back tonight."

⌒

The only good thing about being sent back out in the sleek, slippery, dark night was that Wilder had something on which to focus his mind.

Unfortunately, aside from the hair-raising drive, his thoughts weren't terribly pleasant.

First was the fact that Laney had seen him kissing Tess, which just went to prove that Tess Devine really was his New Year's Eve curse. The gift that just kept on giving. He didn't even try to explain to his date—it was moot. She had a right to be furious, and she didn't give a damn about any bet or curse or anything else.

He knew this because he got an earful *all* the way back to her house. Which took a lot longer than usual because of the weather…which made for an even more unpleasant, tense trip.

He wasn't thinking about kissing Tess, though the hot memory fought him at the edges of his mind. That was one thing he needed to keep out of his thoughts. But that didn't mean he wasn't remembering every other damn New Year's Eve she'd ruined.

Like last year. She'd emailed him, wishing him a Happy New Year. A chatty message, a hey-how're-ya-doing message. Would love to see you kind of thing. He was in Florida, at a party with a date he was sort of into, fully aware Tess was married—and it still screwed his evening because he couldn't help but *wonder*…and that fubarred his night.

When Wilder pulled into the parking lot at the Club, he wasn't surprised to find it empty. He figured that would be the case, but—wait. There was one car. And a dim light from the depths of the building.

Well, maybe he'd get the mink stole after all. At least he'd have something to keep him warm if he ended up in the ditch on the way home—a definite possibility, based on the number of 360s he'd done on the way here.

He trudged through the sleet and ice, nearly falling on his ass because he was still wearing his damned dress shoes. When he passed by the car and noticed the New York license plates, he nearly fell again because he stopped so fast.

Really? What were the chances?

Actually, pretty damn high. And not just because of the curse thing. Tess always stayed late because she arranged for the entertainment, and hung around to pay them and make sure they got packed up. But what the hell was she still doing here?

Unless…maybe she went home with someone else and left her car here. That was probably the case. But he better check anyway.

He relaxed a little and went on toward the Club, expecting to find the door locked and nobody home. Wrong. The door was unlocked and, heart beating, palms ridiculously damp, he let himself in.

Everything was silent and dark except for the faint light spilling from the back of the Club and a quiet rumbling sound. Remnants from the party littered the place because, apparently, even the staff had left early. An ice storm in Henderson was nothing to sneeze at—even though his mother thought it was a walk in the park.

Confetti, champagne flutes (empty and half-filled), chairs in disarray, hats and horns and balloons…geesh. The crew was going to have their work cut out for them when they returned tomorrow. Although it looked as if most of the food was put away. And the band, he noticed, had packed up, for the stage was empty.

Following the glow of light and the rumbling noise, Wilder headed toward the back, where the spa and lounges were…and then he recognized the sound. A bubbling hot tub.

He stopped, wary. But he had to know for certain. Years ago, there'd been that flood. Who knew if the ice storm tonight had caused the pipes to burst and there was another mess that Tess was trying to clean up. On her own.

"Hello?" he called, figuring it was best to announce himself… just in case. "Anyone here?"

He heard a splash as he approached the entrance to the spa area and hesitated. "Hello?" He peered around the corner and froze at the sight that greeted him. *Well.* That was a titillating image if he'd ever seen one.

"Wilder! What are you doing here?" Tess lowered the *gun* she'd been pointing in his direction, and set it on the edge of the hot tub next to her.

But, honestly, he hardly noticed the weapon. Instead, he was looking at her…at his accursed Tess: all flushed and glowing and damp from the hot tub bubbling and foaming around her. The fact that her shoulders were bare and her red gown was slung over a chair told him his teen-aged fantasies had come true…sort of. (A gun had never figured into them when he was seventeen.)

Her hair was still up, all different shades of golden curls and braids, just beginning to sag. He could see that fascinating freckle right next to the hollow of her throat and thought it was one of the most provocative things he'd ever seen. She wore something red and glittery at her ears, and the wide diamond cuff around her wrist…and, he was pretty sure, nothing else.

In that moment, a strange sense of inevitability settled over him.

"So…waiting for someone to join you?" he managed to say, noticing *six* champagne bottles lined up on the edge of the hot tub. Corks littered the floor and the room smelled like champagne. A single crystal flute rested next to her, filled with the sparkling, straw-colored vintage. "Brooks, maybe?" He made his voice casual and easy, but the very thought sent a shaft of deep, dark anger shooting through him. *Better get the hell out of here, Wilder.*

"Hell no," she replied. To his consternation, she seemed utterly at ease. It blew his frigging mind. "But, you know…it could've been you, Johnny Wilder." She lifted the flute in a silent toast, then drank.

"Right." The single syllable came out low and barely audible. Because by now, he was seriously thinking about getting out of his clothes and joining her. He looked away and his eyes fell on her shimmery red dress, along with an unidentifiable flesh-colored article of clothing that wasn't a bra, a sparkling handbag, and her tall, elegant gold shoes. "You going to leave those there all night?"

"There are robes here. This is the spa, you know," she said, gesturing to a fluffy one hanging over a chair on the other side. "Besides, I'm not putting those damn Spanx on again tonight— and I can't get back in my dress without them."

"Spanks?" Finally, he understood. That nude-colored thing must be some sort of undergarment. He couldn't hold back a grin. "My mom claims it takes her ten minutes to get hers on. Is that normal?"

She hooted in delight, a big belly laugh. Her nose crinkled up and her eyes lit and her beautiful, lipstick-free mouth was wide and filled with merriment. Wilder felt a wave of something sad and hot and uncomfortable rush over him…especially when she moved sharply and he caught a hint of breast bobbing beneath the rumbling water.

"I don't know what's normal, but it's a pain in the ass. I heard, though, that Beyonce wears *two* pairs," she told him, still laughing.

"So…what's with the gun?" he said, settling on the edge of the hot tub a safe distance away…but next to where her red-painted toenails occasionally bobbed to the surface. *Do not think about what else is below that water.* "And what are you doing here? Alone?"

"Grab a glass," she said, making a gesture toward the kitchen. "I'll tell you the whole sordid story. But let me start by saying: My Damned Aunt Helen!"

He vaguely remembered the iron-haired lady with the sharp fingernails and violent walking stick. In fact, he'd seen her and his mother in animated conversation shortly after midnight, just as he and an irate Laney were leaving. Something nudged the back of his mind, but he put it away for now. Much more important things at hand. Like keeping his wits about himInstead of going to get a glass, he reached for the nearest open bottle of champagne. It was empty. He started to grab the next one, but she waved him off.

"They're all empty except this one," she said, gesturing to the one beside her.

"My God, did you drink them all?" She should be loaded.

"No," she giggled. "I poured them in here. I've always wanted a champagne bath. Bubbling bubbly!"

He couldn't hold back his own laugh. "Tess…my God, you are a piece of work."

"That's what I'm told." She waved again. "There were a lot left over this year because everyone went home early—and I used the cheaper ones, not the fifty-dollar ones. Daddy won't care." She grinned cheekily. "He's just happy to have me home. I'm stuck here, so I might as well celebrate."

"Celebrate what?"

"A new life. My divorce. Leaving the stage. Doing something that *means* something—to me." She was beaming and glowing, clearly at peace with herself...and he felt something shift inside, at his core...just as it had years ago. *Ka-blam.*

Only this time he knew what it meant. That sense of kismet prickled at him. "So what are you still doing here? Are you going to tell me or what? You can never get to the point, can you?"

"Sure, but...first, what are you doing here? Why aren't you with your...*very sexy date*?" She said these last few words in a breathy, teasing whisper, then waggled her eyebrows.

"As it happens," he said, thinking even more seriously about getting out of his clothes and sliding into the hot, rumbling water, "she saw something that pissed her off quite a bit."

"Oh dear." Tess clearly tried to adopt a sober expression, but a glint of levity danced in her eyes. "Did she see you manhandling me up against the wall, kissing the shit out of me? Or was it someone else you were mauling?"

"Jesus, Tess," he breathed, "are you sure you didn't drink all those bottles of champagne?" His pulse was pounding and other parts of him, which had been more than mildly interested in the situation, rocketed to attention. *So I kissed the shit out of her, did I?*

"Well, that's what you did. Quite effectively I might add. Cheers." She lifted her glass then shook her head. "If you'd played your cards right, you might be in here" —she splashed the water with a firm hand, giving him a flash of breast— "right now."

"So," he said, thinking of the old J. Geils song "Trying Not to Think About It", "I took her home. It wasn't a very pleasant drive."

"No. I'm sure it wasn't."

"Then I got home and my mom sent me back out in this frigging mess to come and get the mink stole that she left here."

Tess raised her brows and her nose crinkled. "I didn't see any mink stoles, and I was looking all over the place...because I couldn't find my purse. That's why *I'm* here."

"Isn't that your bag over there?"

"*No*," she said with a flash of exasperation. "That's my Aunt Helen's pocketbook. That's the problem. I think she must have taken mine by mistake, because they look similar. And the old bat has bad eyesight, even though she claims she doesn't. Mine had not only my keys, but also my cell phone in it. So I couldn't call anyone to come and get me when I realized I didn't have my keys."

"But—are you telling me whoever was here at the end *left* you without walking you out to your car?" He was outraged. "Who the hell would leave a woman here alone on a night like this?"

She looked at him seriously. "I know, right?" She rolled her eyes. "It was Ringlee, the lead singer—he was hot to get home with his latest groupie, and he thought I was right behind him. I thought I was too until I got outside and realized I didn't have the right handbag. But at least I did have this." She picked up the petite gun, waving it around energetically. "Apparently, since she helped solve a murder back home in Maine, Aunt Helen fancies herself quite the detective."

"Right," he drawled. "You do know that's not a real gun."

She rolled her eyes. "Of course I do. But you didn't until you got a closer look at it, and what else was I going to do? Stuck here alone? Anyone could have come in."

"But why didn't you call from the Club's phone? Or is the line down from the ice storm?"

"No, I called…but. Well. I don't actually know anyone's cell phone numbers—they're all in my phone. The only number I know by heart is Mom and Dad's home phone. And Aunt Helen answered and all I could hear was her screeching 'What? I can't hear you! Speak up! The lines must be screwy!' I called a couple times, but the same thing happened. So I figured…I'm stranded here overnight, but at least I have champagne and food…and a hot tub."

"Right."

Her foot, its nails painted bloodred with some kind of sparkly stuff on top, slipped out of the water and settled on the edge next to him. It was an elegant foot, smooth and feminine and quite tiny in relation to his. And there was one small freckle, right at the base between the big toe and the first toe. Very unexpected. And ridiculously sexy.

Before he quite realized what he was doing, Wilder curled his fingers around that warm foot. "Ticklish?" he asked, glancing at her...and looking at the very nice calf that was now out of the water.

"Not a bit," she replied, sinking down lower so the water covered her shoulders and most of her neck. The stem of her glass was submerged in the raging water and she was watching him with those dark brown eyes...just watching.

The moment was surreal to him...something he'd fantasized about for a decade...and yet it no longer seemed so important. Or desperate. Or...earth-shattering.

It simply felt...*right*. As if some cosmic thing had happened to shift his world, his perception.

Hell. Maybe he *had* broken the damned curse. He smoothed his hand along the gentle curve of her instep, unable to keep from touching her now that he'd started. He caught up her foot, positioning it so the sole faced him and used his thumbs to massage the bottom.

"Mmm.... " she sighed, setting her glass on the edge and closing her eyes. "So what's this about a curse?"

Chapter Twelve

TESS COULDN'T remember ever being so turned on.

From the gentle buzz from the champagne to the heat of the bubbly charging up around her, dancing over her breasts and teasing her nipples, to the fact that she was completely naked and a man she'd lusted after for years was completely dressed…and massaging her foot…. She was a live wire.

What the hell did she have to do to get him to join her?

She'd had to put her glass aside for fear it would fall from her nerveless fingers. He made her mouth water and her hormones ping.

And Wilder was just sitting there, on the edge of the tub, massaging her foot, carrying on a conversation as if they'd met on the street. Still in his evening clothes, he appeared relaxed—deliciously rumpled and disordered. His white shirt had splashes on it from the hot tub and the sleeves were rolled up to expose muscular arms. He'd unbuttoned the top two buttons, revealing a vee of dark hair and the curve of his throat. He must have shaved this morning, because the stubble was already darkening the fine, square jaw.

"The curse?" He glanced over at her, his gray eyes contemplative. "You're the curse."

"Me?" That threw her for a loop. "How so?"

He released her foot and it slid back into the water as he rose and walked over to pick up her glass. Now he was standing behind her, so she had to tip her head back and look over. *Why won't he take off his damn shirt?*

He took a drink then refilled the flute from the last bottle she'd brought in here and set it back down next to her. "Has it occurred to you that for the last ten years, we've been…together, or otherwise in touch, on just about every New Year's Eve?"

She thought about that, thought about the last few years. "Well, there was that first one—when we first started the bet. When I kissed you."

"Yes." His voice was hardly more than a breath. "That was the beginning of it. Ever since then, you've totally ruined my New Year's Eves."

She nearly surged up out of the water in disbelief, but caught herself at the last minute. Even though it was getting hot in the tub, she felt a little awkward about exposing herself. This was Johnny Wilder, but this was a different Johnny Wilder than she remembered.

Different from the one who thought of her as intimidating. Who texted suggestive comments instead of whispering them in her ear.

No doubt about it: he'd changed. *Oh*, he'd changed. He'd become a man.

And she realized…*I want this man.* This gallant, brave, sensitive man who'd risked his life for his country but would kiss his mother's feet if she asked him to. Who'd been in her life…but not quite visible enough, not quite assertively enough…for ten years.

She collected her thoughts, drawing in a long, slow breath… just enough to lift the tops of her breasts from beneath the rumbling water. When she saw his eyes go right there, and his knuckles turn white, she knew there was still more than a chance.

"So, I've ruined your New Year's Eves. Want to explain further?"

"Well, there was that first one. And then the year after, we all hung out—you and me and Grat and Cara and my date and your date. And that was fine. But I remembered that kiss, you know."

"Yeah. I think you're exaggerating. How did I ruin that one particularly?"

"Well, I blame you for the fact that I haven't gotten laid on New Year's Eve for ten years. Including that one. At the time, I didn't know it was because of the Curse of Tess Devine, but now in retrospect…. And then the year after," he said, raising his voice to be heard over her protests, "we were here all night—remember? With the flood? I sent Kaylie Schwartz and her 34 double-Ds home alone and came in to help you. You blew my mind that night, you know—out here in your evening gown and boots. You could've been home in bed…but you were here. Working."

"Of course I remember. That was…that was one of my fondest memories. And you were here too, of your own volition. And you know…I almost kissed you that night. When you dropped me off at home? I was just about to lean in, then I thought…no. He's not interested. He's dating Kaylie. And I was afraid I'd ruin our friendship—which I really did enjoy."

The look of consternation on his face was a balm to the fact that she'd just made that confession. "Well, that sucks. Because I was trying to work up the nerve to do the same thing." He sat on the edge of the tub, looking down at her, his feet on the floor.

"What about the year I asked *you* out? How could I have ruined your night?" she demanded, her mouth suddenly dry. His hand was right there, propped on the edge next to her, showing off a strong, sturdy wrist and muscled arm. "You blew me off."

He nodded. "Yeah. I just didn't want to see you, Tess. It was too difficult…especially since you never seemed to respond to my overtures."

"Your texting overtures? Really? You were totally drunk that night—you probably don't even remember what you said to me. How was I supposed to take you seriously? Or the year… the night…you know," she felt her cheeks warm. "The night you stayed at my parents' house. You were smashed. You were saying all sorts of things…you probably don't remember any of it. And it's just as well I didn't fall for it. I know you were just trying to get in my pants. It's what you do. You're an opportunist. I know that about you." Which was why she really couldn't believe anything he said. "You were going off to the service, I was getting married—it was a last-ditch effort. But I knew that." *I wanted to believe you, but I knew better.*

"Tess," he said, his voice a low, careful drawl. "I remember everything I've ever said to you. Or texted you." His gray eyes held hers and she suddenly couldn't breathe—his gaze was deep and intense and hot. Something deep inside her quivered, sharp and hard. "And I meant it."

Then he quirked a cocky grin, his eyelids sliding half closed, his voice dropping even lower. "Trust me, if I'd *just* been trying to get in your pants…I would have."

Tess looked up at him, aware of all sorts of crystalline pieces settling into place in the back of her mind. "The problem is," she managed to say, even though her heart was racing and her pulse had spiked and she felt as if she were about to make some great reveal, "I know you too well…I know how you are with women. I know better. And it's okay. So why don't you climb on in here with me and let's see how *amazing* we could be together. It's been ten years…let's finish it."

His eyes glittered. "Not interested in that, Tess. I might have been once, but not anymore."

Her lungs seized up, tightened, and she couldn't breathe. Her vision turned dark with mortification. Her lips formed a half-smile that she tried to make cool and collected, but inside she was reeling. "All right then," she managed. "Consider the curse broken."

"You don't understand. I'm in love with you, Tess." He said it in that low, sexy drawl.

But he was looking at her, and the words were clear—and this time she knew she'd heard it correctly. But he repeated it, taking her hand and putting it to his chest where his heart thumped madly. "I'm *in love with you*. But I'm no longer intimidated by you. I'm no longer afraid to say it. Being at war changes a man. You learn what's important and to go after what you want—no settling for second best. For leftovers or after thoughts. And so… if I climb in that tub…I expect to spend every New Year with you for the rest of our lives."

"Then what," she said, reaching for his shirt, "the *hell* are you still doing up…there?" And she pulled him toward her, down to kiss her—and he came easily—and then, in a long, slow movement, down into the water.

When their lips parted, damp and hot from the steamy water, she looked into his eyes. "So can you stop calling me your curse now?" she asked, sliding her hand down along a very solid belly to the very interesting package behind his zipper. *Oh yes.* She grinned, exploring behind his wet trousers.

He sighed, the cords of his neck tightening as she found him and cupped him with her fingers. "Right," Wilder said, dipping his mouth to nuzzle a spot right next to the hollow of her throat. "My curse…and my blessing. Happy New Year, Tess."

"Happy New Year, my love."

Read how Tess Devine's spunky Aunt Helen
helps solve a murder in Colleen Gleason's
modern gothic romantic suspense
The Cards of Life and Death.

Available wherever
books are sold.

Annabelle

Dedicated with love to
Harry & Jody Ford
One of the world's great romantic couples.

The Keeper of the Debutantes

Chapter One

New Year's Eve - Noon

"SO HOW MANY laws are we about to break?"

Duncan James couldn't help but smile. Sitting shotgun in his best friend Brooks Bennett's police cruiser, he'd been mulling over that question himself ever since they'd pulled off the road, lying in wait for the target of their bet. He glanced over at Brooks's long, lanky frame comfortable in the police uniform after six years on the job. "Why are you asking me?" Duncan said. "You're the cop."

"And you're the lawyer." Brooks folded his arms over his chest, turned his head and allowed a broad and engaging grin to expand under his mirrored sunglasses and short cropped curly bronze hair. He chomped on his gum a few times before admitting, "Nah, we're in the clear. Mr. Devine gave us his blessing. He knows darn well his baby Annabelle needs to slow herself down a peg on these back roads. You met Harry Devine about a month ago at the Club, remember? Same night we arranged this bet."

"And I'm looking forward to meeting his baby Annabelle who has curled you and Vance around her little finger. This is going to be like taking candy from a baby. And I'm talking about you and Vance, not Miss Devine."

"You, my fancy friend, are about to meet your comeuppance."

Duncan shook his head and glanced out at the pine trees surrounding them. His golden eyes narrowed at the artfully tousled hairstyle he saw reflected in the side-view mirror. He supposed he was fancy compared to his buddies. Neither of them would ever spend any real money on a haircut or shoes or be caught dead wearing a cashmere coat. But this entire week between Christmas and New Year's had been unseasonably cold for North Carolina and he wanted to look official without actually impersonating an officer. "It just can't be that hard to give a woman a speeding ticket. Seriously. I know you've said she's a hottie and all. But it's your job to give tickets. And between you and Vance, you've stopped this woman how many times?"

"Well it's not that easy when you've known the girl all your life. Maybe it will be easier for you."

"Damn right it's gonna be easier for me. I don't care how hot she is, or if she pouts her lips and claims she's racing home to a dying relative. This Annabelle Devine is going down. And you and Vance will be paying my bar tabs for all of next year."

Brooks's grumbled curse was cut off by the hearty sound of Vance's voice coming over the police scanner. "Just spotted Baby D looping around the exit ramp off 85 revving her engines and heading for home."

"Affirmative," Brooks responded. Then he threw a mischievous grin at Duncan. "Buckle up. It's show time," he said as he started the cruiser. They waited patiently until the custom-made, wide-bodied, motor roaring, fire-engine red Camaro flew by.

"Holy shit," Duncan whispered.

Brooks pulled out in hot pursuit, spraying gravel as his tires fought for purchase. "What kind of a woman drives a car like that?" Duncan breathed. He tightened his seatbelt as Brooks hit the siren and they began to gain speed. The Camaro was nothing but an elusive red dot at the end of Duncan's vision. "How the hell are we going to catch her?"

"We'll catch her. Eventually. I know where she lives." Brooks punched the gas pedal.

Duncan was thrown back in his seat, but he kept his eyes trained on the dot on the horizon. "How fast is she going?" He glanced over at the speedometer. "Holy hell, how fast are *we* going?"

"Just sit back and enjoy the ride."

It took a good ninety seconds for the cruiser to start gaining ground. The brief flash of brake lights and gradual slow-down indicated when the driver realized they were behind her. Eventually, a pale, slender arm ventured out the window, waving them around.

"Does she think you're heading to an emergency? Not pulling her over?'

"She knows I'm pulling her over."

"Ah. Her tactics already at work, I see."

Eventually the muscle-bound Camaro slowed to a stop and they pulled up behind it on the shoulder of the road. Duncan could not take his eyes off the souped-up machine and imagined the driver with tattoos and body piercings, dyed black hair and skull and crossbones jewelry. None of which he found particularly hot. This was going to be a cakewalk.

Brooks threw the car into park and said, "Okay Dunc, you're on. The bet is you have to give Annabelle a full-blown speeding ticket. No letting her off with just a warning to make yourself her hero. If you manage that, we pick up your bar tab anytime we're together over the next year."

"Here and in Raleigh," Duncan clarified.

"Here and Raleigh." Brooks nodded. "In addition, if she meets Vance at the courthouse and actually pays this fake ticket, whatever money changes hands you get to keep."

Imagining how the scene was going to play out, Duncan nodded, cleared his throat and reached for the door handle. Then he stopped. "Give me your glasses." Brooks handed them over and Duncan exited the car in one graceful move. He donned the mirrored shades, turned up the collar of his coat and pulled a pair of black leather gloves out of his pocket. He squared his shoulders and applied his gloves like he was strapping on a gun belt and heading for a showdown.

As he approached, a flurry of activity caught his attention through the Camaro's rear window. *What the hell is she doing? Brushing her hair? Putting on lipstick?* As if he were going to fall prey to her heavily mascaraed feminine wiles. Even if body piercings were his thing, he had a bet to win. A very simple bet. All he had to do was give the speed demon a ticket. In his mind, he was already regaling their fraternity brothers at NC State's next Homecoming about besting Brooks and Vance.

Duncan rapped his knuckles on the driver's side window like he'd done this a million times. When the electric window slid down, he put both his gloved hands on the sill of the door and leaned down to get a good look at the driver.

"Danica Patrick, I presume?"

Annabelle Devine's endorsement-ready smile broke wide as she tossed the curling ends of her *Pretty Woman* mass of red hair over one shoulder. Her spontaneous laugh drew Duncan in, and when she pulled off her designer shades, her bright brown eyes and fresh-faced beauty shocked the hell out of him. Where was the nose ring? She was nothing like he'd pictured.

"And you must be Officer Friendly," she drawled.

Quick-witted too!

An unbidden grin crept to life as Duncan leaned in a little closer. "Good a name as any, I suppose," he said, his brain starting to panic. He'd planned to play Bad Cop, but suddenly he found he didn't have it in him. His libido argued that Officer Friendly could give tickets too. "Do you have any idea how fast you were going?"

Annabelle placed one manicured hand over his right glove. "Now, Officer. My daddy is waitin' on me at home just up the road not five minutes from here. And if you'll indulge me, I'll tell you that he and Mother throw a big New Year's Eve ball every year at the Country Club and he relies on me to help him oversee the set-up. Mother can get a little over-zealous with the decor, making it just a teensy bit gaudy, if you know what I mean. Daddy relies on me to be the go-between. I'm sure you can understand. If I'm able to play my part, the entire family arrives at the ball in a good mood and there are no awkward moments for our guests. Now," she said, tilting her head and batting her long, long lashes, "I know you don't want me to be late and disappoint my daddy."

Duncan found her Southern accent charming. And her evasive maneuvers entertaining.

"Miss Devine." When the sparkle in her eyes shifted from amusement to curiosity, he said, "Yes, I know your name. In fact, you've become rather infamous. So infamous that it might be more appropriate to call me *Special Agent* Friendly, because I've been called in to make sure the Henderson Police Department ends the year on a high note."

"Excuse me?"

"You seem to have friends in high places, Miss Devine. And although you've been pulled over on this very road many times during the last twelve months, you've never actually been given a speeding ticket. Isn't this true?"

Annabelle patted his gloved hand. "Oh, you misunderstand, I'm sure. I may have been stopped by Lieutenant Evans or Lieutenant Bennett once or twice, but that wasn't about speeding tickets. That was about catching up."

"Catching up?"

"You know how it is in a small town," she went on. "I live an hour away in Raleigh now, but I was born and raised in Henderson, just like Lieutenants Evans and Bennett. In fact, they are both my sister Tess's age. Do you know either of my sisters, Special Agent Friendly?"

Duncan chuckled at the name. "I don't believe I've had the pleasure."

"Well, I'd be happy to introduce you. Vance and Brooks like to pull me over whenever I'm coming to town so they can hear all about what my sisters are doing. My life isn't very exciting, as you can probably tell, but Tess and Grace are living fabulously exciting lives. Tess is an actress on Broadway. I mean who-the-heck in Henderson has ever done that? And Grace, well she works for the FBI and I'd tell you more but then…you know…"

"You'd have to kill me."

"Exactly," she grinned, tapping his hand again. "I like you, Special Agent Friendly. Seems to me you'd know how to have a good time."

And he was more than certain that the very quick and clever third Devine sister knew how to have a very good time. "I'll take that as a compliment."

"Please do. So you see, I may have been stopped a couple of times, but it was all very social. No tickets needed."

"Are you telling me this is the one and only time, all year, you've flown down this road in this fine piece of machinery and created a sonic boom?"

Annabelle sighed deeply and looked around the interior of her car, caressing the leather of the steering wheel. "She is a beauty, isn't she?" she asked, returning her gaze to Duncan's face.

Duncan couldn't help it. He stared directly into Annabelle's eyes and told the truth. "Never seen anything prettier."

Annabelle ducked her head shyly and bit her lip. With her pale skin, rosy cheeks, pearl stud earrings and rose-scented perfume, she was the epitome of lady-like grace. Duncan felt the urge to pull off his glove and tangle his hand in all that red hair. From there, it was easy to imagine tilting her head and bringing her lips up to meet his.

Whoa. Head in the game, man.

A bit of panic floated around his chest. With thoughts like that this bet was going to go south on him fast. He looked back toward Brooks in an effort to fight the distraction caused by the dichotomy of the seriously pimped-out muscle car and the elegant, astute Southern belle sitting behind the wheel.

He cleared his throat, stood up straight and got back to business. "Your seat belt is fastened," he noted. "The car is obviously in good condition. Is there any sort of emergency I need to know about?"

Annabelle stuttered. "You mean…other than my daddy?"

"License and registration, please."

"Seriously?" Annabelle had the audacity to look appalled.

"Miss Devine. It's noon. Your father's party starts at what time? Eight o'clock? I'm afraid that does not constitute an emergency."

He loved how she hesitated just a moment before leaning over and opening her glove compartment. Clearly, capitulating was not sitting well with her. He almost had to smile, deducing she was too well-brought-up to put up much more of a fight when she was so clearly in the wrong. He watched the cascade of red hair fall over her shoulder and how she tucked it behind her ear as she daintily handed him a small leather portfolio. She glanced up at him briefly, then back to the portfolio. "Everything should be in order."

"Thank you. I'm going to put your information into our computer to see just how many social chats you've had over the last year."

"Is this really necessary?" she asked meekly. Obviously, the fear of a big fat speeding ticket was finally seeping in.

"Just sit tight. I'll be back in a couple of minutes and get you on your way to Daddy."

With a distraught little pout, Annabelle said in a small voice, "I appreciate that, Officer."

Duncan's heart twisted. He'd never felt more like a bully. He tapped her portfolio against his other glove. Standing there. On the brink. Teetering.

The only sound registering was that of his heart pounding in his ears.

Finally, he turned toward Brooks and the patrol car, issuing orders to his legs. *Right, left, right, left...that's it. Keep going. All the way back to safety.* He didn't trust himself around pretty pouty baby Annabelle for one more minute. He opened the door and launched himself inside.

"How'd it go?" Brooks asked.

Duncan turned his entire body to face his so-called friend.

"You have got to be kidding me!" he launched. "Hot? A hottie? That's how you describe a *work of art?*"

"A work of what?"

"You're an idiot, you know that? You and Vance. You two had me thinking Annabelle Devine was a—I don't know…the kind of girl Vance likes to pick up late at night at Spanky's. That girl," he said pointing out the windshield. "That girl is drop-dead gorgeous. The quintessential Southern belle. She's charming, she's witty…my God, she's just as well-bred as she can be, physically, socially and mentally."

Brooks started to talk but choked on his own words as he heard the last part of Duncan's tirade. Sputtering, he coughed out, "What the hell did you just say?"

"She's the one. She's the one I'm going to marry."

The two men just stared at each other. Duncan pissed off, and Brooks looking like he'd swallowed a lizard.

Finally Duncan broke the silence. "How much is the ticket?"

Brooks's mouth just opened and closed under wide, stunned eyes.

"The fine, you son-of-a-bitch. What's the fine for traveling at the speed of light?"

"Three hundred dollars."

Duncan moved his head rapidly in a set of short nods. "Give me the ticket book." As he took it, he glanced out the windshield to find Annabelle climbing out of her vehicle and heading toward them. It was December 31, colder than should ever be allowed in North Carolina, and his future bride was dressed in a tiny slip of white material that barely covered her torso, much less her arms and legs.

Duncan looked over at Brooks with a roll of his eyes. "Been nice if you had told me she was insane." He leapt out of the squad car and rushed forward, taking his coat off as quickly as possible.

"I know it gets hot in those race cars, Danica," he joked as he reached her at the halfway mark, "but it's twenty-eight degrees out here in this crazy cold snap and you're dressed for a summer wedding." He flung his coat behind her and then brought it up over each of her bare shoulders. Grabbing a lapel in each hand, he pulled them together to securely wrap her killer body inside the warmth of the thin, soft cashmere. He knew it was a killer body because she'd stumbled forward as he wrapped her up, landing firmly against him from chest to thigh. His higher brain congratulated him on his dumb luck. He could not have planned this any better. His legs were slightly apart and her pale pink heels nestled right in between his loafers. Instinctively his arms went around her and rubbed up and down her back, trying to warm her as they stood together in the elements.

Appearing a bit flustered, Annabelle looked down at the lack of space between them and then up into his eyes. He was all of six feet, but the look she gave him made him feel a helluva lot taller. "I know I look ridiculous, but there is an explanation," she whispered.

"There is? I'd love to hear it. First, let's get you back into your car. You can roll down the window a couple of inches and tell me."

Now Duncan stood outside without a coat, but at least he had on a sweater, button-down and wool pants. He crossed his arms over his chest and shuffled from foot to foot. Annabelle turned on her car, cranked up the heat, then rolled down her window and passed his coat back to him. He quickly put it back on.

"You warm enough in there? Roll the window back up. Just leave it open a crack so I can hear you." She did as she was told.

"I just came from a photo shoot for work," she explained, her chin slanted up so her voice would carry out of the car. "We had to wear white."

Duncan shook his head like he was trying to clear cobwebs. "And that explains the lack of a coat, hat, gloves and scarf how?"

"Well, clearly I was not anticipating stopping between there and my parents' house."

"Clearly." Duncan took a deep breath. "Okay, Miss Devine—"

"Please, call me Annabelle. That was awfully nice of you to

lend me your coat." Annabelle glanced down at her lap, and after a moment turned her head to the side and smiled at him. "Sort of makes you an officer *and* a gentleman."

Duncan's heart skipped two beats. "My pleasure…Annabelle."

There was a moment then. A long, slow, moment that Duncan would reflect back on in private. A moment when the weather and the car and the bet with his buddies all evaporated and nothing was left except the two of them, smiling at one another. Everything went blank. So when the thought entered his head, it came like the roar of thunder.

I've found you.

Annabelle broke the spell first, shyly glancing down and then back up. "Is that Brooks Bennett in the car with you? I think if we could just get him involved, he may be able to help sort all this out."

"Brooks?" Duncan leaned down as close as he could to the window. He lowered his voice indicating the game had changed. "Brooks can't help you now, darling. This is between you and me."

Annabelle's eyes went wide.

Duncan stood and whipped out the ticket book he'd shoved into his coat pocket. He flipped it open and wrote her name. "Let's make this as quick and painless for you as possible. Like ripping off a Band-Aid. Being as it's December 31, and I know the city of Henderson would love to have your money in their coffers before they close the books out for the year, if you pay your fine in cash at City Hall before they close today, Lieutenant Bennett and I will arrange for there to be no court date or any reporting back to your insurance company. No points on your record either. As a courtesy. For helping out the city. It can't get much cleaner than that."

Annabelle angled her pretty little head at him and rolled her eyes. "A courtesy. For helping out the city." She sighed and checked her watch. "The bank should still be open. How much is the ticket?"

"Three hundred dollars." He slid the ticket through the

opening in the window.

"Three hundred dollars? You've got to be kidding me. For three hundred dollars you should be giving me a police escort to and from City Hall."

"That can be arranged."

Annabelle held the ticket in front of her, saying under her breath, "For this kind of money I could have bought myself an escort for the party tonight." And then her head shot up and she paused for a second before turning toward him, eyes determined. She lowered the window halfway. "Look. I am not going to be the one stuck kissing Lewis Kampmueller!"

"What do you have against—"

"I'll pay your ridiculous ticket, in cash, before five o'clock under one condition. You be my date tonight."

"Tonight?" Duncan took a step back from the car and rubbed a gloved hand over his chin. *Be cool. Do not blow this.* "Annabelle Devine. Do I look like the kind of guy who doesn't have a date lined up for New Year's Eve?"

"Well, do you?" she challenged. "Frankly, I don't care. If this little fiasco is costing me three hundred dollars, I'm going to get my money's worth. You're Officer Friendly, you have a duty to serve and protect. Break your date. I have to be there early, so meet me at the Henderson Country Club at eight. I want full service in return for my cooperation with these shenanigans. It all sounds very fishy to me. "

"Well now," Duncan said, dropping his voice and making it full of promise, "Officer Friendly, at your service. Pay your fine before the close of business today and I'll provide as much service as you can handle."

Annabelle sucked in a breath and blinked several times.

Duncan turned and walked away. Grinning.

He heard her window slide down further and then Annabelle shouting, "Don't you want to know the address?"

He continued to walk toward the squad car. "I'm a cop. With an iPhone. I'll find it."

"Do you own a tux?" she shouted back.

That stopped him in his tracks. He turned around slowly, incredulous. "What? Do I look like I was born in a barn?" That had her smiling, waving him off and turning around to fasten her seat belt.

Duncan headed back to Brooks and the squad car. That, he thought, had gone very, very well. He slid into the passenger seat and asked Brooks, "How fast can this thing get us to Raleigh and back?"

"Why? What the hell is going on?"

"I need to pick up my tux."

Brooks broke into a broad grin as he started the car and spun out on two wheels, turning them around. "So. The Keeper of the Debutantes, huh?" He glanced at Duncan, then shook his head. "Man, I did not see that coming."

Chapter Two
——ᧈ

ANNABELLE MADE sure to drive the speed limit the rest of the way home. The thought of dishing out three hundred dollars on the heels of her Christmas bills sat heavy in her stomach like that god-awful fruitcake Aunt Helen forced her to eat last weekend. She pulled into the large circular driveway of her family home—an impressive red brick, white-trimmed and black shuttered two-story colonial with a wing off each side. Standing atop the brick landing just outside the opened front door was her entire family.

Brooks must have called them.

Her father, Harry Devine, stood a head taller than the women surrounding him. His dark hair had started to fade into a distinguished gray, but his handsome features kept him looking like a man too young to have so many grown daughters. His sharp eyes of deep, dark brown were the origin of the Devine Brown-Eyed Girls, for he had passed them on to each of his three daughters. He was gregarious and kind-hearted, and had more fun at his annual New Year's Eve party than anyone because he loved to dance—and he was good at it. Every woman invited wanted to dance with him.

Her mother, Jody, stood waving Annabelle in, petite and pretty as always. Honey blonde like Tess, but with sea blue eyes which all her daughters envied. Her ever-present three carat diamond studs glistened in the sunlight.

On either side of her mother stood the two best big sisters

a girl could have. She was so proud of Tess and her famous Broadway voice that she could easily overlook the whole bossing around thing she would inevitably do. At least for a few days. And Grace, their superstar athlete, was the best keeper of secrets and hardly ever pinged Annabelle on her head while she was reading anymore.

Annabelle had to laugh in spite of herself as they all started jeering and applauding the moment they saw her. It was like doing the walk of shame in her car. She had to drive by them all before reaching the paved pull-off where she parked. She took a deep breath and sighed heavily before getting out to face the music.

She held up her hands in surrender. "I know, I know. Wow, good news must really travel fast." She managed to smooth the sides of her short shift before Grace, who had bounded down the steps laughing, wrapped her up in a big bear hug.

"Oh, it's a big day when the law finally catches up to my baby sister," Grace said, turning them both toward the rest of the family. She kept an arm firmly around Annabelle's waist as they walked. "Finally you weren't able to flirt your way out of a ticket. Henderson's finest must be upping their game."

"Well, I suppose an FBI agent would think so." Annabelle stopped short. "You didn't set this up, did you?"

Grace laughed, her light brown bangs falling into her eyes. She tucked them back and started walking. "Never," she vowed. "Blood is thicker than water, after all. I've always got your back."

"Just like I'll always sing your praises," Tess added, as the girls approached the rest of the family.

Annabelle squealed and threw her arms around Tess in a tight embrace. "Well, if you're the one doing the singing, at least it will sound good," she said into her sister's neck. They parted slightly so each one could look at the other. "I'm so glad you were able to get home. Grace and I missed you over Christmas and the New Year's Eve ball would be absolutely no fun without you."

"You mean there wouldn't be as much fodder for the gossip mill if I didn't show my face."

"Not at all," Annabelle replied sincerely. "You're Henderson's shining star. Our golden girl. And you're gonna find everyone standing solidly in your corner as the news of your divorce breaks." Annabelle could see the doubt in her sister's eyes, along with lingering hurt and regret. She leaned in and kissed her cheek. "Trust me on this. All is well. You'll see." And then she stepped back and with a victorious grin said, "Besides, since I won't be the one Lewis Kampmueller gets to slobber all over at midnight, I'm sure Grace appreciates you offering some competition."

"What?" Grace shouted.

"I thought you weren't bringing anyone from Raleigh," said Jody.

Annabelle's eyes shifted quickly to her dad, then she threw an arm over her mother's shoulders to usher her inside. "Well...there seems to be a silver lining to this whole speeding ticket debacle. Apparently, for three hundred dollars, I am not only helping out the city of Henderson, but I've hired myself an escort as well."

"Holy hell," her father muttered.

Ignoring that, Annabelle stepped over the threshold saying, "Somebody pour me a cocktail and I'll tell you all about it."

Grace and Tess took a look at each other and burst out laughing. "Oh, this is gonna be good."

———🌑———

Later, when all the catching up was done between the sisters and their mother, and each of them had shuffled off to take care of various errands before the party, Annabelle found her father in his library watching a football game. "Which bowl is this?" she asked, coming in and sitting down on the leather ottoman in front of him.

"The Nissan-Hair Remedy For Men.com-Fly Your Bags for Free or some such nonsense, Bowl. I swear to God. Give me the Rose or the Sugar or even the Fiesta Bowl. But all this sponsorship stuff can make a fan nutty."

"I hear ya. Who do you have in the Orange Bowl?'

"I took West Virginia and the points." Annabelle turned toward him in shock. "Don't look at me like that. I may be Tar Heel born and Tar Heel bred and on and on until I'm dead," he said, making a mockery of the Carolina fight song, "but my money has no allegiance whatsoever."

Annabelle turned back to the TV. "I hear that," she mumbled.

Her dad sprang forward, putting a hand on her shoulder. "What? You didn't take Carolina either?"

She turned and gave him a withering look. "Between you and me, it's a total fluke that they won the ACC. The Mountaineers are going to roll all over them." She turned back to the TV. "And it's gonna hurt."

"I hear that."

They watched a few uneventful plays in silence.

Annabelle finally glanced at her watch. "Do I need to …"

"All taken care of, sugar bee."

She turned her head and asked, "You talk to Brooks or Vance?"

"Vance. He was on his way to City Hall to wait for you. Apparently Brooks had to make an urgent run to Raleigh." That got a smile out of Annabelle. Her father went on. "I told Vance we'd settle up tonight." She nodded at that. Then she got up and came over to kiss her father's cheek.

"Thanks for setting all that up for me, Daddy. You were right. I think I just might like this Officer Friendly."

Her father grabbed her hand as she started to walk away. "His name is Duncan James, sugar bee. And it wasn't long after I met the boy that I thought he might be perfect for my Annabelle. After all, I know just how picky you are. He's got good manners, a firm handshake and solid eye contact. Word is he works hard, but is no stick in the mud. He lives in Raleigh so he can go home to his own damn place after a date. And although he made the poor decision to go to NC State, we won't hold that against him because he got his law degree at Carolina."

Annabelle laughed.

"You go have fun tonight and see what you think." Annabelle nodded and started to walk away. "Gotta be better than swapping spit with old Lewis Kampmueller."

"I hear that," she heartily agreed.

Chapter Three

ON THE OUTSKIRTS of Henderson stood a long and dreary ranch-style house that would only be called a fixer-upper by an optimist. Good thing Brooks Bennett had his share of optimism in spades, because he'd been its proud owner for six months now. Time enough for him to pull down all the wallboard and strip the thing to its studs, opening the kitchen, dining and living room areas to make one big great room. New wallboard was now up, taped, sanded and ready for paint. But all his furniture was crammed into one of the three bedrooms down the hall. The place was clean for a construction site and had a working refrigerator filled with beer—which seemed to be the only requirement for the four men who made do by sitting in three beach chairs and on top of a cooler right in the middle of Brooks's new great room.

"No problem," said Lewis. "Staying with your parents will be a heck of a sight better than this dump. Duncan is welcome to it."

"I appreciate it," Duncan said, popping open a can of beer and handing it over to Brooks before he sat back down on the cooler. "I hate to bust in on this bromance the two of you've got going. I know you don't get to town much these days, Lewis, with all your app inventions and technological leaps and bounds."

Brooks took a sip of beer and then pointed it at Lewis. "You don't know the half of it. He's got something so big in the works right now he's not even telling me about it."

"Not even telling your significant other, Lewis?" Vance Evans goaded. "That's harsh."

"Not as harsh as what the three of you pulled on Annabelle Devine," Lewis said through a laugh. "Explain to me again how a bogus three hundred dollar speeding ticket managed to get Duncan a date with the Keeper of the Debutantes."

"Yeah," Vance said, "because if three hundred dollars was all it took to snag a date with one of the Devine sisters, you would have worked that angle long ago."

"Damn straight," Lewis muttered before taking a swing of beer.

They were a sight, the four of them, Duncan surmised. Him sitting here in his casual business attire and expensive shoes. Vance and Brooks still in their uniforms, stretching their long, lanky, baseball-playing frames out in the beach chairs (clearly they'd done this a time or two)—and Lewis, the one who could buy and sell each of them a dozen times over wearing only a tattered t-shirt and jeans. Didn't anybody dress for the weather around here?

"What have the Devine sisters got against you, Lewis? I heard Annabelle say something about you this afternoon when she was all whipped-up into a frenzy."

"Yeah, what do they have against you?" Brooks teased. He and Vance bumped beer cans and laughed.

"Oh," Duncan apologized. "Sore subject, I see. Sorry I brought it up."

"No," Lewis held up his hand, nodding his head. "It's all right. I feel the wind of change coming, my boys, and tonight is going to be the night."

"The night for what, exactly?" Vance demanded.

"Tonight is the night I'm not only kissing Grace at midnight, I'm also going to tell her exactly how I feel."

The deafening silence that ensued declared Lewis's plan a bad idea.

"For ten years I've been the brunt of their game. And maybe I contributed to it all along," Lewis admitted.

"You think?" Brooks joked.

"But I'm twenty-nine now. I have my own company, a respectable degree of success, and it's time to make a stand. Those girls and I are too old for teenage games, and it's time Miss Gracie Devine put up or shut up. I'm going to make the woman mine… or die trying."

Unwilling to let the poor guy drown in silence again, Duncan spoke up. "Good for you, Lewis." Which encouraged Vance and Brooks to chime in with an "Absolutely" and an "Atta-boy."

"You know, Lewis," said Brooks, "there *are* other women. Other than the Devine sisters, I mean. While you're all manned-up and throwing your weight around tonight, take a look around you. You might have overlooked a pretty young thing you've been missing out on all these years."

"I've had eyes for Grace for so long, I can't even remember when I didn't."

"I hear you. But you and she don't even live in the same state anymore. And you see each other one time a year, at this party. What kind of relationship are you expecting?"

Lewis tossed his arms out in exasperation. "I just want the girl to kiss me, Brooks. Just one time, I want her to kiss me like she means it. That's my goal for the night. Been my goal all year now. If I manage to achieve that goal, I'll just have to figure out the rest."

Brooks nodded his head. "Fair enough."

"So," Duncan asked, in an effort to get Lewis off the hook as well as to satisfy his own curiosity, "tell me more about this Keeper of the Debutantes. Why do you call Annabelle that?"

"Oh, *we* don't just call her that," Vance said flinging his hand around to indicate the group.

"Everyone calls her that," Brooks added.

"It's who she is," Lewis explained. "You see, Annabelle has a lot of interests."

"Yeah, like ballroom dancing and etiquette classes," Vance said as he reached into a bag of Cheetos. "Which fork goes with what course—"

"Thank you notes and penmanship—"

"Proper attire, flowers, social teas, and charity events. She takes after her old Great-Aunt Helen in that regard."

Duncan swore he saw them all shudder at the mention of Great-Aunt Helen.

"Don't worry," Brooks said. "She's actually nothing like her great-aunt. She just appreciates all the old-school ways. Back when Tess made her debut in Raleigh, Annabelle—who is five years younger—took great interest and became an expert on what and who our Henderson debs needed to know. She coached the other debutantes from Henderson right along with Tess. And the powers that be in our little town—"

"Meaning the old biddies who give a rat's ass about that kind of stuff," Vance threw in.

"—asked Annabelle to help out the following year. Eventually, it was Annabelle who met with the debutantes' mothers and oversaw all the party-planning, gown-picking and whatever the hell else goes on with all that."

"She was good at it too," Lewis insisted. "I mean, we all clearly hated the re-establishment of cotillion classes. And since we were over the normal age of all that nonsense, they had special classes for us teens back then. But, the debutante parties went from stale to rip-roaring. It's amazing what kind of behavior you can get away with on the dance floor as long as your manners at the dinner table are impeccable."

"And you're dressed appropriately," Vance added.

"And you've flirted with a few of the wallflowers, along with their mothers, sisters and great-aunts," Brooks finished.

"We all learned something when the Keeper of the Debs was created," Lewis went on. "There is not a man in this town who doesn't know how to tie a bow tie, or dress for a five o'clock wedding. Annabelle upgraded the status of Henderson's social elite in the eyes of Raleigh's blue bloods, and at the same time the town became known for their swinging parties."

"Like the one you've wheedled your way into tonight."

Brooks smiled at Duncan. "The Devine-Kampmueller New Year's Eve Ball is always kickin' ass and taking names."

"So all these years you all have been holding out on me."

Brooks leaned back and took a long swig of his beer. To Duncan it looked like he was hiding a laugh. "Timing is everything," Brooks finally said. "And I'm thinking the time's just about right."

⌐2⌐

Those words rang inside Duncan's head when he got his first glimpse of Annabelle that night.

He stood in the cold, outside on the grand porch of Henderson Country Club. He was purposely early. He thought it would be prudent to re-introduce himself to Annabelle without a large crowd around. Given that he was not, actually, Officer Friendly, or an officer at all—and that he'd given her a hard time and a three hundred dollar ticket this afternoon in order to win a bet—her reaction may not be in keeping with the impeccable manners she was known for.

And, feeling the tightness in his chest, he knew he deserved whatever penalty she dished out. He only hoped she didn't have him thrown out of the party before he could coax her into giving Duncan James, attorney at law, a chance.

He swore he saw snowflakes drifting around him as he stared through the side panel windows of the double front doors of the club. The round foyer appeared to be lit in gold, giving warmth to the scene before him. Annabelle Devine took his breath away. Literally. He stood motionless, not sure if he was conjuring up a character from Homer's *Odyssey*, because the gown Annabelle wore was straight out of Greek lore. Her silhouette displayed a graceful bare shoulder and arm and sheer flowing white fabric cascading to the ground. Her long red hair had been twisted up on her head in a sexy mess he hoped to get a chance to touch. Sooner rather than later.

There was a small crowd in front of Annabelle. Several

younger women, all dressed in white ball gowns, stood in various stages of attention, but all were focused on what Annabelle was saying. She was animated, using her hands to direct her protégés. Behind them, proud parents stood, half listening, half talking amongst themselves. Eventually, the girls held their hands out for inspection. Given a nod, they pulled on their elbow-length gloves, except for one. After a brief discussion, Annabelle nodded and the one girl moved to hand her gloves to the coat check attendant behind Annabelle.

When she returned to the group, Annabelle gathered the girls tightly together and whispered for their ears only. To Duncan, it seemed like a football huddle, a secret game plan for the evening being discussed and agreed on. And then, in one happy moment, laughter erupted from all and the group disbanded, moving about in all directions.

Annabelle watched them go. Beaming, he noticed, like a proud momma. "The Keeper of the Debutantes," he whispered. He heard movement behind him and turned to find Brooks Bennett's parents coming up the porch steps.

"Mr. and Mrs. Bennett," Duncan addressed them, reaching out his hand in greeting.

Mr. Bennett took it and shook it sharply. "Well, I'll be. Duncan James. How are you, son?"

"I'm doing fine, Mr. Bennett. Thank you. Mrs. Bennett, you look lovely, as ever." He leaned in to kiss her cheek.

"Oh, I always love having you boys around." She tapped his cheek. "Are you here for the party?"

"I am.

"Well, good. You have a place to stay overnight? I don't want you driving back to Raleigh after drinking in here."

"I'm staying out at Brooks's place."

"In that mess?" Mrs. Bennett cried. "You come stay at our house."

"Well, thanks for the invitation, but don't you have Lewis staying there?"

"We do, but we have plenty of room. In fact, I don't know why Brooks insists on staying at his place while it's under construction. He could move right back into his old room and at least be comfortable while he's fixin' that place up."

Duncan smiled at being given the perfect opportunity to set Brooks up. "Sounds like the smart plan to me. I don't know what he's thinking."

"Exactly. So we'll see you both later tonight."

"Come on, woman," Mr. Bennett said, placing a hand under her arm and steering her toward the door. He looked back at Duncan and winked. "If we miss you tonight, be sure to stop by for our Rose Bowl party tomorrow."

"I'm looking forward to it."

He stood another moment before following the Bennetts through the door. It was eight o'clock and cars were starting to stream into the circular drive. If Duncan didn't want a crowd when he first spoke to Annabelle, he'd better git-r-done.

Chapter Four

ANNABELLE'S BREATH caught as soon as she spied Duncan coming through the doors. She recognized his luxurious coat and Ryan Seacrest hairstyle. His face was still a bit of a mystery since he'd been wearing those clichéd mirrored cop shades this afternoon. She had the urge to pat her hair and wet her lips just glimpsing his profile. Instead, she took a deep breath to steady herself as John and Ellen Bennett came forward to greet her.

"Annabelle, wait until you see our Darcy this evening," Mrs. Bennett said as she beamed proudly. "I swear since she's moved to Boston her inner debutante has revealed itself. She's transformed, I tell you. She started with LASIK surgery and is ending with a designer ball gown. Trust me, you will not believe your eyes."

"Hardly recognized my own daughter," Mr. Bennett added.

"Well, that is something," Annabelle agreed. "Darcy dragged her feet through the entire debutante shopping experience. I wonder what has caused the change."

Out of the corner of her eye, Annabelle watched Duncan hang back as the three of them talked. She also noticed his slight grimace when he was brought to her attention by Mrs. Bennett.

"Annabelle, dear. Have you been introduced to Duncan James?" Mrs. Bennett motioned for him to come join them. "We've known him quite a while now and we're very proud of him. He's with a law practice in Raleigh. You live in Raleigh too, don't you?"

Game on.

"I do live in Raleigh," Annabelle agreed. "But I'm afraid you're mistaken, Mrs. Bennett. This man is a special agent brought in to work with Henderson's finest. In fact, I believe he was riding with Brooks today."

John Bennett uttered an "Uh-oh," while glancing over at Duncan.

"Well, no, I don't think so," his wife said, confused.

"Yes," Annabelle insisted, turning her attention from Mrs. Bennett to Duncan. "I'm sure this is the officer who gave me a speeding ticket this afternoon. Isn't that right?"

Annabelle felt sorry for Brooks's father. The man immediately started to shift from one foot to the other, grabbing for the coat at his wife's shoulders, trying to turn her attention away from the conversation. "Ellen, sweetheart, let me help you with your coat."

"Well, no, Anna—*John!* What are you doing?"

Annabelle met Duncan's eyes over the Bennetts' tussle. He stood tall, his weight evenly distributed. His hands were clasped behind him making no effort to hide the telltale cashmere coat he had worn that afternoon. The same one, in fact, he had so gallantly wrapped around her. His eyes were yellow-gold and met her gaze full-on, unashamed and resolved to face whatever wrath she chose to dish out.

Brave. She liked that.

"Officer Friendly," she said, tipping her head to the right indicating they should take a couple of steps away to have a more private conversation. He followed her lead.

"Duncan James," he said, his eyes recapturing her gaze and holding it as she offered her hand at his introduction. Her father was right. He did have a firm handshake and solid eye contact.

"Annabelle Devine."

"Keeper of the Debutantes."

"You know about that?" She ducked her chin thinking the title had worn off. At the same time, she felt his thumb move back and forth over her hand. She kinda liked that.

"I know a little. I'm hoping you'll tell me more."

It was how he offered a sort-of apology, combining it with a declaration of interest all put out there with the smoking rich timbre of his voice that had Annabelle feeling lightheaded. She licked her lips, gathering her thoughts.

"And Mrs. Bennett said you're a lawyer. Prosecution or defense?"

"Neither. Corporate attorney."

What a shame for women on juries everywhere, she thought.

He cleared his throat. "Annabelle, I hope you'll forgive me for that little...ah, prank, this afternoon."

"Was I not speeding?"

His body shot to attention, fire amplifying the gold in his eyes. "Hell yes, you were speeding. You and that rocket ship were in ludicrous-speed when you roared by."

"So, I deserved a ticket."

"You did. Without doubt."

"But you're feeling guilty because my three hundred dollars isn't going to *help out* the city of Henderson as you suggested, but *is* going to settle the bet you won with Brooks and Vance."

Duncan moved his head around and adjusted his shoulders. "Ah, apparently someone has sold me out."

"Indeed. But before you go and lose your Man Card by offering my money back, let me tell you that I consider that payment for our date tonight. And as I remember, you—well, you in your Officer Friendly persona—promised me 'as much service as I can handle.'"

The color of his cheeks heightened. Trapped in so many ways Duncan opened and closed his mouth but none of that rich, sexy lawyer talk was forthcoming. She smiled broadly, satisfied to wait as he continued to try to conjure a response.

"I...I simply do not know what to say to all that," he started. "I mean...Man Card? Really? Payment for our date? And...what was that? As much *service* as you can handle? Annabelle," he said shaking his head, "if someone overheard you, your position as

Queen Bee of the Debutantes would be revoked."

"It's Keeper of the Debutantes," she corrected.

"That, too. And Brooks and Vance would have to haul both our asses in. Me for soliciting and you for buying."

"Oh," she said sweetly, "let's not use ugly words like solicitation."

"That's what it is."

"I know, but let's just not call it that."

Duncan pressed his lips into a firm line, saying absolutely nothing. But Annabelle felt the scolding heat of his you're-pushing-it stare slowly penetrate all seven layers of her skin.

Hot, hot, hot. *Seriously* sexy.

And then…then he started unbuttoning his coat. Slowly. Deliberately. Annabelle grew flushed, becoming keenly aware of a smoldering longing flaring up as she watched him disrobe.

He pulled off his coat and carefully folded it over one arm. Then, in his quietest baritone, he said, "I swear to God, if you lick those lips one more time, I'm going to pull you obscenely close and kiss you long and hard right here by the front door."

Her mouth parted in awe. "Was I really licking my lips?" she whispered.

He gave one short nod.

"Well, you can hardly blame me," she said, pointing her finger up and down his body. "Wow."

Duncan James, with his stylishly tossed dark head of hair and angular features softened only by the dimple in his chin, stood one head taller than her five-foot-seven-in-heels frame. He wore a tuxedo that was well-tailored to his broad shoulders and narrow hips. From head to pricey shoes, his style was classic. Impeccable. He knew what looked good on him and he knew how to wear it. She could have wept for the perfection standing before her. Instead, she stopped herself just as she was about to lick her lips.

"Good girl," he said. "Now, let me get rid of my coat and we can move this date to a quieter location."

For a moment she thought he meant they would leave the

party, and it surprised her that she would have gladly followed him right out the door. Not the best form for a hostess. Even though the invitation was officially sent by their parents, Tess, Grace and Annabelle did their part to make the evening the smashing success it was year after year. But, as Annabelle watched the throng of regulars arrive greeting one another with a "Happy New Year," she decided her usual duties as greeter could be forgone this year.

She turned as Duncan approached and offered his arm. She sighed at the gesture, smiling her approval and then pointed the way up the foyer steps. Besides—she thought, while taking his arm—someone really should make sure our newest guest has a very good time.

Chapter Five

WHEN ANNABELLE snuggled her left hand under his upper arm and grabbed his bicep, Duncan felt a shot of adrenaline rush right to those muscles. Like he was Clark Kent transforming into Superman. And when she snuggled her entire body up against his side—so she could top her left hand with her right—he felt the soft mound of breast press against the side of his arm. His brain immediately pictured what she might look like naked from the waist up. As if he'd pulled out his ever-present Swiss army knife and in one cut had the fabric across her shoulder tumbling down, exposing her torso all the way to her hips. If the whole licking-her-lips porn scenario hadn't drained his brain of public decency, what little he had left was now heading south of his waistband, fast.

As they moved together on the staircase and up and out of the now-crowded foyer, his baser instincts had his nose turning toward her profile and drawing in the scent of roses that wafted off her throat. It was all he could do to not press his lips to the intriguing indentation where pale and slender neck met fit and shapely shoulder. He was even starting to relish the beginning sensations of his hard-on when one dreaded word burst from Annabelle's lips.

"Daddy!"

Talk about a cock block.

"Daddy, Mother," Annabelle called while maneuvering him a

quarter of the way down a long, wide hallway lined with couches, tables and chairs. Out of the relative quiet, jarring music erupted from the ballroom to his right, and then—as if Duncan's nervous system hadn't been shocked enough in the last few milliseconds— his source of heat dropped her hands from around his bicep, leaving him internally shaken.

Public place. Parents around. And you don't even know this girl, Duncan's brain scolded as he held out his hand in response to the introductions going on around him. Get your damn head on straight, he thought even as he greeted Harry Devine. "That's correct, sir. Brooks Bennett introduced us back in early November. I think we were all here watching the State-Carolina football game."

"That's exactly right," Mr. Devine said. "I remember you and your boys surrounded by a few shot glasses and a pitcher of beer. Can't blame you. That Wolfpack of yours took a damn beating that day."

Duncan laughed. "That they did, sir. That they did."

"This is my wife, Jody." Harry beamed with pride as he introduced Annabelle's mother. Other than the hair and eye color, there was a very strong family resemblance between mother and daughter. No wonder the man beamed.

"A beautiful party, Mrs. Devine," Duncan said as he took her extended hand.

"Why, thank you, Duncan. We're happy you could join us." He didn't miss the meaningful look Jody Devine gave her daughter.

"And here comes our precious Grace," Harry went on. "Gracie-girl! Darling," he called, motioning a fairy-princess to join their group.

The epitome of Cinderella-at-the-ball started their way, lean and graceful—until she settled directly between Duncan and Annabelle hoisting the strapless ball gown up under her armpits and fixing her bosoms to sit a little perkier under the gossamer fabric.

Duncan had to bite the inside of his cheek not to laugh at Annabelle's horrified expression. "My God, Grace. If you touch the bodice of that gown one more time I'm going to rip it off you. I swear it!"

"I thought it was falling down, Belly. What? You want me running around exposing myself all night?"

"Belly?" Duncan asked.

"I've told you over and over, the dress can't fall," Annabelle insisted. "Pretend it's like your gun holster. *You* wear the dress. Stop letting the dress wear you."

Grace leaned her head to the side, considering. "Huh. Okay, I get it now." She turned to her sister. "Done. And thank you."

Annabelle just nodded in satisfaction.

Mr. Devine picked up the introductions. "Duncan James, my second daughter, Gracie-belle."

"Grace," she insisted, holding her hand out to Duncan. "Just Grace. No belle."

"Got it," Duncan nodded.

"So you're the hero who gave my sister her first speeding ticket," she said, still holding his hand.

Duncan felt another shot of adrenaline, this one heating up his face. His gaze bounced around the members of the Devine family gathered before him, not sure where that prank placed him in their estimation. "I cannot tell a lie," he offered. "I was the one who gave Annabelle the ticket."

"Good for you," Grace said. "About damn time. And what did you think of that car she was driving? Too damn loud. Way too fast. The term *redneck* comes to mind every time I see the damn thing."

"Gracie-belle," her father broke in. "Do I need to remind you we are at a party, not one of your field interrogations? Your language, peanut."

"She does have a broader vocabulary than she's letting on," Jody Devine assured him.

"Sorry," Grace offered. "But that car of hers just makes me

crazy. It's absurd for Belly to be riding around in that thing. She's going to kill herself."

"I like the car," Duncan confessed with a quick wink to Annabelle. "Call me a redneck, but I'm trying to figure out what I need to do to be able to test-drive that machine."

Harry laughed as Grace groaned. Annabelle stepped in between Duncan and Grace, securing his bicep in her left hand again. "Well, I don't know about a test drive, Mr. James. But that comment certainly gets you a free drink at the bar," she said, turning him away from the ballroom and her family, toward the open doors on the other side of the hall. "We'll see ya'll a bit later on," she said in parting.

"Stop on by the house tomorrow," her father said to Duncan as they headed off. "We'll talk more football during the Rose Bowl."

"Will do, Mr. Devine. Thanks." Duncan let Annabelle lead him away. He didn't know why she and her family were letting him get away with impersonating an officer so easily, but the fact that they had lulled him into a wonderful sense of security.

Met the parents. Check. Met the tough, gun-toting sister. Check. The night had hardly begun and Duncan felt buoyant having managed his perceived mine field so quickly and easily. His ego was puffed up and in full riot gear when Annabelle stopped him far short of the two very secluded seats he was spying at the far end of the bar. "And this is my sister, Tess," she announced.

Tess.

Beautiful. Vibrant. Sultry, bedroom-eyed Tess.

Who was also, very obviously—if not to Annabelle, then at least to himself—pissed off at the world, Tess.

The daggers her chocolate brown eyes shot at Duncan ripped his riot gear apart and had his ego lying at her tiny, little high-heeled feet.

Seated on a tall chair at the center of the bar and draped in wine red, Tess's lush and curvaceous body was turned sideways, her slender arm dangling over the back of the chair. A large cuff of sparkling diamonds circled her wrist as she pointed directly at his heart. He wasn't certain daggers weren't going to shoot from her fingertip as well.

"Dun-can Jaaames," she sung at him. "Man among men! Infamous," she pronounced. "Tell me, Duncan James, with your GQ hair-style and your thousand-dollar tuxedo," she said, swirling her pointed finger all around him. "How is it, exactly," she said as her eyes narrowed, "that you are able to give my baby sister an outrageous speeding ticket in the afternoon, and then dare to have your hands all over her at our father's party tonight?"

So much for not stepping on a fucking land mine.

"Don't mind, Tess," Annabelle said turning toward him with a light-hearted smile. "She has a wonderful sense for the dramatic. Which serves her really well in all her roles on Broadway. Doesn't it, Tess?"

Tess threw Annabelle a sarcastic grin.

"Since she's the one Devine sister without a date tonight, it appears she's taking her frustration out on you. I'm guessing she's been imagining Lewis Kampmueller's hands all over her during their kiss at midnight. Am I right?"

Tess turned back to the bar and lifted her drink. "At least we know he's a good kisser," she said before taking a gulp. "Who knows about Officer Friendly there."

Duncan slipped his arm around Annabelle's waist and looked down into her pretty brown eyes. "She's got you there." Then he lifted his attention to the back of Tess's head. "His bank statement beats the hell out of mine as well, but I guess you Devine sisters aren't worried about all that. However…" He took a step toward Tess, bringing Annabelle with him so he could whisper in Tess's ear. "It's my understanding that the highly respected Mr. Kampmueller is interested in only one of the Devine sisters tonight. Forgive me for saying this, *Tess*, but you're not the one he's picturing getting his hands on at midnight."

Tess turned her head sideways and gave him her first honest smile. "Grace has always been the one he thinks he's in love with," she said kindly, showing her true feelings about Lewis. "And if Annabelle and I have our way again this year, he'll be kissing the one he wants come midnight. Michael-schmichael."

"Grace's date," Annabelle explained.

"Ah. A stumbling block for Lewis."

"Perhaps," Tess said. "We'll have to see how it all works out." Then she waved them away, a queen dismissing her court.

With a hand on the small of her back, Duncan directed Annabelle to the farthest two bar chairs tucked close to the back wall of the room. "Your father seems awfully relaxed for a man who has three gorgeous daughters," he said.

"That's sweet of you to say," Annabelle responded as he helped her into the last chair. It was an intentional move. Duncan hoped that his body would block her from view for a while. He was as social as the next guy, but having survived the last half hour, he needed a breather before encountering any more family or friends. Besides, he thought as he took a serious look at the elegance settling herself beside him, he needed all the time he could get to make a lasting impression on this particularly beautiful Devine sister. He wanted a second date on the books by the end of the night.

"So what's your drink, Annabelle?"

"Bourbon and Ginger Ale."

"Is that right? A true Southern belle."

"Uh-huh. And how 'bout yourself?"

"Beer, generally," he said. But when the bartender stepped toward them he ordered, "Two tequila shots."

The young, dark-headed bartender stopped dead in his tracks. From the expression on his face he was obviously trying to figure something out. "You want them with the cut-up limes and a shaker of salt?"

"That'd be good," Duncan nodded. "First night on the job?"

A magical smile lit up the young man's face. "Something like that," he said. "Two shots, coming right up."

"Tequila shots?" Annabelle threw Duncan a sideways glance.

"Hey. Midnight rolls around and I'm lucky enough to be kissing you, I want you just tipsy enough that you aren't comparing me to Lewis Kampmueller."

Annabelle burst out laughing. "Are you actually worried about outshining Lewis in the kissing department?"

Hell yes! "No."

Annabelle leaned her shoulder over and nudged him in the arm. "Really?"

He wobbled his head from side to side, causing her to grin. At least it looked like a grin from his peripheral vision. At the moment, he found himself unable to face her. What if he didn't kiss better than Lewis?

Jesus, he cursed at himself. *Man up, dude.*

As the bartender arranged the shots in front of them, Annabelle noticed his name tag. "Your name's Harry?"

"That's right," he said, wiping his hands on the towel tucked into his waistband. He held out his hand to Annabelle and the cuff of his white shirt pulled up. Duncan noticed a tattoo on his wrist. It looked like a quiver holding six arrows.

"Harry," she nodded, taking his hand and shaking it. "That's a good name. My father's name in fact."

"Is that right?"

She nodded. "Harry, would you bring another round of shots when you have a chance? Sounds like Mr. James needs help with his performance anxiety."

Duncan slapped his hand on the bar, turned his head and laid a disbelieving stare on Annabelle. He could hear the mirth Bartender Harry tried to smother as he headed off to do her bidding, but he didn't take his eyes from the one he wanted now more than ever. God, he could never have conjured up all the perfect pieces that made up this woman. The same thought he'd had hours before rang out clearly in his mind.

I have found you.

He had. He knew it. And maybe, just maybe, Annabelle Devine knew it too. Because without a doubt, she had just thrown down the gauntlet…and he was more than willing to pick it up.

Duncan nodded his chin at the set of shot glasses. "Let's see who has performance anxiety."

Annabelle's eyes sparkled as she turned her attention to the tequila. Duncan followed just a split second behind as they licked the skin between their finger and thumb, poured on the salt, licked it clean, downed the shot, and then bit into the wedge of lime. He was certain the grimace on her face was far worse than his own.

He wiped his lips with the back of a hand while The Keeper dabbed hers with a cocktail napkin. It reminded him of something. "Pretty impressive. Where did you develop your expertise?"

"Tequila Shoot-Out. Zate House. Fall semester, sophomore year."

"Ah." Duncan nodded knowingly. "Wild night?"

"Can't say for sure. But nothing ended up on Facebook, so except for the insane hangover the next day, I think I made it through relatively unscathed."

"Miss Manners. At a tequila shoot-out." He tried to imagine Annabelle the debutante coed.

"But you're more than a book on manners, you know. You are gracious."

"Thank you. Isn't that one and the same?"

"Not at all," he stalled while Bartender Harry and his quiver full of arrows set up a second round. "For instance," he went on quietly as the bartender moved away, "our young friend here offered his hand to you. You know that a book of etiquette says a gentleman never offers his hand to a lady, but waits to have her hand offered to him," he said drawing on his own cotillion experience. "And yet you don't stand on principal. You shook his hand without pause."

"Well, of course. Otherwise it would have created a terribly awkward moment."

"Exactly my point. You were gracious. You *are* gracious."

She fed him a brilliant smile, and leaned in closer. "And you are going to get a hell of a kiss come midnight."

Oh, I'll be getting more than a kiss, he promised himself, glancing at his watch discreetly. Maybe the tequila had already started talking. More likely it was Annabelle's easy humor and the way his body simmered in a state of rapt attention wherever she touched him. And, he noted, she was touching him a lot. But most likely, it was the mounting anticipation of getting his hands on the bare flesh of all those curves covered in just the sheerest of fabrics—so sheer he swore he saw the dark coloration of the tips of her beasts when he dared allow his glance to go there. In his mind, she wore nothing underneath that dress, and he was starting to get just a little desperate to find out if he was right. Hell with a damn kiss at midnight. He wanted some time alone with Miss Devine and he wanted it as soon as he could get it.

Chapter Six

THE BAR AREA with its masculine wood architecture and hunter green accents had filled up nicely, and the conversations which ensued created a lovely warm hum that had Annabelle sinking cozily into their little twosome at the far end of the bar. Her body was now turned sideways in her seat, her back literally against the wall. Duncan's frame had likewise turned towards her, and his broad shoulders and taller height blocked her vision of any guest coming or going. It was perfect.

It was perfect how her knees fit between his and how his inner thighs would brush against her outer thighs as the two of them conversed with an extraordinary amount of animation. It was perfect how his arm laid along the back of her chair, and his fingers would stroke her bare skin from time to time. His touch created the perfect little goosebumps on the outside of her skin and the perfect blast of heat that ran itself ragged on the inside. But the most perfect thing of all was the moment right after their second shot, when they laughed and caught each other's happy gaze. The world around them stopped, going quiet. That moment…that perfect moment…when their lips were only inches apart and her heartbeat pounded in her ears, when Duncan laced his fingers with hers and brought her hand up, turning it slowly, and placed a kiss on the sensitive skin of the inside of her wrist.

It was romantic and subtle and stole her heart. And it was then that Annabelle realized she had better get to know a little more about her Officer Friendly if she was going to go home and announce to her sisters that she planned to marry Duncan James.

"So growing up in Richmond, you decided to go to NC State?"

"I didn't have the grades to get into Chapel Hill. I figured it was the next best thing. And don't laugh, Little Miss North Carolina. In the end, it truly was the right place for me. I met Brooks and Vance and we formed a close-knit group, bonding over our college experience. We shared a lot of good times. But more than that, they always had my back. And they still do today. Best thing that ever happened to me."

Annabelle loved the way he spoke about his friends and their solid relationship. "But you went to UNC for law school?"

"Well," Duncan said, eyeing her over a sip of water, "I'm stupid but I ain't crazy." She laughed. "I set my sights on law school at Carolina before I set foot on campus at NC State. I like the south, and staying in North Carolina kept me closer to home. So, my goal was to get straight A's because I was not going to be turned down again."

"And you got them."

"I got them," he acknowledged.

"So are you a hard worker or are you just that smart?"

"Well, now." He leaned in close, his light Southern accent noticeably heavier. "I'm sitting here with you, aren't I?"

Annabelle bit her lip, trying not to show the pleasure that his answer gave her. "Well, unless you majored in drama, I'd say playing the part of Officer Friendly today was pretty hard work."

"But gettin' you to insist I be your escort tonight…now that was brilliant." He flashed an arrogant grin before adding, "And thanks for goin' easy on me about all that, by the way."

A pang of guilt about what had really gone down threatened to intrude, but Annabelle shoved it away. Things were going too well to jeopardize the evening with a confession. "Am I detecting a slightly heavier Southern drawl?"

Duncan sat back with his arms crossed over his chest,

grinning broadly. With each word he sat up a little straighter and moved in a little closer. "I'm pretty certain that a couple of tequila shots and a pretty Southern belle could reduce me to sounding a lot more like Redneck One and Redneck Two than usual."

"Brooks and Vance?"

"You catch on quick."

"Those two are sort of celebrities around here."

"And don't I know it. They took State to three College World Series. Won one of them on a no-hitter from Brooks. Man, those guys could play."

"So how is it you knew you wanted to go to law school before you even started college?"

"No choice in that." Duncan shrugged. "I was born to it. My dad is a criminal defense attorney, and if that's not bad enough, my mother is a judge."

"Your mother is a judge?" Annabelle exclaimed wide-eyed.

"That's right. And we aren't talking Judge Judy, although at home she settled our disagreements about the same way, I suppose."

"You have brothers and sisters?" Annabelle asked, finding all of this fascinating.

"Three sisters and one brother. I'm the oldest. Then the girls—Molly, Lacey and Abigail. Then Jesse."

"Your brother's name is Jesse James?" When Duncan nodded, Annabelle laughed so hard she snorted.

"Oh my God, that's the first unladylike thing I've seen you do," Duncan said, grinning from ear to ear. "You are a mere mortal after all, aren't you?"

"I am indeed," she agreed. "Seriously, Jesse James?"

"My parents might be lawyers, but they are lawyers with a sense of humor. And they probably needed a good reminder of that when kid number five arrived."

"Annabelle!" A deep-pitched baritone from the other end of the bar caused Duncan to turn. Annabelle probably wouldn't have noticed it—so enthralled with the man in front of her—but following Duncan's lead, she looked down the bar as tall, blond and long-ago heartthrob, Stubs McKenna started to call her name again.

"Anna— Oh, there you are," Stubs said as he spied her down the way. He pointed his finger at her and started muscling his way through the crowd gathered at the bar to get to them.

Duncan's disgruntled protest gave her great satisfaction as she assured him this would only take a minute. With eyes only for Annabelle, Stubs landed a heavy hand on Duncan's shoulder, only acknowledging him with a quick "Hey, Bud," before shoving his head in the space between Duncan and herself to plant a big ol' kiss on her cheek. Annabelle was pretty sure she saw her date stiffen. Another boost to her feminine pride. "Come on now," Stubs said, holding out his hand, "the band is kicking serious ass. Why are you crammed back here in the corner? You know you're my go-to gal on the dance floor."

Duncan, whose arms were crossed over his chest, glanced down at Stub's big hand sitting on his shoulder, then up into Stubs's face as he blurted all this out. Then he rolled his eyes dramatically toward Annabelle, giving her a direct look that said, "You have got to be kidding me."

She winked and held up one finger to Duncan, seeking a little patience. "Well, bless your heart, Stubs," she started, turning her full attention to the man. "How thoughtful of you to come find me when there are so many other pretty girls just dying for you to ask them to dance. In fact," she went on, turning Stubs's attention where she wanted it, "Katherine Stuart was asking about you the moment she arrived. See her over there, just out in the hallway?" She gave him a little push in the right direction. "Now you be the gentleman and go on and give that girl a thrill."

Annabelle and Duncan watched as Stubs ambled away. "Well, I'll be," Duncan whispered, then turned his attention back to Annabelle. "It was like you put that lummox in a trance and he didn't have the capability not to follow your orders."

She took a sip of water. "Oh, he's just a big ol' sweetheart.

Probably didn't even realize he was intruding. Now, where were we?"

Duncan took her hand in his and bounced it up and down. "You know, I was thinking," he said, "you were probably an undergraduate while I was in law school at Carolina. We were on the same campus. I wonder if our paths ever crossed."

"I highly doubt it," Annabelle scoffed. "Sounds like you were probably in the law library, and I have to admit, I was rarely in any library at all. I did not go to college to make the dean's list, much to my parents' chagrin."

"Is that so?" Duncan's expression was priceless. A combination of amusement and wonder.

"Well, of course I wanted a good education, and I got it. My only redeeming academic achievement is that I never ever missed a class. Which I repeatedly pointed out to my father whenever he started ranting and raving about my grades and the cost of tuition. I assured him I was getting his money's worth, and I did. More than most students, because I filled every hour with a group or club. There were just too many enticing activities and too much stuff to learn to justify spending more than the minimal amount of time necessary studying for tests."

"Is that a fact? So what sorts of things, pray tell, enticed the youngest Devine sister?"

"Basketball. I wanted to make sure I got inside the Dean Dome for every home game, so I finagled a job babysitting the VIP alumni. You know, show them to their seats, make sure they have everything they could want, schmooze them into bigger donations." She flashed him a cheeky smile. "I was good at that."

"I don't doubt it."

"Then, of course, the sorority. Which has become my career. I'm our acting Field Representative for all the Atlantic Coast colleges, keeping all the garish behavior of uninspired coeds out of the public's eye. I've become very good at putting out fires," she smirked.

"And inspiring better behavior?"

"They don't call me Keeper of the Debutantes for nothing. But back in college I served as Rush Chairman, was our Panhellenic Delegate junior year and then was the Philanthropy Chair. Other than that..." She sighed, thinking, counting the rest out on her fingers as she spoke, "I participated in the Synchronized Swim Club, the French Club, the Auto Mechanics Club, and then all the usual. You know, Habitat for Humanity, Big Sisters of Durham, and Santa Claus Anonymous."

Duncan stared at her blankly. "Is my head actually spinning? Because who the hell knew there was synchronized swimming and I just can't picture you in the Auto Mechanics Club to save my life!"

"And yet, you've seen the car I drive."

"Good point."

Archibald Reynolds jostled his way up to them, looking like he'd been on a roll shaking hands and kissing babies all night. "Hey there, Buddy," he said taking Duncan's hand and shaking it. "How you doin'?" The expression suited whether he was supposed to know the person he was addressing or not. Duncan didn't appear to be amused. Especially when Archie turned his back on Duncan, essentially blocking him from Annabelle. "Now you know, sugar, if you sit in this corner all night your momma's party is just gonna roll over and play dead. Sweetheart, you need to come with me and be seen on the dance floor. Now don't try and tell me no."

Noticing Duncan's hand landing on Archie's shoulder, Annabelle gestured. "May I introduce my date," she said quickly as Duncan spun Archie around. "Archie, this is Duncan James. He's a good friend of Brooks Bennett and Vance Evans. Duncan, this is Archibald Reynolds, a family friend."

Duncan eyed Archie as the other man's whiskey came dangerously close to sloshing over the rim of his glass. "Brooks, you say? Well, any friend of Brooks..." He turned back to Annabelle. "Find me later on, honey, and I'll give you a twirl." With that, he downed the last of his bourbon, toasted the couple with his empty glass and brought it down heavily on the bar in between them. He scooped his long blond bangs out of his face before turning and dissolving into the crowd.

"Give you a twirl?" Duncan squinted. "What the hell does that mean?"

"I'm sure he meant a twirl on the dance floor."

"Yeah. Right." After holding her gaze, Duncan rubbed his jaw, glancing around the room. "I have to give you credit, Annabelle Devine. You sure know how to handle the awkward social situation."

"Well, as the expression goes, 'This ain't my first rodeo'."

"Ha," Duncan let out a short laugh. "I bet. Seems about time to order up a real drink. Bourbon and Ginger?"

"That'd be perfect," Annabelle said, realizing how utterly tempting he looked now that the polished sheen had worn off. His hair was a little tousled and the color in his cheeks had risen. He'd unbuttoned his jacket and didn't look disheveled as much as loose. Or, was that his body spoiling for a fight? A tiny thrill rent its way through her, from front to back. Her breath hitched thinking about his annoyance at the interruptions. Dear Lord, there was something about this combination of impeccable manners and male aggression that had her softening into very malleable putty, longing to be in his hands.

Heaven help her, she was getting turned on just thinking about it.

When Harry the magical bartender delivered their drinks, Duncan handed him a tip and then lifted Annabelle's glass to her. As she sipped, he seemed to be trying to figure out something. Finally he tilted his bottled beer, took a swig, and then pointed it at her.

"You've given me something to think about, Annabelle. Something to look at differently than I have ever before."

"Really? What's that?"

"Something you said about your college experience. The way you looked at it. See," he said, glancing around the crowded room again before resting his gaze back on her. "I joined the Phi Deltas for a lot of reasons, but one of them truly was their motto: 'Become the greatest version of yourself.' To me, it seemed, I had already embraced that. Get the straight A's. Leave no question about getting into law school. Throw in civility, loyalty, respect for women and elders, that kind of thing, done. But you," he said, pointing the tip of his bottle toward her again, "you went and explored everything you could get your hands on. You..." he said thoughtfully, "you didn't let grades get in the way of your education. There!" he congratulated himself. "That's it."

"I had no use for grades because I wasn't going to law school. Or med school. Or any sort of graduate school. So, I had the luxury."

"Indeed. And now you can, what? Speak French?"

"Mais, oui!"

"And build a car from the ground up?"

"Maybe...with the proper tools."

He spread his arms wide. "And you're funny and clever and not only Keeper of the Debutantes, but the sorority girls as well. And," he said, "apparently you are a hell of a dancer because it seems everybody and their brother wants to give you a twirl."

"Oh, no."

"Oh, yes."

"No, I mean...oh, crap."

It was all the warning she could give before another hand landed hard on his shoulder, and another good ol' boy called him Buddy.

"Hey, Bud-dy!" Tucker Davenport put a big ee sound on the end of his greeting and Annabelle wasn't sure if that was what set Duncan off or whether it was the fact that he'd been knocked so hard his beer splashed out of the bottle. "Annabelle," Tucker said as he circled her wrist with his hand pulling her off her chair, "you've played wallflower long enough and it's time to come—"

Tucker stopped short when a large hand landed flat, hard and square in the center of his chest. He looked down at the hand,

and then at the man attached to it.

"Release. My. Date."

Annabelle had never heard three words promise more. She actually had to choke back a laugh at the expression on Tucker's face. Tucker, who had a good fifty pounds on Duncan, looked as if a gun was being held to his head. In fact, after he released her wrist, he held both hands up and backed away.

Duncan said nothing more. The incident seemed to go unnoticed by anyone except the three of them. They both eyed Tucker until he finally turned and picked his way through the room and out the door. Hearing his long release of breath, Annabelle glanced up at Duncan.

"Are you okay?" he asked.

"Never. Been. Better," she said slowly and honestly, looking him straight in the eye. It was the best she could do to convey that he'd just handed her one of the biggest thrills of her life.

If his smile was any indication, he understood. "Really?"

"Really."

"Well then," he breathed, taking her by the hand. "Let's take these drinks and head on over to the dance floor. Maybe that will keep the goddamn vultures at bay."

Chapter Seven

IT DIDN'T ESCAPE Duncan's notice that Annabelle had to bite her lips to keep from smiling too big. Well, good, he thought as he led her through the bar. The last thing he wanted to do was embarrass her or himself. But he'd be damned if he was going to step aside tonight. Not for one minute was he willing to give up his time with Annabelle. He certainly hadn't intended to go all Neanderthal on her father's guests, but he was not about to step the fuck aside. Not now. Not ever.

He was rolling with a good head of steam when he saw them. Probably had every thought showing on his face too when, just across the hallway and standing at the entrance of the ballroom, Duncan spied the two biggest assholes on the face of the Earth. Son of a bitch, he thought, as Vance and Brooks burst out laughing the moment they saw him.

"You two," Duncan pointed. "Later," he promised.

"Why are they laughing?" Annabelle asked as they entered the ballroom. "You don't think they set all that up, do you?"

"I'm certain of it," Duncan said, raising his voice to be heard above the band. He continued to hold Annabelle's hand as he turned to face her. Behind her, the room was rocking. The large ballroom was jammed with party-goers, most of whom were dancing—and, from the looks of all the discarded jackets, sweating as well. Beyond that mayhem, the band put on a show. With a brass section and backup dancers, no wonder everyone wanted to be on the dance floor. "Man, this is some party," he said over her head.

"Why would they do that?"

Duncan looked into Annabelle's upturned face and couldn't help but smile. She was indignant on his behalf. Almost made it all worth it. He carefully took the glass out of her hand and held up a finger indicating she should wait there. He stashed their drinks on a side table littered with purses, cocktail napkins, half-finished drinks and even ladies' shoes. When he came back, he slid an arm around her waist and pulled her in close to speak against her ear.

"Brooks and Vance think I don't like to dance."

Annabelle pulled back and looked up at him with a cautious expression. He tugged her back to him intending to say more. But her heat and her scent had every neuron in his brain zeroing in on the soft, pale skin just below his lips. As if in a trance, he closed his eyes and leaned in to bite the tender spot between her neck and shoulder. Abruptly, he caught himself, his body immediately pumping adrenaline at the misstep. *Jesus H. Christ. Sweet Mother Mary.* He felt his heart pounding against his ribcage. His brain had shut down and his libido had gone commando. *I am a complete goner.* He swallowed before he could remember what he'd intended to say. When words came out they were thick, and full of want. "What Brooks and Vance don't know is, I actually *do* like to dance. It just has to be with the *right partner.*"

Almost afraid to look at her, Duncan unwrapped himself and started to back up, slowly pulling Annabelle onto the dance floor. When his eyes finally made their way to her face, he was richly rewarded by the soft, tender expression waiting for him. Well, dang. Apparently he did have a way with words.

Duncan acknowledged that a lot of things had to be in alignment for him to have a good time on any dance floor. Two shots of tequila and a beer didn't hurt. A kick-ass band could get him most of the way there. But he'd told the truth—having the right partner was key. Because while his attention was on

Annabelle, thoughts of looking like an idiot out here didn't bother to intrude.

While dancing over the course of the set, one of the things Duncan found wildly entertaining was watching Annabelle and her sisters dance around each other. They had this habit of hiking their gowns clear up to the tops of their thighs—and we're talking some sweet-looking thighs. He expected Mrs. Devine to run out and swat all those dresses down at some point, but then he saw the darnedest thing. Mrs. Devine came running all right. But they must have been playing the family theme song because all the girls gathered where he and Annabelle were dancing, and even Mrs. Devine had the hem of her dress swishing around some very shapely thighs. Huh. It wasn't quite ten o'clock and the Keeper and her mother were flashing the crowd. Damned if Brooks wasn't right. This New Year's Eve ball was kickin' ass and taking names.

And as much fun as all that was, the elation he felt when a slow song began to play could have raised the Titanic. Because there was nothing he wanted to do more than get his hands on the ball of fire in front of him.

However, he was not going to swing her into his arms like an eager teen. No. He was of a mind to savor this coming together. Savor the first time he'd take this fast-drivin', law-breakin', debutante-makin', quick-witted beauty into his arms. So he maneuvered slowly, with great intent and purpose. Stepping close and sliding one arm around her waist. Feeling the heat of her body, noticing her labored breathing. He bent one knee to fit between the two of hers before wrapping his other arm around her back, slowly pressing the solidness of his chest against the softness of hers. Her head tilted up. Her lips waiting just below his own. Like the start of a whirlpool, the blood in his head began to circle, threatening to take him under.

His eyes darted away from her face and around the room. "What?" he heard Annabelle's soft rustle of laughter. "Who are you looking for?" she asked.

"Your father," he confessed, then drew his attention back to her upturned face. "God, you're beautiful," he sighed. "But that guy scares me." His gaze shot out around them again.

Annabelle tucked her forehead against his chest. She was laughing at him but it couldn't be helped. He was dying to kiss her and just wasn't willing to ruin the moment by worrying about her daddy as he did. Luckily, there was no sign of the man. But as relief started to flow, he caught movement out of the corner of his eye. The WTF, you've-got-to-be-kidding-me kind.

He cleared his throat. "Annabelle," he said, causing her to look up in surprise. "The thing you are about to find out about me? I've got a temper."

She saw them then. Brooks, Vance and three others moving in their direction.

"I swear to God, if one of them so much as hints at breaking in on this dance, it's gonna get ugly."

She looked between him and the approaching band of buffoons. "Now might be a good time for that test drive," she said.

She took his hand and quickly led him away, bobbing and weaving through the couples slow dancing, heading straight toward the band. *God, how great is this woman?* They turned left at the stage edge, stooping low in front of all the dancers until they hit the outskirts of the crowd, then shot left again and broke into a run toward the far back door. When they hit the hallway, it was less crowded, and there was no sign of Brooks or Vance. Annabelle motioned for him to follow her to the right and then down a set of stairs. The music and party chatter kept receding as they descended, lingering over their heads as a heavy beat when they crossed back under the party and moved down a long, dimly-lit hallway that traversed the back of the clubhouse.

At the sight of the exit doors, Annabelle started laughing and broke into a run. Duncan followed in chase, hitting the door along with her and bounding up a short flight of concrete steps, free at last.

After working up a sweat on the dance floor, he found

cool relief in the frigid night air. Annabelle continued to laugh, saying, "I can't believe we just ran away from them." She turned to Duncan, walking backwards into the light cast from a street lamp at the entrance to the parking lot. "Like playing hide and seek when we were kids."

Duncan allowed his steps to slow into a lazy gait, enjoying the scene before him. Annabelle flushed with excitement, her eyes sparkling, her cheeks rosy, that dazzling smile turned on full wattage and directed right at him. The light behind her showing through her white gossamer gown giving him a full view of just how little she wore beneath it. In two quick steps he caught her up in his arms and pressed her to him, thinking he might owe Brooks and Vance a little gratitude for forcing them out here, finally alone under the dark of night. Because he was now going to be able to do the one thing he'd been thinking about for most of the day.

Drive Annabelle's car.

"Ah, damn it to hell," he uttered shaking his head. "And it was such a clean getaway, too."

"What?" she laughed at him. "What could possibly be wrong now?"

"Besides the fact that for the second time today you are standing in the freezing cold wearing next to nothing? We need your car keys, Danica Patrick. Unless you have them strapped to your inner thigh, I'm guessing they are back inside, tucked into some flimsy little purse."

"Ooh," she said, backing out of his hold and turning toward the parking lot. "There is so much you have left to learn, Officer Friendly," she said, her voice trailing behind her. He caught up with her in time to hear, "We always leave the doors unlocked and the keys under the driver's side mat."

The idea left him dumbstruck as he halted and simply stared after her. Finally he shrugged, "I guess that's good to know. In case I ever need to make a quick getaway."

Impressed that her big bad muscle car was tucked into the end of a row, protecting at least one side from dings, he herded her around to the passenger side and opened the door, helping her in. The bitter cold was starting to seep into his awareness and he would have felt sorry for any Greek Goddess draped only in chiffon if it weren't for the saliva-producing way her nipples responded.

He shut the door and practically growled as he headed to the driver's side.

The inside of the machine was spacious due to its wide, low ride, but the leather bucket seats molded around his thighs, supporting him front to back. He started her up with a roar, and gave the gas a punch just to hear it again. He smiled the exhilarated smile of a kid strapping himself into the latest high-tech roller coaster. Thank God whatever weather system the newscasters had been yammering on about hadn't started yet, because this was gonna be good.

After adjusting the mirrors and fastening his seat belt, he cautiously maneuvered Annabelle's baby out of the parking space, down the lot and out onto the long front drive of the Henderson Country Club. He hit the gas and felt the power surge throw him back as the Camaro went from zero to sixty in one crazy nanosecond. He was braking before his thoughts could catch up to him, and sat for a moment at the end of the driveway, wondering why the hell he didn't have one of these. Finally he turned his head toward Annabelle and said, "Awesome." She simply nodded.

He fumbled in his jacket pocket for his cell phone and handed it to her. "Call Brooks," he said. "Tell him I wanna open her up along Lake Road. See if any of his cop buddies are patrolling there this time of night."

"Really? You want me to call Brooks and tell him where we are?"

"Haven't we had enough tickets today, Little Miss Speedy Gonzales?"

"Are you kidding me? Brooks will be calling everybody on duty to nail your ass coming and going. You'd be handing him the revenge he needs after you won the bet today."

Duncan stared at Annabelle, open mouthed.

"At least that's what I'd do." She flicked her shoulder. "But it's your money," she said, starting to dial.

Duncan grabbed the phone out of her hands. "It's exactly what I'd do, too," he muttered. "And what Brooks would do," he assured her. "And did I just hear the word 'ass' come out of your mouth?" he said, stuffing the phone back in his pocket. "The Queen of Etiquette?" he said, putting the Camaro in gear and moving out onto the open road. "Or was that the hot babe in the Auto Mechanics Club talking?"

Annabelle just smiled into the night whizzing by her. "Take your pick," she said.

I want both.

It was then that the thrill turned from the drive to what might be found at the destination.

Chapter Eight
—

LAKE ROAD was the perfect place to open her up, but Annabelle knew that speed was one thrill, and handling another. So after Duncan hit somewhere around one hundred-twenty on the speedometer, Annabelle directed him to a winding country road leading up a small pass to a park that overlooked the lake. The back and forth turns could have been taken with a bit more speed in the light of day, but Duncan's expressions and occasional outbursts assured her that he was having a good time playing with her car.

The road dumped into a small parking lot, which was apparently just large enough for Duncan to gun the engine, spin them around and skid into a stop. All of which was a little more daredevil than Duncan probably had intended, producing a short scream from Annabelle and some wide eyes and heavy breathing from him as the car settled beneath them.

"Oh my God!" "That was close!" they said at the same time.

"I got a little carried away," he said sheepishly.

"Believe me, I understand," she assured him. "Would you mind taking off your coat before we start back?"

Duncan looked down at his tuxedo jacket. "I am so sorry," he said, quickly stripping the coat from his arms. "You must be freezing."

"No," she said, folding his jacket and holding it over the back seat. She let it drop behind them.

"No?" he said, his eyes shifting back and forth between hers.

She shook her head as she reached for his right hand and started to unfasten the cufflink she found at his wrist. Duncan watched in silence as she dropped it into the cup holder. But when she leaned over him and started to unfasten the other one, he dragged in a slow breath and caught the back of her head in the palm of his hand. She finished pulling the cufflink free just as he turned her face to his.

"Annabelle," he whispered, his breath labored. "Annabelle, I…"

At a loss for words he brought his other hand up and captured the side of her face, pressing her back a little before his mouth caught up to his hands. He pressed his lips to hers in a slow, soft kiss.

It was just a tease, a tender touch, but oh how it shot rockets of desire through her body. He angled his head and kissed her again, this time allowing his tongue to sweep gently across her upper lip and then her lower one. He turned his head the other way and Annabelle's hands moved up of their own volition to grab onto his wrists as his mouth toyed again with delicious tenderness.

"Annabelle," he whispered, balancing his forehead against hers. "I was trying to hold out until midnight."

Deliberately licking her lips, she whispered back, "I got tired of waiting."

"I was trying to mind my manners," he grunted as he hauled her over to the driver's side, and settled her onto his lap. "Something I'm aware the Keeper of the Debutantes is all about." With her back to the door and her legs draped over him and the center console, he hit the seat adjustment button to move them back from the steering wheel as far as possible.

Annabelle's fingers started in on his bow tie, pulling it loose with expert hands. "First my jacket. Then my cufflinks. Now my tie? What am I? Your little Ken doll?"

Annabelle stopped her fingers on the second stud of his shirt, slanting her head to consider. "No. You're more like my Officer

Friendly action figure. And I've been dying to see you without a shirt ever since this afternoon when you wrapped me in your coat and pulled me up against this chest." She rubbed her hands down his shirt, over his pectoral muscles and his rib cage then back up and over his shoulders. She stopped at his biceps and squeezed.

Duncan watched her ogle him, his grin spreading from ear to ear. "I guess a girl who drives a muscle car might have an appreciation for…" His words fell off while he moved his fingers into Annabelle's hair. "I had this crazy urge this afternoon, too," he said slowly, as if remembering. "I wanted to run my hand through your hair. Like this," he said threading his fingers up the back of her scalp. "And then pull you close," he whispered as he did. "And kiss you," he went on as he touched her lips with short, soft kisses. "Like I meant it," he breathed before he deepened the kiss.

The thrill of his tongue finally demanding its way into her mouth shot a branding heat throughout her chest and down the center of her rib cage. Her body grew heavy and warm and then seemed to fade away. Her mind fell into a blissful state of semi-consciousness while she kissed Duncan James.

Like rising through the fog of a dream and entering slowly back into a state of awareness, Annabelle found herself in Duncan's arms, her body tingling in arousal, his mouth trailing its way from her lips, down her throat and over to the sensitive spot just above her clavicle. She felt his tongue swirl across the indentation there and his hands moving up on both sides of her rib cage, his thumbs brushing the underside of her breasts at first…then finally moving across the peaks of her nipples.

She heard a sound escape, though she was unaware of making it, so focused on her core being melted, tipped, and now cascading down to pool at the southernmost region of her body.

"I want…" she started, eyes closed, licking her lips. "I need to…" she tried again, but had no ability to find the right words. "Here," she finally breathed, gripping the back of his seat and leveraging herself around Duncan's legs. She pulled at her gown, gathering it high so her legs could straddle his, bringing them face to face. She eased her body down to his lap and bit her bottom lip when the throbbing aching need of her met the rock-solid heat of him.

Duncan rolled his pelvis in response. His hands slid down to grip her hips. "Jesus Christ," he cursed as he rocked himself against her again. His hands slid under her gown and up her parted thighs, feeling their way to the soft curve of her behind, moving her forward at the same time as he ground himself against her. His mouth sought hers and she feasted on his lips, tilting her pelvis to help create more friction.

The deliciousness of her body moving against his, of his arms tightening around her, of the way their lips played, the way their tongues tangled, the joy of being alive and having found the One bubbled up inside Annabelle and it all came out in a yummy, humming sort of groaning approval that vibrated against his lips.

"I know," he breathed, a hand coming up and sweeping the hair back from her face. "This feels really…" He kissed her again. "Really…" He got lost in her lips, and his hands groped around for purchase between the sides of her thighs, her lower back, sometimes skimming her aching breasts but not settling anywhere for long. Finally, he set both hands on either side of her face and put some distance between their lips. He looked at her, then closed his eyes, panting.

"This…" he started, opening his eyes and staring at her seriously. "We…" His chest heaved with a large intake of breath as he managed to continue, "are not making this a one-night stand."

Annabelle leaned back a little. "Are you asking me out on a second date?"

He nodded, still holding his hands to her head. "Are you accepting?"

She nodded back.

"I'm serious," he told her.

"I believe you," she said.

His hands fell from her face in exasperation. "And I probably am going to have to turn in my Man Card for this, but I have no intention of making love to you for the first time in this car. It just would…" his voice began to trail off, "set the wrong tone for a relationship." He turned his head and looked out into the darkness.

The silence pounded heavy and long, matching Annabelle's heartbeat. She wanted to respond with a gift of words equal to what he'd just bestowed upon her. But her mind could find nothing worthy. Emotion swelled within her and before she could lean into him, he turned his face back and barked, "Don't you debutantes have a five date rule or something?"

She nodded briskly and saw his features soften. Inches apart, he had to have noticed the tears in her eyes. "We should," she sniffed, nodding again. "We really should." She eased herself down against him, pressing her cheek against his shoulder.

His arms closed snugly around her as he said, "So let's count this up. We have tonight, date number one. Your daddy asked me over tomorrow for the Rose Bowl, so maybe we can count that as date number two." Annabelle simply snuggled down lower. "Tomorrow night we both will be back in Raleigh and I'm thinking I'd like to take you to dinner, if that's all right." She nodded her head against his chest. "That's date number three."

He rubbed his cheek. "Friday night is always a good movie date night," he said. "You free this Friday?" He tucked his chin to look down at her and she nodded against him again. "Okay, good. Date number four."

A comfortable silence settled around them, the heater still pouring out warmth, the headlights still shining on the road back down the hill. When Duncan started to talk, it was as if he were constructing a poetic invitation. "For date number five," he breathed, tilting his head and kissing the soft spot behind her ear, "I will discover, through my own devices, your favorite flower and present you with a bouquet when I arrive to pick you up. We'll take my car—which is not as fast as this one but a little more luxurious—to The Capital Grille where we'll enjoy a steak dinner by candlelight at a very secluded table. I'll order a fine cabernet and we'll share the chocolate soufflé for dessert. And while we're at dinner, we'll make plans for Valentine's Day weekend. And then," he said, leaning down and catching her lips up with his, "I will take you home and make love to you," he said between kisses, "all…night…long."

Chapter Nine

—ᦔ

THEIR ABSENCE wasn't noticed until Annabelle and Duncan arrived back at the party hand in hand, moonstruck by all accounts. If anyone had been watching—and no one was, due to the shenanigans on stage—they'd notice that the kiss they shared at midnight was both hungry and eager. In high spirits, watching Annabelle say goodbye to friends and relatives as the party began to dwindle, Duncan's only pang of uncertainty came when he overheard Annabelle tell one of her debutantes about instituting a "five date rule". He had a sinking feeling that that whole thing was going to come back and bite him in the ass.

—ᦔ

Duncan's concern about getting along with Mr. Devine and gaining his favor was short-lived. The man seemed genuinely delighted to have a bit more testosterone around the house watching football during date number two. It was the Devine women who threw Duncan a curve ball from the moment he arrived.

It was hard to miss that Mrs. D was all grins and sighs whenever Duncan spoke about anything. And likewise, Grace— no longer the fairy princess but still a knockout in her faded blue jeans–stared at Duncan wide-eyed in wonder for most of the day. Tess…Well, Tess didn't pay him much mind, though when she did deem to acknowledge his presence, it was always with a great amount of personal satisfaction. As if Annabelle had told her that he did, indeed, kiss as well as Lewis Kampmueller—and that in some way Tess was pleased for her sister.

Annabelle, herself, was simply *more*.

More sporty—in jeans and a Carolina blue v-neck sweater— her red hair in a high pony-tail with a twist that bounced with so much life he couldn't help but tug on it.

More playful—as she interacted with him and her family. Her knowledge of football and sports in general, setting her apart from the other females.

More handsy—touching him casually in front of her parents and in more shocking ways when she pulled him into the kitchen to prepare a plethora of snacks.

She was a handful, this Annabelle Devine, stealing kisses and insinuating about Saturday night every chance she got.

The complete package was more to his liking than Duncan could have dreamed. Annabelle was a rose, with more soft and intriguing petals than he could count. He definitely did not want to blow this. But after stopping in at the Bennetts' before heading back to Raleigh, he began to worry that he already had.

"Aren't you a little young for needing Viagra?" Vance started in on him by the beer refrigerator out in the garage. "I mean, just because you can't get it up doesn't mean you have to ruin things for the rest of us."

Duncan squinted at the fool in front of him. "What the hell are you talking about, Evans?"

Vance just looked disgusted and took a swig from his bottle.

"He's just a little pissed at this five date rule," Brooks offered. "Oh shit."

"Oh shit is right," Vance agreed, popping Duncan's chest with the lip of his long-neck bottle. "I don't care if you want to play the gentleman for Ms. Devine or if you're covering up the fact that you've been neutered. Leave the fucking rest of us out of your insanity, Dunc. Some of us are interested in getting laid before the fifth date. Before any date," Vance spat.

"How the hell did this get out?"

"Oh, bro. It's out. It's out and alive and crawling all over the place," Brooks said. "The women of Henderson are loving this. They'll probably have a statue erected in your honor. Anyone with a daughter is singing your praises right about now. Of course," he said, taking a swig of beer, "anybody with a pair of balls would like to cut yours off."

Duncan squeezed his eyes shut and stood contemplating all the ramifications of his conversation with Annabelle. And the one he focused on was the horror of Annabelle finding out the actual truth. Because for someone who prided himself on valuing truth above all else, he'd gone and bent it twice in one day. And he knew himself and his temper well enough to know that, had Annabelle been the one doing the truth bending, he'd be walking away and not looking back.

He knew he should keep it to himself, but the guilt had started to grow the moment he'd seen the emotion in her eyes. He couldn't do it. He couldn't keep this in. He had to tell somebody.

"Look," he said, releasing a huge breath. "I wasn't trying to be a gentleman. The truth is, I just couldn't find the damn zipper on her dress."

～

By the time Duncan stood on the doorstep of Annabelle's condominium in Raleigh, ready for date number three, he'd considered and rejected a million ways to tell her the truth.

What he'd said was true. He damn well didn't want a one-night stand. And he had no intention of making love in that crazy-ass car of hers. But he was only a man for God's sake, and a weak one at that. Things had heated up faster than he could keep ahead of, and his saving grace was that her dress had zipped up the side, not the back. So he'd fallen back on Plan A and told her the truth. But when she didn't respond, he'd felt vulnerable and threw out the five date rule bullshit. And now she'd gone and told the debutantes and who knew who the hell else. No wonder her mother and sisters were looking at him with big ol' eyes all afternoon.

He wanted Annabelle to fall in love with him, but not under false pretenses. He had to tell her the truth.

But date number three at the sports bar went so well—eating hamburgers and discovering more and more about each other— including a bunch of mutual friends—that Duncan literally forgot the dark cloud hanging over everything. Who would have guessed that a red-headed Southern belle liked to ski the double black diamond slopes, or had her own bookie?

The date went later than either of them planned and for the second night in a row, at the stroke of midnight, there was a kiss that set off fireworks.

◦——

OMG falling fast. Annabelle texted Grace and Tess the next day. *Sending pictures of possible lingerie for Saturday night. Stand by.*

Annabelle snapped pictures of a combination camisole and boy-shorts, nude in color and adorned in French lace, a baby pink bra and panty set, and a sexy but fun black strapless negligee that tied under the bust with a big red bow.

Your signature white? Grace texted.

Wearing a killer white dress, she texted back. Her phone rang and Tess was on the other end.

"I like the red bow. Like he's opening a gift," Tess teased.

"Yeah." Annabelle smiled into the phone. "I thought so too. It's flirty. I just want to make sure it's not too flirty. Too much."

"Annabelle, you are planning to consummate this relationship, right? I don't think anything is too flirty at this point."

"I know," she said, moving to a corner of the store so her voice wouldn't be overheard. "It's just that Duncan is such a gentleman and I basically threw myself at him the other night.

I'm nervous. Everything about him, us, seems so good. What if it doesn't hold up in the bedroom? What if he expects me to be all prim and proper? Or worse—what if *he's* all prim and proper?"

"You told me there was plenty of chemistry."

"On my side, yeah. My body is having its own nuclear meltdown. But he was the one who put on the brakes. I was a sure thing after one long kiss. I was the aggressor. What if that turned him off?"

"Little sister, this is music to my ears. I didn't think you had it in you."

"Oh, it's in me. Apparently Duncan brings it out with a vengeance. I just…I just don't want to be the only one losing control. I want him to be, you know, crazy for me."

"Trust me on this," Tess said. "I've seen the way he looks at you. You have nothing to worry about. Buy the lingerie and call me on Sunday." Tess hung up.

Annabelle looked at her phone. "And then there is that pesky little detail of how we met," she said to herself.

—⟲⟶

Annabelle had an agenda all worked out for their movie date. Come clean, then seduce the hell out of Duncan.

Duncan, on the other hand, had his own agenda. Keep his hands as far away from Annabelle as he possibly could. After their last date, where he had to bite his own tongue in order not to beg her to let him escort her inside, he was determined to make it to tomorrow night. If nothing else, he hoped by then she'd be as horny as he when he told her the truth about the five date rule. He was fully prepared to give her the full-court press seduction and push not taking no for an answer within an inch of propriety.

During the action-packed thriller, when Annabelle's hand crept onto his thigh, creating the beginnings of a raging hard-on, he intertwined his fingers with hers and relentlessly held on to them for the rest of the movie. The only time he let himself go was when he pressed her up against the car door and took her mouth with his own, letting her feel the effect she had on him—promising her that tomorrow night would be worth the wait.

It wasn't until he was alone in bed that he remembered Annabelle saying, "I have something I need to tell you," right before he'd cut her off by maneuvering his way into her arms.

⟶

To Annabelle, the beginning of date number five was as poetic as Duncan had described. Her mouth watered when she opened the door to find him looking ridiculously handsome in a traditional blue blazer and gorgeous lavender Façonnable shirt and tie. She'd worn her hair up just in case he did bring her favorite flower, so she was delighted when he presented her with a gardenia, and promptly added it to her coiffure. Their elegant circular booth at The Capital Grille was cozy and secluded with an already decanted bottle of Rubicon cabernet awaiting their arrival. When she found the second gardenia artistically arranged among the votive candles, she fell in love. And as they sat side by side, enjoying a glass of wine after first indulging in a Stoli Doli, Capital Grille's signature cocktail, Annabelle was smiling inside and out because Duncan James couldn't keep his hands off her.

"When I first saw you tonight…" Duncan whispered, kissing the indentation beneath her ear, his fingers brushing tendrils of hair back from her neck, "you took my breath away." His mouth trailed down her throat. "You'd think I'd get used to it because it happens every time I see you." He brushed his lips and tongue over the tender spot at the base of her neck that so fascinated him. "Annabelle," he breathed, "I've been longing to bite you right here ever since New Year's Eve."

She tipped her head giving him better access, pressing a hand against his thigh in response to the heat and sensation. "That's good to know," she whispered. "I worried I may have been too forward."

He choked a stilted laugh and sat up, handing over her wine

glass. "Finish your wine," he said. "I have a confession to make."

She eyed him suspiciously, taking a sip. "Is it so bad you have to ply me with fabulous wine? I know you're not married," she teased. But as their waiter approached, Duncan silently waved him off. That's when her stomach sank. "Okay, now I'm getting worried."

"I want to straighten out a misconception, before…before we…you know."

"Have sex," she supplied.

Duncan leveled her with that reprimanding stare. The one that let her know she was precariously close to crossing a line. His body became a fortress. One strong arm resting across the booth behind her, his broad shoulders hemming her in at the side, and his other arm tense on the table in front of her. He spoke in that quiet no-nonsense baritone that made her insides weep with longing and anticipation.

"Annabelle." God, she loved how he said her name. "Every word I told you in your car New Year's Eve was true. I wanted a second date. I wanted a chance at a relationship. I did not want a one-night stand." His upper body angled closer, causing her heart to pound. His gaze drifted to her mouth for a moment, then back to her eyes. "But with you on my lap, I was perfectly willing to take advantage of the situation anyway." His voice dropped to a whisper. "At one point, all I could think about was stripping you naked and,"—his gaze dropped briefly to her thighs—"sliding you down onto me."

Her eyes went wide as every bit of pent-up desire slid south and turned hot and moist. Her breath caught in her chest, her heart pounding enough to make her pulse points throb. She licked her lips and Duncan leaned closer.

"The truth is, the only thing that stopped me was that I couldn't find the zipper on your gown. It was much later that night when I realized the damn thing zipped up the side."

The sexual tension was too taut for her to laugh. The only thing she could think to say was, "Oh?"

Duncan eyed her mouth again before leaning back. "I got frustrated when I couldn't find the zipper," he said, moving his hand off the table and on to her thigh, "and that made me stop and realize where we were heading. I didn't want to give you the impression that sex was all I wanted. I didn't want to do anything to embarrass you or make you want to avoid me the next morning. But the point is," he said eyeing her heavily, "had the zipper been in the back where it normally is, I wouldn't have stopped. And this whole five date rule? Complete bullshit."

Annabelle felt her head nodding but her mind had shut down after the words "sliding you down onto me." With her body vibrating so intensely, the only thing she could think about was how she had to tell him the truth about how they met. Her heart squeezed at the thought of his rejection. God, she didn't want to ruin this.

Finding no way to avoid the inevitable, she finally pointed to his glass of wine. "Drink up," she insisted.

Duncan looked a little stunned. A little confused.

"Drink up," she repeated, motioning him toward the wine with her hand. "Because if that's the extent of your confession, I assure you it's a sonnet compared to what I have to tell you."

"Tell me?" he questioned, releasing her thigh and reaching for his glass. "Wait! Before you say anything. Are we good? I mean, are you okay with what I just said?"

She licked her lips and leaned in to kiss him, whispering, "I'm *very* okay with *everything* you just said."

His relief turned into a big, sultry grin. "Okay then." He took up his wine and downed what was left like it was cheap beer at a keg party, then all but smacked his glass on the table. "Your turn."

Tears threatened as Annabelle described how her father had overheard Brooks bet Duncan he couldn't give her a speeding ticket. How he'd come home that night and told her all about it. And then how he'd recommended she play along so she could meet Duncan and see if he was the kind of guy she'd be interested in.

While Annabelle talked, she saw Duncan's expression shift the moment he figured out where her story was heading. He sat there in silence through its entirety, staring at her. When he started to drum his fingers on the table, she wrapped it up, figuring no amount of talking was going to put the cat back in the bag.

"Are you done?" he said, his eyebrows lifting. Annabelle nodded a weak little nod, terrified of his next words.

Duncan turned to the waiter hovering in the distance. "Check, please."

"Oh my God. Duncan, no!" Annabelle pleaded, throwing her hands up to his shoulders trying to turn him around to look at her. "Please, don't be mad..." she went on, becoming aware of a suspicious shaking under her hands as he turned around. Laughing.

She threw him her very best pout, but he said, "You deserved that. You and your father. I cannot believe I was set up."

"Believe it," she groaned. "And it was brilliant...all except for the part where I started to fall for you. Then it became weird and twisted and this big fat lie that I had to live with—"

She saw the poor waiter scurry off again as Duncan pulled her close and shut her up with one long, hard kiss. Her toes literally curled. "You started to fall for me?" he asked against her lips, sounding very pleased.

Annabelle simply nodded against him.

"Okay, then. How 'bout that steak?"

Chapter Ten

"NERVOUS?"

Annabelle responded with a quick smile as Duncan unlocked the door. Yeah, she was nervous. The two of them were never at a loss for words, but the drive home had been noticeably quiet. Just like their walk from the car to Duncan's townhouse.

And now, she thought, now they were literally standing on a threshold.

"Come here," he said, reaching out, taking one of her hands and slowly moving it up to his shoulder. He stepped in like he was pulling her close for a slow dance when her feet came out from under her and, like Scarlett O'Hara, she found herself airborne and being carried off in the arms of her own Rhett Butler.

"Duncan James," she said, "you've been sweeping me off my feet all week."

Once inside, he backed up against the door, closing it with his backside, and asked her to lock it by throwing the deadbolt. Then he said, "How 'bout I give you a tour in the morning?" She simply nodded as that delicious nervous angst bloomed inside her chest.

He walked to the stairs and set her feet down on the first step so they stood more or less eye to eye. His hands moved into her hair on either side of her face. "I'm crazy about you, Annabelle Devine." With exquisite concentration, he took his time kissing her lower lip, lightly running his tongue across the upper one.

"I want you in my bed something awful," he drawled, his Southern accent growing heavy, his voice going sleepy. He trailed his lips across her jaw line. "I'm completely healthy," he assured her, moving down her neck toward that one little spot she was growing so fond of. "I'm prepared. I'll protect you," he promised, his mouth settling on top of her shoulder then trailing a path to the sensitive place where he nipped at her flesh.

Moving a hand to the banister and another to her hip, Duncan nudged her backward up the next step while his mouth played again with hers. "There's no zipper on this dress," he said between kisses, moving them further up the steps. The pressure of his hand on her hip was tantalizing. "So I'm gonna watch you take it off," he said pulling her firmly against him halfway up the stairs.

His tongue slid into her mouth and plundered. Annabelle moaned against him as the wave of passion tossed her under its magnificent surge. Gone again was conscious thought. Her mind drifted to another dimension while her body remained anchored by the onslaught of chemical combustion. Her breasts felt engorged and begged to be touched. Her thighs quivered with need. Her tiny lace thong grew damp from arousal. And just as it had been on New Year's Eve, she longed to feel the firm, steely heat of him rubbing against the soft throbbing ache of her.

"Annabelle…baby," Duncan whispered in her ear. "Take your dress off for me, please. Right here. Right now." He held her by her shoulders until she was steady. Her dress, created by rings of fabric, needed to be pulled over her head. So she licked her lips and watched his expression through lowered lashes as she slowly drew the gardenia from her hair and let it drop to her feet. She noticed his jaw tighten as she deliberately removed the tiny hairpins one by one, making a great show of letting them fall from her fingertips. She watched him swallow when the tight white fabric started to inch up her thighs, saw that his eyes were trained on the apex of her legs. She hesitated on the brink of exposing her pink lace lingerie, causing Duncan's eyes to flick from the tops of her bare thighs to her face and back again.

When she continued to stall, he closed his eyes and licked his lips. "Sweet Jesus, Annabelle. I swear to God, one slice down the middle is all it will take." He started reaching for his back pocket but froze to watch Annabelle pull the dress up and over the moist heat hidden behind her pink lace thong...then fully expose her hour glass figure and lacy push-up bra. She drew the dress over her head, then shook out her red curls and combed her fingers through her hair before tossing the ball of fabric to land behind him on the foyer floor.

Duncan growled as his jacket hit the floor. And, as he loosened his tie, he backed her up the next two steps while pulling his shirttail from his pants and unbuttoning the cuffs. "Still wanna see me with my shirt off?" he asked, stalking her.

Annabelle could only nod, reaching out to steady herself with the banister. Her red heels started to slip, so she took one off and then the other as he backed her up the steps. When she looked up again, Duncan's chest was exposed. And boy, oh boy was it *magnificent.* She stifled most of a squeak as her eyes feasted on his tanned and muscled torso with its sexy smattering of curly dark hair which dipped and narrowed, disappearing beyond the waistband of his slacks. Her eyes drifted there just in time to watch Duncan loosen the buckle and pull his belt out of its loops with menacing slowness. He held it over the banister and let it drop to the floor below.

Annabelle came to a dead stop short of the top of the stairs. Her eyes took in the length and breadth of the ill-concealed hard-on behind Duncan's pants. She glanced up only when she heard him say, "You are welcome to lick your lips all you'd like."

She felt her face flush and was at a loss for a pithy comeback, suddenly realizing she was in way over her head. Duncan. Older and obviously more experienced. She. Four years his junior and far, far less experienced, she was sure. And this—her heart caught in her chest—this meant so much. This...being with him, meant...everything.

Frantic, she turned to run from the realization. Run from

the emotion boiling up inside her. Run from the fact that she was in love with Duncan James and couldn't bear to make one false move and jeopardize it all. She sprinted up the rest of the steps and ran down the hall, but Duncan grabbed her up by the waist and hauled her in the opposite direction saying, "The bedroom is this way."

Short of kicking and screaming, she flailed enough so that he put her down as soon as he managed to get her through the door. Then he shut them inside, turned his back to the door and folded his arms across his chest. Annabelle's breathing was heavy and labored and it cost her every ounce of courage she had to meet Duncan's eyes.

"You freaking out?"

"Little bit."

He nodded. Then looked down at the floor. Realizing he still had his shoes on, he toed them off. "Okay," he said through a thick release of breath, running a hand through his hair before looking back up at Annabelle. He spread his arms in quandary. "Well... you look beautiful," he said, indicating her partially naked state with a quick gesture before reaching up and rubbing his jaw.

"It's just..." Annabelle started. "It's just that..." But the swell of emotion grew so intense that the only place she could imagine finding solace was in Duncan's arms. So she moved to him, wrapped her arms around his waist and laid her cheek against his chest. His strong arms engulfed her upper body and held her tight. "It's just that it's all fun and games until someone gets hurt," she whimpered.

Duncan rubbed her back and kissed the top of her head. "No one is going to get hurt."

"You don't know that."

"Yes," he said, lifting her chin so he could see her eyes, "I do."

She believed him. She trusted he believed what he was saying and that was all she could ask. She reached up and placed a hand at the back of his neck, coaxing his lips to hers. Tentatively she pressed her tongue between his lips to meld with his own and offered up not only a sweet kiss, but her trust and belief as well. Both arms came up to circle his neck and she stood on tiptoe as he pressed her pelvis to his, letting their heat meld there as well.

"Touch me, please," Duncan breathed. "God knows it's all I can think about." He took her head in his hands and devoted exquisite attention to her mouth while her hands drifted over his shoulders, slid down his chest and worked together to unfasten the waistband and unzip his pants. "God, yes," he moaned into her mouth, kissing her with greater intensity as she slid one hand down between his pants and his boxer-briefs that covered the taut, firm shaft of his erection.

He pushed himself against the heel of her palm as she slid it down the length of him, and then groaned his approval when she used her fingers to massage his balls through the fabric. His lips kept their connection as he removed his pants. Then he took her hand and moved it inside the elastic band of his shorts and she followed his lead, slowly exposing his erection as the heat of her hand came in contact with the engorged shaft of his cock. He sighed her name in appreciation.

As his legs worked to disengage his boxers, Duncan slid the straps of Annabelle's bra off her shoulders, biting the smooth skin at the side of her neck. He unhooked her bra and pulled it down between them, his mouth eagerly following his hands to her aching breasts. She sighed, closing her eyes, biting her lower lip as she guided his hands to use more pressure. Her need swelled in delight and she rocked her pelvis against his shaft, stroking both of them where they needed it most.

Her legs instinctively circled Duncan's waist when he lifted her up, backing her to his bed where he lifted one knee, guiding them both on to the top of his comforter. Annabelle slid backward to the head of the bed, digging her fingers into the end of the comforter and pushing it under her body as Duncan helped drag it down beyond them. He laid her down, her head on his pillow and took his time to look his fill of her naked breasts, narrow waist, and long shapely legs.

"How the hell did I get so lucky?" he asked, sliding one hand up and down the side of her body as his eyes roamed freely. "Underneath all your stylish perfection, there is this sinfully, smokin' hot body." He lowered his head, closed his mouth over a nipple and sucked hard, causing Annabelle to gasp and buck her pelvis. He covered her lower body with his own, feasting on her breasts while drawing her hands up over her head.

His own hands slid back down languidly, caressing the sensitive insides of her arms, the ticklish depression of her underarms, the rounded sides of her breasts, and the indentation of her waist before tucking themselves under her back and massaging her buttocks. "I've been dying to get my hands on your shapely derrière," he said leaving a trail of kisses down her stomach and over her navel as his hands fondled her hips and rear-end.

He pulled the silky threads of her G-string down her hips and off her legs. Annabelle closed her eyes, feeling the contrast as cool air hit her warm, wet pubic hair, leaving every part of her exposed. Duncan traced his thumb through the thick of it, making her body bow when it slid over her clitoris and continued down her slick center. "So perfect," he said, his breath tantalizing the engorged nerve endings. His mouth lowered and he lovingly kissed her right where she could feel it most.

"Oh baby, there's so much I long to do to you," he moaned, lifting up and crawling forward over her body. "But I can't get what you did to me the other night out of my head," he said looking into her eyes. "Here," he offered his hand and helped her sit up. Then he moved back against the headboard and fumbled with a condom before taking her hand and bringing her to him.

"Just like you did before," he begged, clasping her hips and maneuvering her on to his lap. "Rub yourself against me," he pleaded as she slid her body along the back side of his erect shaft. "God yes," he breathed, his head thrown back as Annabelle started to rub her aching center up and down the long length of his cock, her body providing lubricant for the condom. "I fantasized about this," he said bringing his gaze down between them to watch the action. "Every night since." He cupped her ass with his hands and set the rhythm for the both of them. "Feel good?" he asked when Annabelle started to moan.

"So good," she said, closing her eyes, licking her lips. He smiled. She could hear it when he spoke.

"That mouth of yours is one hell of a turn-on," he said, moving her body a little faster. She tilted her hips and pressed harder, targeting her swollen nub. Duncan's hips started to pump causing an "even better" to spill from her lips.

"You like this, baby?" Duncan asked, his breath coming faster. His fingers gripping her ass tighter. His cock sliding quickly within the folds of her flesh. "Is this what you needed? Finish what you started New Year's Eve, Annabelle. Come on, baby. Come for me," he breathed, "Come for me so I can take us where we both want to go."

He reached between them to press his cock hard against her. When Annabelle first started to spasm and shake, he moved his thumb over her nub and manipulated her into a soul-wrenching orgasm. And as the hollow need inside her grew desperate to be filled, he lifted her up and then slid her down, sheathing his erection. Another orgasm erupted immediately, causing her body to go loose everywhere except where it counted for Duncan. Her internal muscles milked him hard, setting off a wild chain of events.

Duncan pushed Annabelle to her back while she still came, whimpering his name, squeezing his cock inside the very core of her body. "Holy shi—" he began, but the blood drained from his head down to his groin, erasing all thought. His hips worked like a piston, ferociously fucking the girl of his dreams. Every muscle from his toes to his forehead strained, his shoulders and neck were rigid, his jaw clenched. He heard himself grunt louder and louder, out of control with every pump, until his entire body shook uncontrollably with a long, hard climax.

"Holy Mother of God," he panted, lying on top of her, sweaty and spent.

Moments later, still breathing heavily, he reached for Annabelle's hand and squeezed it.

She squeezed back.

Finally finding the strength to move, he rolled off and sprawled flat on his back, both their heads at the end of the bed. "Annabelle, sweetheart," he whispered, his heart rate still off the chart, "I'm afraid you're gonna have to marry me." His other hand collapsed on top of his stomach and he closed his eyes as Annabelle rose up on an elbow to peer down at him.

Through labored breathing he told her again, "You're gonna have to marry me, baby." He opened his eyes and wiped sweat from them. "Because there is no doubt you have just ruined me for all other women. And, more importantly," he went on, "I know damn well there isn't a condom in this world built strong enough to survive a fuck like that."

He glanced over as Annabelle choked out a laugh at his ungentlemanly choice of words. Giving his spent body a long, cool once-over, she shrugged a shoulder. "Okay," she said before flopping back down and snuggling in against him. "I'll call Daddy."

He smiled at that, his arm going around her, his fingers playing over her deliciously soft skin. And then he smiled broader because he was a lawyer. And although Miss Devine might be somewhat unaware, she'd just entered herself into a verbal contract.

And he had every intention of holding her to it.

Interested in what romance has is in store for Duncan's friends Brooks and Vance? Visit my website www.LizKellyBooks.com to read an excerpt from *Loving Lolly*: Part One of the Good Cop Bad Cop Series coming in early 2013.

Grace

For Scott, with love

Kiss of a Lifetime

Chapter One
⎯ ℭ ⎯

December 12
Arlington, Virginia

"I HEAR," Leo Ramos said as he pulled Grace toward his chest with one arm, pivoted, and expertly rolled her body over his hip, "that you're kissing Lewis Kampmueller on New Year's Eve."

Grace Devine landed flat on her back on a mat that really needed to be softer. She had to wait a moment before she had enough air to speak. She'd been at the FBI's Washington Field Office for six months and hadn't mentioned the annual Devine-Kampmueller New Year's Eve Ball to anyone. She had done her absolute best to not even think about it. "There's no way you can know that," she finally wheezed.

"And yet," he squatted next to her, forearms resting on his thighs, "I do." Ramos's brows quirked over amused eyes, his irises a shade of deep, rich brown.

Grace rolled to her side and came up on her knees, facing him. He was close to laughter, his black silky hair mussed and his skin damp from exertion. For a crazy half-second, she was tempted to lean over and brush her lips against his, just to see if his smile tasted as good as it looked.

Yeah, and he'd probably fall over flat on his back in shock.

Grace was one of the guys. She sweated with the squad during workouts, outshot most of them at the firing range, won her share of Friday night poker games and never, absolutely never, ordered a sweet drink at the Pub.

In the testosterone-fueled world of FBI special agents, it worked for her.

Or it used to.

Their off-site training facility, affectionately nicknamed The Pit, was empty now except for the two of them. While much of her work on the counterterrorism squad involved field interviews, computers and too much late-night coffee, their squadron leader, David Carter, had the whole squad train together twice a month to keep their defensive skills sharp. Tonight, Ramos had stayed late to help her with the Koshinage hip throw, a seemingly simple move that she'd mangled every time she tried it. Damn it. She didn't want to leave until she had it mastered. Ramos knew that about her. He was the same way.

"Why so quiet, Devine? Are you getting all dreamy about Kampfiller?" Ramos's lips curved into a taunting grin. A smile of one kind or another was rarely off his face. Sometimes she wondered if he used it to keep people at a distance. Nobody asked you what was wrong if you were smiling.

"Kampmueller. And no, I'm not." She tilted her head. "Have you been messing around in my file?" And had her background check really included the New Year's Eve Ball? Ugh.

"I'm hurt, Devine. That would be against regulations." He placed a hand over his heart. "I'm a by-the-book kind of agent."

"I don't doubt that. Exactly what book is the question." Whatever one it was, it definitely wasn't an open book. For all his friendliness, Ramos remained a mystery to her.

He ignored her jibe and leaned slightly forward on the balls of his feet, balance still perfect. He studied her. "Devine has a boyfriend. Surprise, surprise."

"What are you, twelve?" She lifted a hand to touch her ponytail, suddenly conscious that her makeup must have sweated off. Her faded, baggy t-shirt, a relic from Academy training, hung past her hips. Gray gym shorts hit her legs mid-thigh and were ugly as hell, but easy to move in. She was not the type of woman most men dreamed of at night, but she lifted her chin, pricked by his teasing. "And your surprise is not very flattering."

A dimple flashed in his cheek. "I'm surprised that my expert FBI deduction skills failed me. You never talk about a man in your life. Nobody ever meets you at the Grub Pub when we all go out. You never blush when reading a text and, most importantly, office gossip is silent about you."

"Oh." Stupid of her to suddenly feel like the most boring person alive. She pushed quickly to her feet, wanting to get some distance from him. "So you found out about Lewis how?"

Ramos rose more slowly. "Baxter and I were going over some reports from the Raleigh office this morning." Roy Baxter had the desk behind hers. "We overheard you on the phone saying something about Kampfooler and New Year's Eve and kissing."

"Kampmueller. You listened to my phone conversation?" That was so not allowed. At least not without reasonable cause, reams of paperwork and the proper court order.

"After the first couple of words, both Baxter and I stuck our fingers in our ears and hummed. Honest."

The angelic look on his face made her struggle to keep her frown. Exactly what had she said on the phone this morning while talking with her little sister? They'd discussed their older sister Tess and her impending divorce, but mostly Annabelle had been bubbling over with news about the New Year's Eve Ball, now only three weeks away. And, as usual, she couldn't resist teasing Grace about the stupid bet that had been started years ago.

The Devine sister who didn't have someone to kiss at the New Year's Eve Ball at midnight had to kiss Lewis.

Of course, there were all sorts of potential problems with that. What if more than one sister didn't have a date? What if Lewis *did* have a date? Not that any of that mattered because she was the only one whose date always disappeared before the stroke of midnight, and Lewis had never once brought a date to the Ball.

Her newest strategy for dealing with the fact that she lost

the bet every single year was to make losing sound really good. Unfortunately, once she started rhapsodizing over the rare wonder of kissing Lewis, Belly had started laughing uncontrollably. Belly had the kind of laugh that filled a room with warmth, and once started made a person want to feed it like a roaring fire to keep it going. So Grace had gone on a riff about how Lewis had a talent for kissing that was so amazing, someone should market his gift. She'd then spewed some nonsense about developing a new sex toy called KampKiss—vibrating lips guaranteed to make rabbit ears obsolete and revitalize the economy. Empty car factories in Detroit would convert to K-Kiss production. Unemployment would plummet. Depression would become a forgotten diagnosis.

Dear God.

"Exactly how loud were you humming?"

Ramos grinned. "So what's the big deal? Why are you keeping this Kampdrooler a secret?"

"Kamp—" She paused. There was no way she was going to explain the whole Lewis thing to Ramos. "When you start sharing your private life, I'll start sharing mine."

His smile faded. "Fair enough."

Okay. That had sounded harsher than she intended. He'd just been ribbing her, a standard form of guy communication. "Ramos …."

He held up his hands. "Not a problem, Devine. Let's run through this one more time and then go meet the rest of the squad. I have someone waiting for me at the Pub."

Of course he did. She'd put money on the fact that Ramos always had a date on New Year's Eve too.

"One more time." She nodded at Ramos and took a step back. "You attack me."

He came at her panther-quick, before she had time to set her feet in the proper position. His hand circled her forearm and she jerked him toward her, pulling him slightly off balance while she turned her backside into his pelvis, bent forward and let his momentum propel him over her hip and onto the floor.

Unfortunately, this perfect move was ruined by the fact that his hand still gripped her arm. Her body followed his and smashed into six feet of muscle and bone.

Sprawled across his chest, breath knocked out of her lungs again, she silently blinked. His eyes were only inches away, liquid darkness. Her pelvis rested against his stomach and she could feel the regular rise and fall of those hard muscles as they slowly lifted her, lowered her. Her legs, slightly parted, aligned perfectly against his.

Little flashes of light started to stab across her vision and she realized she wasn't breathing. She sucked in air and stopped mid-motion when her breasts pushed more firmly against him.

"Breathe," he ordered gruffly.

She gingerly released her breath and took a few more shallow gulps of air. "Well. That certainly wasn't supposed to happen." She tried to sound brisk and analytical, as if her only thought was to figure out how the Aikido move had gone wrong. She would be in big trouble if his attack had been for real.

Ramos's body heaved and twisted and she was suddenly no longer on top of him, but trapped beneath, one arm still firmly locked in his hand, the other wedged between their chests.

Okay. She was in big trouble anyway.

"Treat an arm grab like a wrist grab," he instructed, his face close to hers, his breath a warm brush on her cheek.

"A wrist grab." She nodded. His eyelashes were the exact shade of his hair. Small smile lines radiated from the corners of his eyes, even though he wasn't smiling.

"When I grabbed your left arm, one of your possible moves was to step toward me with your right foot, rotate your left arm within my grip to weaken my hold and then strike my attacking arm with your right elbow."

She could feel his heart beating. Or maybe that was hers. No, the rhythm was too slow and steady. He turned to look at her arm and raised it slightly, as if to bring his grip to her attention. Did he think she'd forgotten he was holding her?

What he actually brought to her attention was his neck, which was very, very close to her lips. The skin was smooth beneath the dark wave of his hair. She lifted her head slightly, as if to look at her arm. Her lips brushed the area beneath his ear, and without her consciously directing it to do so, her tongue lightly flicked against his skin.

His body froze.

Grace carefully lowered her head. She held her breath. She hadn't just done that, had she?

"Right." Ramos finally moved. He released her arm with a jerky motion, put both hands against the floor and lifted his chest, his knees still on either side of her hips. She shivered. The room suddenly felt twenty degrees colder. "We should head off to the Pub now."

"Right," she echoed. She waited for him to demand why she'd licked his neck. Then again, the movement had been so quick, he might not have noticed. In fact, she was sure he hadn't noticed. Those moments he'd gone scary still had only been a perceptual trick, like the way time doesn't really slow when you're watching a bullet speed toward you, it just feels like it because your senses are sharpened. Not that a bullet had ever sped toward her—her job was not as dangerous as her mother believed—but she'd watched a lot of movies, and they couldn't all be wrong.

Okay, her brain had officially derailed. She shut her eyes and tried to focus on saying something reasonable. Her tongue felt strange and she rubbed it against the roof of her mouth, savoring the subtle flavor of him.

"Are you okay?"

Grace's eyes flew open. Ramos's gaze had settled on her mouth. He abruptly stood and stepped to one side of her body.

"I'm fine." She scrambled to her feet and smoothed a strand of hair behind her ear. "Thanks for staying to help me practice." She made herself meet his eyes. She was acting like an idiot. Ramos was her friend and an agent that she admired. He always went the extra mile with any of the squad. He was well respected and as much a leader as Carter.

He nodded, his face oddly serious as he stood there.

She tugged at the bottom of her shirt. Ramos didn't usually look at her in such an intently brooding way and she didn't know how to respond to him. Saying "I just licked your neck and am interested in tasting more of you," seemed wildly inappropriate.

Unfortunately, it was true.

He was part of her squadron. Work relationships were messy. He was also a wicked charmer who was attracted to gorgeous women like her older sister Tess, not to sweaty jocks like her.

"I'll head to the locker room and I'll see you over at the Pub." She waited a second. When he didn't respond, she lifted her hand and waved. She turned and walked quickly toward the women's locker room. Good Lord, had she really waved, like she was Queen Elizabeth or something? She felt a blush heat her cheeks. When she rounded a mat and broke into a jog, she hoped she looked athletic and not as if she was running away.

Chapter Two

THE GRUB PUB was warm, noisy and smelled of fried food and beer, two of Leo's favorite things. He stepped inside the restaurant, a homey mix of vinyl-topped tables and roomy booths, and took a deep breath. It didn't help. He still couldn't get Devine's scent out of his head. Her skin had smelled faintly of lemon and a tantalizing hint of some spice. He'd wanted to bury his nose in the spot where her neck met her shoulder and breathe her in.

Which was so fucking wrong.

Devine was…Devine. His friend, his colleague and the woman who had wormed her way under every damn protective shield he'd erected. He'd known he was in trouble her first day at the field office when he'd looked up from a conversation with Carter and had seen her stride into the room with the confidence and graceful rhythm of an athlete. Carter's voice, the noise of the office, had faded. For a moment, there had been just her—a smiling woman with hair the color of spiced rum and a face filled with intelligence and curiosity. Then Carter had touched his arm and the world came back into focus. Thankfully, weird shit like that had never happened again.

Sometimes, though, he caught himself thinking about her when they were apart, wanting to share a joke, wondering about her opinion on certain situations. Wondering how that hair would feel under his fingers and across his chest. How that body would feel beneath him.

He pulled his brain up short and forced himself to remember another woman he'd worked with, Katherine Dill. Immediately, guilt and pain knotted in his chest. His hand groped into his pocket and he felt the reassuring weight of his phone. Hawk was on speed dial. He'd never called him. But he could. If he needed to, he could.

Leo flexed his shoulders and relaxed his tense muscles. Devine was an excellent agent with a whip-smart brain. He liked and respected her. Nothing more. And she regarded him as one of the guys, no different than any other man on the squad. Which was exactly what he wanted.

Except, she'd licked his neck.

"Leo!"

He turned at the sound of his name and walked toward the large double booth crowded with the squad and a few of their significant others. Mandy Jenkins, a beautiful blonde lawyer in the Justice Department, scooted over to make a spot for him. They'd been seeing each other for a few weeks. This was her first time at the Pub and, while she had only met a few members of the squad, she seemed comfortable with the group. She was sophisticated, yet warm and friendly, exactly the type of woman he liked. She rested her perfectly manicured nails on his arm and he stared at her hand, seeing Grace's slender, strong fingers and short, naked nails.

What was it about naked nails that made him hard?

"Leo." Mandy snapped her fingers in his face with a laugh. "Are you all right?"

He shook his head and smiled. "Sorry, my mind was still on work." He looked down the length of the booth. "Did I get here before Devine?"

Lisa Roberts, the only other woman on the squad, snorted. "Nope. Michael Wolfram snatched her up the minute she walked through the door." She leaned forward, a gleam in her eyes. "Could our newbie have a secret boyfriend?"

Roberts was the squad's prime source of office gossip. Leo

thought the woman was wasted on them and should have been placed in Intelligence. If the CIA had recruited her years ago, there was no way Bin Laden would have stayed hidden for so long. Roberts heard everything, sometimes before people even said it.

She gave a sigh and raised her beer. "Wolfram looks like the Swedish GQ version of a special agent. We should use him on recruitment brochures for the Bureau." She nodded to a point over Leo's shoulder. "The two of them are seated at that booth over there."

Leo didn't turn his head. Wolfram had mentored Devine in the Chicago office, her first assignment out of the Academy. He was in Washington for a couple of months to receive additional training at Quantico. Word was also circulating that Wolfram was forming a special task force to go after one of the most hated domestic terrorist groups in the country. A long line of agents would give their eyeteeth to be part of that team. Wolfram could choose from the cream of the crop.

"You could be right, Roberts." Roy Baxter, one of Leo's oldest friends in the Bureau, blew a silent whistle. "Our skirt is looking mighty friendly with the Big Bad." His eyes narrowed. "Shit, that table is full of HBOs. She's moving in elevated circles."

Telling himself he was curious about the High Bureau Officials, Leo turned to look. At the far end of the room, he saw the back of Devine's head. Her ponytail was gone and her hair looked thick and shiny under the Pub's bright lights. She was seated in a booth on the same side of the table as Wolfram, their shoulders touching on a seat that had plenty of extra room. She tilted her head back as he watched and she laughed—a clear, happy sound that cut through the chatter and noise of the bar. Wolfram bent his blond head and whispered something in her ear. David Carter, their squadron leader, sat on the other side of the table along with Jim McDonald, the ADIC and Teri Murphy, an Assistant Special Agent in Charge. Not that Wolfram and Devine were paying much attention to anyone else.

It was a day of discovery about Devine. She had two men

dangling from her string, Kampmueller and Wolfram.

It was also a day of discovery about himself. He didn't like it.

Mandy's hand covered the fist resting on his thigh. "Hard day?" she murmured in his ear.

He breathed in her light, floral scent. "I don't think I'm going to be good company tonight. I'm more tired than I thought."

She ran a nail along his knuckles. "Want to go home and have an early night?"

The invitation was clear. They hadn't slept together yet and she meant for tonight to be the night. Leo looked down into her face and felt absolutely nothing except a dull thread of pain that snaked through his head and began to throb at his temples. Great. He could just imagine telling Mandy he didn't want sex because he had a headache. He looked toward Baxter, sitting across the table from him.

Baxter lifted a surprised eyebrow, but shrugged. "Devine wear you out with all those hip flips, Ramos?" He easily joined the conversation as he poured a beer from the pitcher on the table and shoved it in front of Leo. "That woman is a tiger. What our boy needs is some food," he said to Mandy, as if he hadn't picked up the subtext in her invitation. "He'll feel better in no time."

"Food." Leo grabbed the menu he knew by heart. "That's exactly what I need." He was hungry. That was the reason for the headache, the burn in his belly.

A hum of awareness at the back of his neck pulled his gaze to Devine as she wove through the tables toward them, her fluid stride mesmerizing. Her brown leather jacket hung open over a pair of tight jeans and a soft-looking yellow sweater. Brown leather boots reached to her knees. Her smile took in the table. "I'm about to head for home." She ruffled Baxter's hair in an affectionate gesture. "Some of us put in extra work and trained late."

"I'll have you know we've been working hard at hoisting these beers while you and Ramos probably spent half the time on your backs in the Pit." Baxter swiped imaginary sweat off his brow.

"Please." Devine crossed her arms and shot Leo a mischievous grin. "Ramos spent most of the time on his back. I got my daily deltoid reps just helping him up."

She was teasing him, treating him just the way she always did. He stared at her silently and her smile faltered.

"Hold on, Devine." Roberts leaned over past Baxter. While Devine was one of the guys, Roberts was all female. She wore a snug cashmere sweater, her red hair and makeup perfect despite the fact that she, too, had come from the Pit. "You can't leave without giving us the scoop on the Big Bad. You've been holding out on us, girl."

"The Big Bad?" Devine looked confused.

"The Big Bad Wolfram." Roberts fanned herself.

Devine's smile widened again and she glanced over her shoulder to the table where Wolfram still sat. "Wish I'd thought of that handle. He was my supervisor at the Chicago field office. He's a good buddy."

"You've got a lot of those," Leo commented.

"What can I say?" Devine shrugged. "Men just fall at my feet, wanting to be my pal. I think it has something to do with the fact that I'm the only woman they know who can tell them which college football team signed the best recruiting class this year."

Roberts snorted.

"Hey," Baxter began, forgetting to take a swig of the beer almost at his lips.

"Alabama," Devine answered before he could ask. "They just got a commitment from Rodney Stark, a five-star running back out of Plainview, Illinois. Everyone was sure he'd go to Notre Dame." She shifted, stuck her hands in her jacket pockets. Leo felt the weight of her gaze. "Ramos, can I talk to you privately for a moment?" She smiled an apology at Mandy. "I won't keep him but a minute. Work consult."

Ramos didn't want to be alone with her right now. Not until he could safely cage this damn inappropriate possessiveness. The thought of Devine with Wolfram or Kampmueller shouldn't make him want to bash heads.

She shifted her weight again, a frown beginning to form when he continued to say nothing. Then she cleared her throat, a vulnerable sound that socked him in the stomach. Hell. He wasn't going to embarrass her with his rudeness, just because he was a damaged prick who wanted what he couldn't have.

He rose from the suddenly quiet table, aware of the curious eyes that followed them to an empty two-seater tucked against the wall in the corner. He waited until she sat before pulling the chair out across from her.

"What's the problem?" He eased down and put his elbows on the table. She ran a hand through her hair and tugged at the strands near her neck.

"I'm nervous," she admitted and looked him square in the eye. He liked that about her, her honesty and directness. "Ramos," she started again, then paused with a brief shake of her head. A small smile tilted her lips. "Leo." Her voice softened on his name in a way that twisted his gut.

He was drowning here and couldn't seem to do anything to save himself. The water just kept getting deeper and deeper.

She fidgeted, as if she couldn't get comfortable, then stilled herself, squaring her shoulders. "I don't know if you noticed, but I sort of licked you at the Pit." She folded her hands on the table in front of her. Actually saying the words seemed to settle her.

Unfortunately, they didn't have that effect on him. She watched him now with a calm that told him she was totally unaware of the impact of her simple words. He closed his eyes and muttered a short, fervent prayer, asking for strength. Asking to be transported to a safe, Devine-less environment where he could forget her scent and the feel of that tentative touch against his neck. Instead, when he opened his eyes she still sat across from him.

Chapter Three

GRACE GRIPPED her hands tighter. Exactly why had she thought this conversation would be a good idea? She should have texted Tess or Annabelle first. They would have told her to keep her mouth shut, that she was making way too big a deal about a little tongue flick.

"Sort of?" Ramos opened his eyes after briefly closing them and mumbling something in Spanish. He looked almost angry as he stared at Grace.

"Well, not sort of. Definitely. I definitely licked you." Who knew semantics would be so important to him.

"Okay." He nodded as if that was all he needed to hear. He turned away from her and looked toward the booth where his date was talking with Baxter.

"You don't want to know why?" she asked after several moments.

He turned back to her, his expression grim. "No. I don't want to know why."

"Oh." She bit her lip, not sure where to go with that. "Should I apologize?"

"No, just stop talking about it." His voice was tight, not at all Ramos-like. "What did you want to consult about? I'm hungry and want to order some dinner."

The idiot. Did he really think she'd wanted a consult? She'd wanted to talk about the now off-limits lick and, hopefully, their mutual attraction which—it was now painfully obvious—was not mutual.

Right. She needed to salvage this situation and keep them on a friendly footing. "I just said that about the consult so I could talk to you privately," she said with an easy smile.

Ramos stiffened and his eyes darkened.

"Uh, but I do need some career advice," she added quickly.

He looked at her in silence for a full ten seconds. "Career advice." He seemed to say the words very carefully. "You're asking me for career advice."

"Well, yes. Yes, I am. You've been around here for a couple of years and I'm still relatively new on the squad. Here's the thing. Michael has asked me to be part of his new task force. What do you think? Is it a good idea?" She'd had no intention of discussing Michael's offer yet, not until she'd had time to consider it first. But it was all she could think of, spur of the moment, and it was a heck of lot better than a pathetic "I wanted to tell you I like you. Do you like me?"

Especially since he was telegraphing the answer to that question, loud and clear.

"It's the opportunity of a lifetime." His voice was flat, matter-of-fact.

"Of course." She widened her smile. "You certainly helped me put the offer in perspective. I'm glad we had this little talk." She slapped the table with her hand, prepared to stand and get the hell out of Dodge.

His hand snapped out and circled her wrist. "Devine."

Her heart stuttered in her chest and she slowly sank back into her chair. She cleared her tight throat. "Yes?" Shadows seemed to pool in his dark eyes.

"You and I. We wouldn't work. I don't do long-term romantic relationships."

"You don't do long-term relationships? Ever?" Grace found it easier to focus on the last part of his statement.

"Ever."

His assurance rankled. "So how does that work? What's the tipping point? How many times can you date a person before they move from short-term to long-term?"

He shrugged. "There's no exact number."

"Ballpark figure, then."

His eyes narrowed. "I don't date a woman longer than a month."

Grace nodded over toward the booth. "What week is she on?"

"Three." The word came out sharp and short.

"That has got to be the most asinine rule I've ever heard. What if you really like a woman and think she's the greatest thing since …" Grace waved her free hand, "hot fudge sundaes? You would stop seeing her after four weeks simply so the relationship doesn't cross your line into long term? How does that make any sense?"

"I've never met a woman equal to a hot fudge sundae, so I can't say." The shadows in his eyes gave way to amusement.

"And the women are all okay with this?"

He shrugged. "They all think they'll be the dessert that destroys my diet."

She regarded him with a bit of awe. "I see the brilliance of this. You only date successful, driven women. Setting a time limit on the relationship taps into their competitive spirit. You're the ultimate challenge. Women probably line up for a chance to make it to week number five."

He gave her an odd look. "Not one woman has considered this brilliant, Devine. Most often I'm called a jerk."

"Well, that goes without saying. You're emotionally stunted and in serious need of psychological help."

"Tell me something new." His tone was dry. "And just so you know…I have another rule."

"I feel like I'm in school again." And she hadn't particularly liked most of those rules, either.

"I don't date women from the field office. Not special agents, not support staff, no one."

"Why is that?"

His fingers, still circled around her wrist, tightened. He could probably feel the rapid beat of her pulse. "Doesn't matter. I just don't."

She thought it mattered very much, but didn't pursue his reasons.

"One more thing."

She gave an exaggerated sigh and gazed around the bar as if none of this really concerned her and she was getting a bit bored. "Yes?"

He tugged hard on her wrist. Startled, she looked at his face. Emotions she couldn't begin to name sharpened his features. His lips twisted and his dimples briefly flashed, but not in a smile. He slowly lifted her wrist and pulled her arm toward him. Grace watched, not resisting, as if her hand had a will of its own.

His eyes didn't leave hers until her hand was cradled, palm up, in his larger one. One finger slid along the pad of her thumb tracing the lines of her palm, easing open her fingers. Then he lowered his head, black silky hair falling across his forehead, and his tongue swiped across the pulse in her wrist. Not a quick swipe, but a slow, flat-tongued lick.

She couldn't speak. She wasn't sure she could move. He set her hand down gently on the table.

"We're even now." He placed both his hands against the table and pushed out of his chair. He walked to the booth, to his beautiful date, without once looking back.

⌒

Leo didn't go home with Mandy. He didn't go home at all. Instead he went back to the Pit, swiped his security card, and spent forty minutes trying to beat the stuffing out of a leather punching bag. The bastard bag defeated him. His arms felt like spaghetti noodles when he finally tossed the gloves aside, but he still hadn't succeeded in easing the knot in his chest.

"I haven't seen you this wired since right after New York." Roy Baxter's voice caused him to jerk his head around. Baxter was sitting against the wall of the weight room, legs stretched out in a relaxed pose, bottle of beer in hand.

"How long have you been here?" Leo bent to grip his thighs and pulled in a couple of deep breaths. Then he straightened and wiped the sweat from his forehead with the towel he had stuck in the waist of his sweats.

"I came in about fifteen minutes ago. I drove by on my way home from the Pub and saw your car in the lot. You want to tell me what's got your panties in a twist?"

"No." Leo walked over to the water cooler and filled a paper cup full of water.

Roy didn't take the hint and shut up. "Your little consult with Devine didn't have anything to do with vampires did it?"

Leo shot him a frown. "What the fuck are you talking about? How much have you had have to drink?"

Roy grinned. "Not enough to blur my vision. I saw you sucking at her wrist. And she looked a little pale when you walked away."

Devine. That's what this was all about.

"Mandy wasn't too happy with that little performance either, but that won't stop her from saying yes the next time you ask her out." Baxter looked disgusted. "What is it about you, Ramos?" He frowned. "Must be the whole Latin Lover vibe you've got going. Women go for that shit. And Wolfram's got the whole Viking Marauder Vibe. Why the hell is that sexy? I had to wipe the drool off Roberts's chin. Hell, if—God forbid—I tried to toss Roberts over my shoulder to ravish her, she'd cut off my balls, yet the Big Bad has her panting." He shook his head, took another drink. "The real problem is that dudes with German heritage don't have any vibe going for them. Unless it's the whole Anal-Retentive Vibe, which, I gotta tell you, isn't a chick magnet. My degree is in accounting, you know. That got me no mileage in college."

"Jesus, Baxter. Do I have to put a two-beer limit on you? What the fuck are you talking about now?"

"Shit." Baxter looked as if he suddenly had a light-bulb moment. "You've got a thing for Devine, haven't you?" He knocked the heel of his hand against his forehead. "Of course."

"No." Leo said the word forcefully.

"Anal-retentive people are very good at small details." He shot a look at Leo. "Which makes us very good lovers, in case anyone asks."

"Why would anyone ask me how good a lover you are?"

"Well, the least you could do is start the rumor. Shit, tell Roberts. It'll be around the entire Bureau by Christmas."

"Devine." Leo refocused Baxter. "What small details?"

"You were the only one who went to see that romantic comedy with her last month. Even Roberts wouldn't go."

"Devine went to see the Kurosawa retrospective with me. I owed her."

"You know she doesn't like to sit next to Jagger when we play poker so you always take that seat."

"Jagger eats M&Ms all through the game. Devine can't resist them if they're in front of her and then she feels guilty all weekend and only eats lettuce."

"She volunteered to take the field interviews over at the Lakeland Senior Home two weeks ago, even though Carter originally had you going. You told her how difficult going into those places is for you since your grandma's dementia, didn't you?"

"Carter had me down for those interviews?"

"And when she went on the late beer run last Friday, she bought the Bell's Hopslam, your favorite, even though she's a wheat beer girl."

"She said she wanted to expand her palate."

"I've been blind. True love has been blossoming before my very eyes." Baxter put a hand to his heart. "Are those violins I hear playing in the distance?" His blue eyes lost some of their humor. "She's family, Ramos. Treat her like shit and you're a dead man."

No idle threat. Baxter was their best man at the firing range.

"There is no Devine and me." If he said it enough, he might believe it. "You know why that isn't going to happen."

Baxter's face went totally sober. "Are you thinking about New York? Dill was totally fucked up. Nothing that happened was your fault."

"She's dead, Baxter."

"So? Death doesn't make her a saint. Didn't Hawk say she had some kind of personality disorder shit? Anyway, that was years ago, man. Move on."

Move on. Hawk's words, too. Accept the past and leave it in the past. He rubbed the back of his neck, suddenly bone-tired. "Wolfram asked Devine to join his task force."

Baxter whistled. "Devine's good, but she's not tested yet. Has he got a thing for her?"

The knot in Ramos' chest tightened. He'd had no business visualizing Wolfram's face on the punching bag. "I don't know."

"Well, good for her, bad for us. I'll miss her here in Washington." Baxter's gaze was steady. "Sucks for you."

"She hasn't given Wolfram an answer yet." She'd be crazy to turn him down.

Baxter watched him. "You going to give her a reason not to go?"

"There is no reason not to go. I told her to take his offer."

Baxter set his beer aside and lumbered to his feet. "That's that, then." He picked up his jacket. "You didn't eat much dinner. Let's go get some nachos."

Chapter Four

Henderson, North Carolina
New Year's Eve

"DO YOU KNOW what I hate more than anything in the world?" Grace flopped back on her sister Annabelle's bed and contemplated the ceiling. It was a spotless shade of Moonlit Lace. Grace knew this because on one lost-forever break from college, Annabelle had waved so many paint cards with different shades of white in front of her eyes that she thought she'd go snowblind.

"Losing." Annabelle didn't even look up from her iPad. She was no doubt typing a list of Dos and Don'ts to email to this year's herd of debutantes before tonight's New Year's Eve Ball. Her perfectly shaped pink nails tapped the screen with industrious precision. A slight frown wrinkled her usually smooth forehead.

"Besides that." Grace did a sit-up and scooted against Annabelle's bleached oak headboard. She loved Annabelle's room. The décor was an ultra-feminine mix of green, pinks and yellows and the room was always in perfect order, unlike the obstacle course that her room usually reverted to less than thirty minutes after she cleaned it.

"The thing you hate wouldn't have anything to do with a certain kiss at midnight, would it?" Tess asked from the doorway. Tess was older by two years. When she strolled into the room, the space immediately felt smaller. Despite the fact her long blond hair was tied back in a ponytail and there wasn't a brush of makeup on her face, Tess filled the room with her presence. She always had. Her success on the Broadway stage had come as no surprise to Grace.

"Of course not. I've told you, I don't hate kissing Lewis." She actually liked Lewis, something she'd never admit or her mother would have the wedding planned and future grandchildren named. She crossed her legs, making room for Tess to sit on the foot of the bed. "Wouldn't surprise me if he's written an equation for the perfect kiss."

Tess's brown eyes were full of amused disbelief. "Is that so? Well, you would certainly know." She snickered. "Belly told me about the KampKiss. I think you should ask Dad to fund the start-up."

Grace reached behind her back for one of the five million decorative pillows that Annabelle kept on her bed and tossed one that looked like a yellow tootsie roll at Tess. "I do not want to be responsible for Daddy's loss of innocence. Can you imagine his reaction to the idea that one of his daughters even knows what a sex toy is?"

"I refuse to believe Lewis is that good of a kisser anyway." Annabelle didn't look entirely certain.

"You'll never know for sure unless you kiss him." Grace tried for a mysterious smile.

"We wouldn't dream of depriving you of the pleasure." Tess tossed a pink and white pillow at Grace. She wrinkled her nose when Annabelle opened her mouth to object. "What? They're called throw pillows, aren't they? So, what do you hate, Gracie, if it's not kissing Lewis?" Her tone was light, but Grace recognized the bulldog glint in her eyes. Tess had picked up the fact that something was seriously bothering her.

Annabelle set her iPad aside and leaned forward. "Spill, Gracie."

Grace took a deep breath. "I've got a big decision to make about my job. I've been asked to join a task force led by Michael

Wolfram, the special agent who mentored me in Chicago. I told him I'd give him a decision when I go back to work next week."

"Michael Wolfram?" Tess's brow furrowed. "I remember him from when I came to visit you in Chicago."

"He's driving down from Washington tonight. He's my date."

"Way to go, girl." Tess looked impressed, and then worried. "He might actually kiss you at midnight."

Grace pumped a mental fist in the air. No losing for her tonight.

"This sounds like a no-brainer. Is there a problem with joining the task force?" Annabelle asked.

Grace tugged at the ends of her hair. "No. Well, okay. Maybe just a little problem. His name is Leo Ramos. He's a special agent assigned to my squad in Washington." She scowled. "We're good friends."

"Ah." Annabelle didn't have any problem understanding her explanation. "That's a bitch."

"And a recurring theme for you," Tess added.

Grace nodded. "I'm not a girly-girl. Men automatically put me in the friend category."

Tess gave a short laugh. "Men never automatically put women in the friend category. You put yourself in that category." She tilted her head, her look assessing. "You don't have to be a girly-girl to be a hundred percent female."

Sometimes when Tess spoke with that rhythmic musicality in her tone, Grace expected her to break into a song, in this case, maybe Rodger and Hammerstein's "I Enjoy Being a Girl," or Shania Twain's "I Feel Like a Woman."

Tess threw another pillow at her, ignoring Annabelle's huff. "Quit humming, I'm not about to sing. Here's my advice. Grab him, kiss him blind and he'll stop thinking of you as a friend. Then have your way with him. If you're enough of an idiot to let him break your heart, simply listen to Adele—once in the morning before work and once before bed for two weeks. Then you can head off to the new task force, strong and fierce, Ramos forgotten."

A startled silence settled over the room. Before her marriage, her sister hadn't been such a cynic. Tess must be having a harder time with the divorce than Grace realized. About to probe more deeply, she caught Annabelle's quick headshake.

Right. A lot of eyes would be on Tess tonight. They always were, but tonight, in her hometown, at the celebration she'd made the backdrop for her wedding, the focus would be relentless. Tess didn't need to delve into a discussion on the psychological consequences of her failed marriage hours before stepping onto that stage. Grace would corner her tomorrow for a heart to heart

"Okay, Dr. Tess," Grace said slowly. "Not a bad plan, except he refuses to become involved with FBI employees."

Tess shrugged. "That just makes it more of a challenge."

Annabelle looked confused. "Is this guy going to be here tonight?"

"No, of course not." Ramos as her date tonight was something she wouldn't even let herself fantasize about.

"Then forget about him for now and focus on the guy who will be. Did I ever meet Michael?"

"I don't think so," Grace said. "You'll love him, though. He's probably got almost as many clothes in his closet as you do."

Annabelle folded her arms across her chest. "Then I hope you're wearing something appropriate tonight."

Grace winced. "Actually, I was hoping you might have something I can wear."

"Grace Elizabeth Devine, are you telling me that you have no idea what you're wearing and the party is tonight?" Annabelle stood up and marched toward her closet. "I cannot believe we share the same DNA."

"Mom made the mistake of stepping inside a Wal-Mart while she was pregnant with me. My Niemen Marcus gene was damaged beyond repair."

Annabelle ignored her and walked into her closet.

"You might want to leave a trail of bread crumbs so you can

find your way back out of there," Grace called.

The rustle of clothes hangers was Annabelle's only response.

"So you're thinking of transferring again after only six months in Washington?" Tess asked quietly. "I thought you loved it there."

"I do. I love the excitement, the feeling that I'm at the hub." There was always something happening. She sighed and rubbed her forehead. "A new joint task force is going after the group responsible for the Isaac Massacres." Several months ago, a suspected domestic terrorist group in the Idaho wilderness had shocked and horrified the nation when each family in the sect had killed off their eldest child in what was believed to be a twisted loyalty ritual.

"I didn't sleep for a week after I watched the news coverage. I almost envy you the chance to go after them." Tess's beautiful brown eyes narrowed. "Tell me about Ramos."

Grace hesitated and finally settled for a simple description. "He's smart, tough, and is an excellent leader because he doesn't have to constantly prove he's an alpha male with a bigger dick than the rest of us."

Annabelle's voice floated out of the closet. "Do I need to keep reminding you that you don't have a dick?"

"Trust me, I've had to grow that and a pair to go along with it."

"Good thing I made sure the dress I chose isn't too short or tight in the crotch area," Annabelle said as she came to the closet door. She carried an alarmingly big dress bag draped over one arm. Setting the dress bag across a chair, she walked to her dresser and opened a case filled with nail polish bottles.

Grace tucked her toenails under her thighs. "I'm not putting that stuff on my nails."

Annabelle sighed. "The pair you grew is only metaphorical, right?"

"Girls!" Jody Devine popped her blonde head around the door. "Here you are." She paused and a warm smile spread over her lovely face. Jody's sparkling blue eyes, the envy of all three of her brown-eyed daughters, filled with emotion. "Seeing you all together up here reminds me of when you were little. How did you grow up so quickly?" Since it was a frequently asked question, no one attempted to answer. "Tess, there's a phone call for you on the house phone. Apparently you ignored your cell." Mom thought it was the height of rudeness not to answer your phone. She still operated on old landline rules in a mobile tech world. She held out the handset. "It's on hold."

Tess jumped off the bed. "Thanks, Mom." She took the phone from her mother and gave her a quick peck on the cheek. "It's probably my publicist. I'll take this in my room."

"Tess." Grace scrambled off the bed and grabbed her sister's arm, unable to stop from asking one question. "Wait a sec. Are you going to be okay tonight?"

Tess had her stage smile firmly in place. "Of course. I'm fine."

"Barry is a dickhead. You want me take some of my boys and go rough him up a bit, just because?"

That got a flicker of Tess's real smile. "That's Mafia-speak, not FBI."

"Oh, right. I keep getting those two mixed up. In that case, how about if I let you kiss Lewis tonight. It will make you feel better, trust me."

Tess actually laughed.

Her mother's eyes brightened. "Lewis? Tess, I always thought he'd make a good match for you. He's such a nice boy."

Both Grace and Annabelle laughed as Tess escaped down the hall.

Chapter Five

DAVID CARTER tapped his finger against the forms on his desk, the ones that wrapped up an extortion case on which Leo had taken the lead. His steady brown eyes held a smile. "You did an excellent job as supervisory relief."

Leo leaned back in his chair. "It wasn't hard. You've developed a hell of a squad." His mind drifted to Devine before he pulled it back.

"The best. But even the sleekest ship takes a steady hand to steer it. You've got that." Carter glanced at his watch and a harried expression crossed his usually placid features. "I have a full schedule today and my wife is expecting me to pick up the babysitter on my way home. Let's schedule a meeting for next week and I'll update you on some phone calls I've made. There is a supervisory position open that may be a good fit for you."

"I'll have Joan schedule me in on your calendar." Leo had met with Carter a couple of weeks ago to begin discussions on his next career move.

The phone on Carter's desk rang and he held up a finger as he picked up the receiver, indicating Leo should wait. "Yes? Put him through, Joan."

Leo stood and walked over to the window that looked out onto a gray, overcast sky, unsettled and on edge. Grace Devine didn't belong in any decision making process about career. But honesty forced him to acknowledge that six months ago he'd been ready to approach Carter about this move. His busy schedule wasn't the only thing that had prevented him from finding the time.

The woman had short-circuited his brain, something he'd been able to deny until that day at the Pit.

His fingers curled into a fist as he remembered the electric shock of her tongue against his skin and the taste of her when he'd retaliated. Some switch in his brain had permanently flipped and a new neural pathway had been forged. He couldn't think about her without getting hard. Since he couldn't get her out of his head, he walked around in a perpetual state of semi-arousal, with about as much control over his hormones as a teenage boy. He'd been responding to old fears that night at the Pub when he shut her down cold. He and Devine needed to have a serious discussion.

He turned from the window when he heard Carter hang up the phone.

Carter sighed. "I swear to God, something always comes up on a holiday when you're rushing to get out."

"Anything I can help with?"

"That was the Raleigh resident office. Devine is apparently friends with a man the NSA is hot to recruit. The SSA at Raleigh wants her to contact the guy since their boys haven't had any luck."

"Who's the potential recruit?

"A mathematical genius named Kampmueller. The cryptanalysts at Fort Meade are hyperventilating over an algorithm he's developed for a video game called *Code Breaker*."

"Kampmueller developed *Code Breaker*? Hours of my life have been spent playing it." Leo might have to kiss the man himself. He loved that game.

"You, my son, and half the world's male population—not to mention a good portion of the female population, as well. The NSA requested an initial background screen from Raleigh. Then, when they were unable to close a deal with the elusive Kampmueller, they figured the Raleigh agents who did background might have an easier time contacting him. Raleigh hasn't been any more successful than the NSA. Kampmueller doesn't pick up phone calls, return messages or keep appointments." Carter's phone gave a beep and he grimaced. "Five minutes until my next meeting. Anyway, Raleigh just made the connection between Kampmueller and Devine. Now they're salivating at the opportunity to dump the NSA request in Devine's lap. She left last night for her parents' place in Henderson, North Carolina, right? "

"I'll do it," Leo said abruptly. "I know where Kampmueller is tonight. I'll find him and arrange a meet with the NSA. If for some reason I can't, I'll pull in Devine and use her influence."

Carter gave him a long look. He didn't question Leo's willingness to take on the shit task. He didn't ask how Leo knew where Kampmueller would be. He simply wrote down the NSA contact information. "Call this person when you're ready to set up a meeting."

Leo took the paper and shoved it in his pocket. The gray day suddenly seemed brighter. He stopped at Joan's desk on his way out, gave the attractive older woman a New Year's kiss on the cheek, and asked her to put the meeting on Carter's calendar for next week.

Then he stopped by his desk to pick up his jacket and headed for the elevator. Henderson was about a three-and-a-half-hour drive from Washington. He had time to go home and change before leaving for the party.

The elevator opened and he stepped in. A single occupant filled one of the corners, blond head bent over his phone. "Wolfram."

The other man looked up and nodded a greeting. "Ramos."

Leo crossed his arms and took up position in the elevator's opposite corner. He and Wolfram had been introduced several times and had shared drinks with a joint group of friends once or twice as well. "Enjoying your Quantico holiday?"

Wolfram grimaced. "I feel like I'm back in college. Advanced Psychology and Geographical Topology intermixed with Tactical Strategy. I'm brain dead."

"I hear you're pulling together a task force to go after the Isaac Cult."

"The local office in Salt Lake City is swamped and doesn't have the time or resources to close this case." Wolfram's face was grim. "Pulling this together has been a lesson in bullshit bureaucracy." He gave Leo a thoughtful look. "I want Grace Devine on the team. She asked permission to discuss it with a few people and she mentioned your name."

"She told me." Leo met the man's straight blue gaze, his own eyes narrowed. "Devine's still relatively new. I heard you were looking for experienced agents."

Wolfram shrugged. The elevator door opened and both men headed toward the entrance doors. "Devine's got special skills. She's one of the best field interviewers I've seen. She connects easily and quickly with people. Men, women, and children want to be her friend when she flashes that warm smile of hers. We'll be interviewing in some remote regions where folks don't easily talk to strangers. She'll fit in well with the team I'm assembling."

"She fits in well here, as well." Leo kept his tone mild.

Wolfram must have caught some inflection, however, because he swiveled his head sharply to look at Leo. "Rachel Sherwood has already been assigned to the task force. She'll be the perfect mentor and role model for Devine."

Leo couldn't argue with that. Sherwood was a legend in the FBI. Working with Wolfram and Sherwood would be an invaluable experience for Devine. "What exactly is your relationship with Devine?" Leo asked as he pushed through the glass door out into the brisk afternoon air. Both men came to a halt beside an empty concrete planter.

"That's a personal question only someone close to one of us has a right to ask." The hint of amusement in Wolfram's expression irritated Leo.

"She's on my squad," Leo said. In his book, that meant he had the right to watch her back, regardless of any personal feelings. "I don't want her hurt."

"I don't have the ability to hurt her, Ramos. You might. So tread carefully." Wolfram's phone beeped and he glanced down. "I have to take this call." He headed off toward Fourth Street then paused and looked back. "We have more to talk about. I'll be in touch next week."

Leo nodded curtly and watched him stride away, phone to his ear. Wolfram was an excellent choice to head this new task force and a smart man to want Devine on his team. The question was whether he also wanted Devine for himself.

His gut clenched at the thought of the two of them together. Wolfram was an honorable man. He had more to offer a woman like Grace than the month of empty sex that constituted most of Leo's relationships. That knowledge acted as a cold slap of reality. Was he asshole enough to drive all the way to Henderson on New Year's Eve and crash the Devine-Kampmueller Ball on a flimsy excuse when he wasn't sure what he had to offer her?

The phone in his pocket buzzed, signaling a text message.

A full-length picture of Mandy Jenkins appeared on the screen in a shining silver dress cut to her navel, full breasts barely covered. What kept the material sticking to her? He squinted to get a closer look. A small silver bell hung against the taught muscles of her abdomen, attached to a silver loop through her navel. She held a flute of champagne up to the camera. Underneath were the words: *Reconsider. Party is at my place.*

He shoved the phone back in a pocket and headed for his car.

Chapter Six

GRACE PULLED her battered leather jacket tight around her chest as she stepped carefully out of her Jeep at the Henderson Country Club. Only a few cars were parked in the large, blacktopped lot this early in the evening. Her family always arrived first. The valet staff wasn't even on duty yet. She should be able to get inside and have her jacket safely stowed away before she ran into anyone, and by anyone, she meant Annabelle. Her sister would not be pleased to see her carefully executed ensemble covered by worn leather.

Grace took a step, felt her ankle buckle, and immediately grabbed the roof of her Jeep. Ramos would laugh if he could see her now, the tough agent playing at being the belle of the ball. She pulled back her long, champagne-colored skirt and considered her shoes. She had no idea why women wore these kinds of things. What if she needed to chase down some criminal, or execute a defensive move?

Annabelle, fashion tyrant, hadn't bought that argument. She'd commandeered Grace's perfectly nice pair of flats and had hidden them in her magic closet. They were probably somewhere in Narnia by now.

The shoes she currently wore were deceptively pretty instruments of torture. Sparkly confetti in shades of pink, blue, gold and silver shimmered on the peep-toe sling-backs. Despite several laps around her room, she still wobbled when she walked.

She was about to take a few more practice steps when

headlights appeared on the road leading to the clubhouse and a white Maserati roared into the lot. Her parents had arrived.

Her mother slid out of the passenger side and walked around the front of Grace's Jeep, moving quite easily in her heels. Maybe Tess was right all those years ago.

"Mom, am I adopted?" Grace asked the approaching woman.

Her mother raised one lightly penciled eyebrow. "Twelve hours of labor, ending in a C-section. You're all mine. I have the scar to prove it."

"I was there. I can confirm that." Harry Devine joined his wife. "Why? Are you thinking of disowning us and ditching the party? Tired of losing the bet?"

"You know about the bet?" No one but the three sisters was supposed to know. They'd sworn a secrecy oath, hadn't they? She frowned. Her memory was fuzzy on that part. She'd talked one of the young wait staff into a couple of glasses of real champagne that night instead of her usual sparkling white grape juice.

"Gracie-belle, most of Henderson knows about it. Your annual bet is one of the highlights of the Ball." Her dad patted her arm.

An acid burn started in her stomach. Losing to her sisters was one thing. Having the whole town watch her dates dump her every year brought her failure to a whole new level. Okay, that settled it. If for some reason Michael didn't come tonight, she would kiss Lewis and then she would drown herself in the nearest punch bowl. Ramos would attend the funeral and hear what an amazing young woman she'd been, loved by all, except on New Year's Eve.

She felt better for having a plan.

"Are you waiting for someone, sweetheart?" her mother asked, eyeing Grace's hand against the car. "Your date from Washington?"

"No, Michael won't get here for a couple of hours. He got held up in a late meeting." She cleared her throat. "I was just standing here admiring the...evening sky." Okay, that was weak.

But she really didn't feel like adding shoe klutz to her title of dating loser. Tess had danced on several Broadway stages in heels and Annabelle…well, Annabelle probably slept and took showers in hers.

Grace had every intention of mastering these suckers, even if they maimed her. She just needed her parents to go inside so she could have a few moments in private to find her balance.

"The overcast, starless, moonless sky is very lovely." Her mother glanced up. "And the nip in the air is certainly refreshing. However, I think we should all go inside."

Since the temperature was close to freezing and the wind was painfully cold, not nippy, Grace unfortunately couldn't argue.

The parking lot was located to the left of the clubhouse, a gracious old Southern mansion only slightly faded in glory. Warm yellow light, glowing from every window, beckoned a welcome. The pavement that stretched between the parking lot and front doors did not. Grace squared her shoulders and slowly removed her right hand from the roof of her car. She could do this.

Her father stepped forward and with a courtly bow, offered her his arm. "May I?" he asked. Taking her left hand, he tucked her fingers in the crook of his arm. Her mother smiled and took his other arm.

"Two beautiful women. I'm a lucky man tonight." Harry pulled his arm tight against his ribs, allowing Grace to lean slightly against him as they began to walk.

Squeezing his arm, Grace kissed his cheek. "I'm the lucky one."

Her mom leaned over with a mischievous grin. "I bet that's exactly what Lewis will think when he sees you walk in tonight without a date."

⌒

Since Lewis hadn't arrived yet, one could only guess what his thoughts would have been on her dateless entrance. Grace released her father's arm once they had navigated the steps into the clubhouse and made her way over to the coat check on her own. She handed her jacket to one of the two teenage girls sitting behind the half door that led to the coatroom. Grace had a vague memory of babysitting for both of them in middle school. How had they grown up so fast? "Hi, Ann. Hi, Jen." *Thank you, nametags.*

"What an absolutely gorgeous dress, Grace," Ann breathed, eyes wide. "That's one of the newer Thela designs, isn't it?"

"Look closer, Ann." Jen squinted her eyes. "That's definitely Vera Wang. And those shoes!"

"Are those Kate Spade's Charm shoes?" Ann looked like she might faint.

Her shoes had a name?

"Ann, did Annabelle teach you nothing?" Jen threw her a disgusted look. "Those are Jimmy Choos. I've wanted a pair of those forever but my mom won't buy them for me. You are so lucky, Grace."

"I have a job," Grace said sternly. "Get good grades, work hard, earn money and you, too, can have Jimmy Chews." Or, screw that advice and borrow them from Belly.

The girls gave her an odd look but nodded. Her duty to the future generation done, Grace turned to walk across the lobby toward the long, wide hallway that led to the back of the building. On the left of the hallway was an open room dominated by a polished wooden bar. Hors d'oeuvres were set up on tables against the walls. On the right, a long row of doors led into the ballroom. Tonight they were wide open and Grace could see the twinkling lights of what looked like a blue and silver fairyland. She glanced down at her full skirts and suddenly felt like Cinderella at the ball.

Until midnight, she would dance, visit with old friends and forget Leo Ramos. At midnight, she would kiss Michael and break her New Year's Eve dating curse. This would be the perfect start to a fabulous new year. Really, it would. The fact that Leo was no doubt at some party not even thinking about her didn't matter a single bit.

She'd only made it three steps toward the ballroom when her dad called her over to a small group composed of her mom, dad, Belly and a man who must be Duncan James, Belly's date. As soon as she saw Annabelle eyeing her critically, Grace tugged at her bodice.

"My God, Grace. If you touch the bodice of that damn dress one more time I'm going to rip it off of you. I swear it!"

"You and what army?" Grace asked and then shrugged. "I thought the dress was falling off." She was not quite as blessed as her sister in the breast department.

Belly started spouting some idiotic nonsense about wearing a dress like a gun holster (as if she had any idea how to wear a gun holster) and her dad began introductions.

Grace ignored them both and gave Duncan her FBI stare, to which he responded with a barely concealed grin. He wore a tux like Annabelle wore a pair of heels—as if born to it. His brown eyes held a hint of devilry and more than a hint of intelligence. "You're the hero who gave my sister her first speeding ticket."

"I cannot tell a lie. I was the one who gave Annabelle the ticket."

"Good for you." Grace liked the look of him. He might be just the man to shake up her little sister's well-ordered life, but he should know that if he hurt her, he'd have Grace to deal with. She held his gaze until he gave her a slight nod.

Annabelle rolled her eyes, fully aware of the unspoken communication, and pulled Duncan off toward the bar. Grace shared a smile with her parents then turned to head to the ballroom.

Inexplicably, her heartbeat quickened. Anything could happen once she stepped into that magical blue and silver world. Her aching feet and the awkwardness of her strange clothes faded and she felt transformed from a plain and sturdy agent into a princess.

Anything could happen. She blinked. Including a

hallucination of a dark, lean Prince Charming who looked remarkably like Ramos. She closed her eyes and opened them more slowly this time.

The hallucination didn't disappear. Leo stood with one shoulder propped against the wall, looking gut-wrenchingly handsome in a tux. Hands in his pant pockets, a half-smile on his face, he watched her approach with lazy intensity, his eyes never leaving her.

Chapter Seven

"RAMOS! WHAT are you doing here? What happened? Is something wrong?" Grace held up her skirts with both hands as she hurried toward him. Then logic returned. He wouldn't take time to dress in a tux if this was an emergency. She took a deep breath and spoke more slowly. "Why are you here?"

"I'm on assignment." He sounded different, distracted.

"Assignment? Here at our ball?"

He didn't respond. His gaze slowly travelled her body. Starting at the softly curled hair that Annabelle had pulled back and secured with small shiny clips, he appeared to take in every detail of her appearance. He lingered on the curve where her neck met her bare shoulders, and paused again on the strapless sweetheart bodice hugging her breasts. His stance was relaxed, yet she could sense the tension in his body as he studied the snug material that defined her waist and the wide sweep of a skirt that belled to the floor.

He finally raised his gaze to hers and spoke in a slow, low drawl. "Devine, you're taller."

The look in his eyes made her breath hitch. "No, you've just started to shrink."

He grinned and the two small dimples creased his cheeks. They were so not necessary. He didn't need their help. It was like putting chocolate frosting on chocolate brownies. Total overkill.

He hitched up his slacks and sank into a crouch. Before she

could protest, he lifted the hem of her skirt. His dark head bent over her feet for longer than she thought the shoes warranted. She sucked in a breath when one finger traced the bone of her ankle and moved up the back of her calf. Heat shot directly up her thigh and she concentrated on not letting her knee buckle.

"Hot damn, Devine." He dropped the skirt and rose slowly.

She shrugged. "Standard FBI issue. No big deal." Her voice almost sounded normal.

"There has never been anything standard FBI about you." He held her gaze until she glanced away, unsure how to respond.

"What did you say you're doing here again?"

Her repeated question seemed to wipe some fog from his brain and he gave his head a quick shake. "I'm on assignment. I'm here to see your kissing buddy."

"Lewis?" A surge of unexpected protectiveness flared. She crossed her arms under her breasts. "Exactly what do you want Lewis for?"

"Whoa, Mama Tiger." His tone cooled. "Exactly who is this Kamptooler to you?"

"Kampmueller. He's a friend." She leaned into him just a little, an intimidation tactic learned in training.

"A friend who kisses you every New Year's Eve." He leaned a little towards her, the downside of standardized training.

"I'm well aware of that fact," she hissed, tired of the reminders. "Let's take out an advertisement in the *New York Times*. Post it on Facebook. Tweet about it. Give 'The Kiss' its very own Wikipedia page."

"I have my own Wikipedia page," boomed a too-familiar voice. Grace sighed and backed away from Leo.

"Aunt Helen?" She turned, hoping she was mistaken.

"Who'd you think I was? Sophia Loren?" Her great-aunt, who was seventy-five but looked at least a hundred, cackled and stomped her cane twice on the floor. She wore a simple full-length black dress with a cowl neckline. On another person, the dress might have an understated sophistication. Aunt Helen looked like she should be stirring a black cauldron while holding a vial of bat eyes. Her laugh ended abruptly and she turned a hard look on Leo. "I'll have you know I could have passed for Sophia in my day."

"I have no doubt of that. Your eyes remind me of hers." Leo smiled.

Leo obviously had no idea who Sophia Loren was. Grace, having been raised with repeated showings of *Man of La Mancha* and *Houseboat* while Aunt Helen babysat during her mother's weekly golf date, knew that Sophia Loren's big slanted eyes bore no resemblance to Aunt Helen's beady orbs.

"*El Cid* was Tío's favorite," Leo continued. "We watched it at least once a month."

"*El Cid's* not bad, but it's no *Houseboat*," Aunt Helen grumped.

"So true." His dimples deepened.

Even Aunt Helen couldn't hold out against that smile. The wicked witch seemed to melt into a softer, kinder version of Aunt Helen. She raised a pink-tipped hand (Annabelle had obviously been at work) to her chest and giggled.

At least Grace thought the rusty, grating sound coming out of her aunt's throat was a giggle.

"Who's your young man?" Her aunt's cane wacked Grace's leg, which was thankfully padded by layers of skirt.

"Aunt Helen, allow me to introduce you to Special Agent Leo Ramos." Definitely not her young man. "Ramos, this is my great-aunt, Helen Galliday."

"Does Lewis know you brought him?" Aunt Helen demanded with a stern look.

"I didn't bring him, and even if I did, why would I tell Lewis?" She felt a twinge of guilt even though she knew she shouldn't. Aunt Helen had that power.

"You kiss him every New Year's Eve. Since you finally snagged a date who don't look like the running-type, seems only polite to inform the boy."

Grace needed alcohol, or a wall to bang her head against. She contemplated the sturdy plaster of the clubhouse wall. Definitely alcohol.

"Grace Elizabeth, you look at me while I'm talking to you. You always go off in some kind of daze. Makes people think you're a little touched in the head." Aunt Helen gave Leo a pitying look. "You got your hands full with this one. She don't have the manners of the younger gel or the talent of the oldest."

Grace felt heat rise in her cheeks.

Ramos stepped over to her side and his fingers curled around hers with a firm grip. He smiled easily. "Grace got the courage. Your niece is one of the best FBI agents I've worked with, Ms. Galliday. Our agency motto is *Fidelity, Bravery and Integrity*. She sets the standard for all three of those qualities. The country is damn lucky to have her enforcing its laws."

His hand tightened on hers and she blinked, momentarily bereft of speech.

"And don't you forget it, young man." Aunt Helen thumped her cane in front of Leo with a pleased expression on her face. "I've got my eye on you." She lowered one lash in a flirty wink.

"Yes, ma'am." Leo's wink back was much more successful.

The weird noise gurgled out of Aunt Helen's throat again and she turned and took off toward the ballroom, dragging her cane behind her.

"Your aunt needs to take care of that phlegmy throat." Her mother paused in front of them, her gaze following Helen. "I'll make her a doctor's appointment while she's here." She turned to Leo and smiled. "You must be Michael, Grace's date. Welcome. I'm Jody Devine, Grace's mother."

"It's a pleasure to meet you, Mrs. Devine. I'm Leo Ramos. I work with your daughter."

"Oh, I apologize." Her mother gave their clasped hands a curious look that meant questions would follow when they were in private. "Of course, you're welcome as well. I'm glad to have the opportunity to meet one of my daughter's colleagues. I worry about her."

"Mom, I've told you that I mostly do field interviews and computer work. Don't believe everything you see on television and in the movies."

Jody turned to Leo. "I remember a few years back there was a female agent who got killed in New York. It was all over the news."

"Katherine Dill." Leo said the name stiffly. He dropped Grace's hand and the shadows she had seen before flickered across his face.

"Yes, that was her name." She shot Grace a triumphant look, as if Leo's confirmation gave weight to her argument. "Grace had only been in Chicago about year when that happened. I was an absolute wreck."

"Mom. The Dill situation was unusual. You don't need to worry."

"Wait until you have children." One of her mother's favorite responses. Jody put a light hand on Leo's arm. "I'm sure your mother worries about you, too."

Leo smiled, no trace of the earlier darkness on his face. "If I don't text her daily that I'm still alive and breathing, she will be on the phone to the Special Agent in Charge wanting to know what happened to me."

Jody flashed a look at Grace. "I want that phone number." Then she opened her clutch purse and pulled out her camera. She waved it at Grace.

Her mother took a picture of her every year at the ball. She claimed it was the only time Grace ever dressed up. "I want to get a shot of you next to the poinsettia. This will just take a second." Jody flashed a smile at Leo. "It's a tradition."

"Traditions are important." Leo stepped behind Jody as her mother positioned Grace next to one of the huge potted plants. A sudden commotion at the club's entrance caused him to turn his head, then he moved out of Grace's line of sight.

"What happened?" Grace craned her neck and tried to see

past her mother and the plant.

"Don't fidget! You'll ruin the picture." Jody ordered. "Someone tripped. Your friend is helping out."

"Is Aunt Helen anywhere near the scene?" That woman and her cane were dangerous.

Her mother glanced over her shoulder and frowned. "I think the poor dear forgot her glasses. Probably threw off her depth perception."

"Who?" Aunt Helen didn't wear glasses.

Her mother, busy channeling Annie Leibovitz, didn't answer. At her command, Grace dutifully turned, cocked her chin, and smiled, all the while wondering about the look on Leo's face when he spoke Kathryn Dill's name.

By the time her mother finally tucked the camera away, Leo was striding back across the floor toward them. Several sets of female eyes followed his progress.

Jody beamed a smile at him. "All done. Now, why don't both of you get some food before the dancing starts?" She put an arm around Grace's waist and gave her a quick hug. "I'm going to go find your father."

Grace waited until her mother was far enough away that she wouldn't hear. "Are you familiar with the Katherine Dill incident?"

"I worked with her." His face gave nothing away. "I was in that apartment when she died."

Oh crap. "I'm so sorry, Ramos. That must have been an incredibly difficult time. Another agent died as well, right?"

"Yes." He nodded once. When it became apparent that was all he had to say on the subject, Grace reached out and rested her hand on his forearm in silent comfort. Then she changed the subject. "What do you want with Lewis?"

Leo ignored her question. He covered her hand and brought it between them, his long fingers wrapped around hers. "Who is this Michael your mother mentioned?" His brows drew together in a sudden frown. "Is Wolfram your date tonight?"

Really? The murder of an FBI agent and her friend's

involvement with the NSA were on the table and this is what the man wanted to talk about? "My date for the evening is none of your business, Ramos."

"I'm getting tired of people telling me your personal life is none of my business."

She stared at him, not sure she'd heard him correctly. He stared back.

"Where we can talk without interruption?" He bit out the question.

She took a deep breath and turned swiftly. Conscious of his silent presence at her back, she led the way out of the ballroom, carefully negotiated the stairs at the end of the hallway and opened the door of the first room she came to. Ramos followed her into the exercise room and shut the door behind him with a loud click.

Chapter Eight

LEO STOOD with his back to the door, his arm bent behind him, his hand still gripping the knob. He needed to get his balance, find his control. Which was difficult when he felt like the world had narrowed to the space filled by one lean, five-foot, seven-inch woman. She overwhelmed his senses—the rustle of her skirts, the clean, citrusy scent of hair, the memories of the silken feel and the salty, sweet taste of her skin. But most of all, she filled his vision. He couldn't stop looking at her, couldn't see past her.

And she, apparently, was not experiencing the same shock to her system. She spun to face him with a graceful swirl of skirts and put her hands on her waist. "What is wrong with you? Why have you been looking at me like you've been looking at me all evening?"

Trust Devine to get right to the point. Amusement helped him pull it together enough to straighten and take a step away from the door. "You have a dress on, Devine. I've never seen you in a dress. Of course I'm going to look at you differently."

"The sight of a woman in a dress immediately makes you think of sex? Because you are definitely thinking about sex." She hesitated. "I think."

"No, the sight of a woman in dress doesn't immediately make me think of sex. The sight of *you* in a dress makes me think of sex." He took a step closer. "The sight of you in *that* dress makes me want to fight dragons for you." He touched her soft cheek. "Even worse, it makes me want to fight dragons with you."

For a moment, he thought she'd walk into his arms. Her eyes got liquid soft and her lips parted. Then she opened her mouth. "Shut up, Ramos. Just two or three weeks ago you clearly warned me off. Now you're going to fight dragons for me? I don't have any dragons." She glared at him. "And if I did, I'd fight them myself."

"We all have dragons." He shoved his hands in his pockets.

She frowned but didn't say anything.

"I've been thinking a lot about that night at the Pub, a lot about you." He met her eyes and went for it. "I think you're the greatest thing since hot fudge sundaes, Grace Elizabeth Devine." He moved forward and leaned down to speak softly in her ear. "And I want another lick."

⟶

Grace retreated a step. He didn't mean what she wanted him to mean—that she was special enough to make him forget his stupid relationship rules. No, Ramos was all about the licking. She took a deep breath. He tracked her movement, eyes focused on the neckline of her dress. Her breasts felt plumper, the material of the dress too tight. Nerves fired along every inch of her body at the same time she felt her muscles loosen. How could he do that to her, without even touching her? "Everywhere you look at me, my skin gets hot. Confess. You're one of those experimental government agents with superpowers. You've got a pair of high-tech ocular laser implants."

Leo choked out a half laugh, half groan.

The sound was like a rough caress. Grace shivered and rubbed her hand against her arm. The touch felt so good her palm kept moving in a slow glide to her bare shoulder. Leo's jaw tightened and his eyes narrowed as they followed the motion of her hand. Fascinated by his reaction, she let her nails scrape lightly across her collarbone and slid a finger down to the single, cream-colored pearl that rested just above the quick rise and fall of her breast.

His body stilled. Her adrenalin surged, and it wasn't because of fear.

"I want to watch you touch yourself everywhere, Devine. And then I want to follow your hand with my tongue, tasting every inch of you."

She fisted the pearl to keep her hand from jerking down her neckline.

He sucked in a deep breath. "Privacy was a mistake. We need to get out of here." He didn't move. "You're not a quick fuck in an exercise room."

"I could be." Yes, that had come out of her mouth. She hadn't even had anything to drink and she meant it.

He gave a huff that could have been laughter. "Damn it, Devine. I like you too much."

"And you only have quick fucks with people you don't like?" He said nothing, his gaze fixed on the wall over her shoulder as if he couldn't trust himself to look at her. "What's too much?"

For a moment she thought he wasn't going to respond to that question, either. Then he sighed and met her eyes. "Too much is when I can't stop thinking about you. Too much is when I don't care about anything but this." His hands were suddenly on her bare shoulders. He yanked her against his chest, bent his head and covered her lips with his.

Sensation, like a hot tendril of smoke, curled through her body. Despite his swift move, there was nothing hurried about his exploration of her mouth. He kissed her slowly and thoroughly, as if he had done so a thousand times before, as if she belonged in his arms. One hand cradled the back of her head, holding her still as his tongue teased the corner of her lips and then plunged into her mouth, deepening the kiss.

Grace didn't melt against him. The emotions that ripped through her at his forceful move were not soft and gentle; they roared—a forest fire, all-consuming, uncontrollable. Her hands gripped strong muscle. If she didn't have the damn Cinderella dress on, she could straddle his waist.

She unhooked his cummerbund and flung it, lips never leaving his. He worked the zipper at her side, lowering it to her waist. She pulled the shirt out of his pants, desperate to touch his skin. He pushed her bodice down and his hand came between them to cup one breast still encased in a strapless bra. Grace reached for his trouser zipper. His hand smacked against hers, stopping the action, molding her palm against his hard length.

He broke the kiss and she took several quick breaths, her gaze caught in his.

"You are so beautiful." His free hand shaped her breast. Grace shivered at the flair of pleasure. His hand slid to the front clasp of her bra and he unhooked it. The bra fell to their feet.

He pulsed and hardened under her hand. His eyes were dark, almost black. He dipped his head, and his tongue—slightly rough and damp—dragged across her nipple.

Her head fell back and she pressed her hand harder against him. "Damn it. Let me get this zipper down."

He groaned something in Spanish and then he lifted her hand and pressed it against his chest. She could feel the steady thunder of his heartbeat. "I'm an asshole, but I'm not this big an asshole." That was English, but still incomprehensible. He backed a step away.

Her body shook in protest and her heart actually hurt. "What does that mean, Ramos?"

"It means we need to talk." His eyes were dark and serious. His hair was disheveled and his shirttail was only partially tucked into his pants. Several buttons of his shirt were undone and his bow tie was missing, though she had no memory of yanking it off.

The man who'd slept with half of Washington, D.C., wanted to talk when she stood half-naked in front of him. This, combined with her inability to keep a date on New Year's Eve, would undoubtedly drive her to therapy. Or to a Victoria's Secret catalog. No, the therapy would be cheaper.

She picked up her bra and fumbled with the catch until she got it latched. With a quick yank, she pulled up the bodice of the gown and zipped it. She couldn't think, but her lips still formed sentences. "We have nothing to talk about. You're not an asshole, you're a true gentleman. I get it. End of conversation."

"Devine." His tone was almost gentle.

She held up her hand, determined to stop the embarrassing excuses. "I work around men. I understand testosterone."

He put his hands in his trouser pockets, not bothering to tuck in his shirt. "You do?"

"I know what just happened doesn't mean anything. I understand men's bodies and their brains don't always work in tandem and sometimes hormones win out."

"Who's been feeding you that bullshit?" His voice was dry. "I'm not sixteen. My brain has been determining my behavior for a long time now."

"Obviously." Grace took a deep breath. Her heart beat so fast she was starting to feel dizzy. If Ramos had his way, they'd leave this room the way they entered—good pals, friends without benefits. In a couple of months, she'd join Michael's task force and leave Washington. The impossible, infuriating, fascinating Ramos would just be a memory, a lost opportunity, a what-if fantasy for lonely nights.

"C'mon." He turned toward the door with an unusually jerky movement. "I need a drink and I think it's safer to talk in the bar."

"I have a proposition for you," her voice rushed out when his hand closed over the door handle.

"What now?" Leo turned toward her, impatient and apparently eager to be out of the room.

"To recap," she talked fast, before her nerve left her. "A quickie in the exercise room is too short for your sense of honor, and I'm not a candidate for your usual flavor-of-the-month relationships."

"Correct. You will never be one of my flavor-of-the-month women."

She ignored the jolt of pain at his firm declaration. "Yes, well, you've been quite clear on that point. So I'm proposing something different."

"What?"

Hell if she knew. "A micro-relationship," she blurted.

"A what?" An oddly arrested expression settled on his face.

"We'll have two hours together tonight where I'll be Grace and you'll be Leo." Her voice was firmer now. She actually liked this idea. "We'll dance, tell each other things about ourselves the other doesn't know, and do things like …." She paused, considering how to make this different than one of their movie nights. "Flirt!"

Okay, maybe that wasn't quite how Tess suggested getting him out of her system, but since kissing him had caused him to turn tail and run, she was out of options.

"That's ridiculous. Whoever heard of a micro-relationship?" He actually looked upset.

"You're the one who puts time limits on relationships," she pointed out.

"Even I never put a two-hour time limit on a relationship."

"I'm an innovator. Look at it this way—we get the thrill of a new relationship and the drama of the break-up all in one evening. None of the boring you-leave-your-socks-on-the-floor stuff that happens in the middle. It's pure excitement from start to finish. What's not to love?" Grace spread her arms and smiled. There was so much not to love about it that she could fall asleep counting the reasons. But if it was two hours or nothing, screw the reasons.

◌2—

Leo's hand tightened on the door handle. How had the evening turned into such a cluster fuck? He wanted to start this relationship the right way, build it into something solid, and she was talking about a micro-relationship. "What about sex?" he gritted out, since it was all he could think about anyway.

"Excuse me?"

Give a girl a princess dress and she starts talking like a Brit. The imperious tilt to her chin disarmed him, even though he wanted to shake some sense into her. "When do we get to have sex?"

Her eyes widened. "Do you have multiple personality disorder? Aren't you the same man who just two minutes ago refused to have sex with me?"

"I've changed my mind." If he only had two hours, he needed to lead with his strong suit.

"Sorry, I'm not in the mood anymore. Rejection does that to me. Sex is excluded from this micro-relationship."

"Says who?"

"Says me. Since I invented the concept, I get to make the rules. You have sex with every single woman you date, don't you?"

"Not every single woman." He hadn't had sex with Mandy.

"Almost every woman then." She paused. When he didn't say anything, she continued, "This is two hours, Leo. If we have sex, we won't be able to go back to just being friends. Besides, I don't like the idea of being one of the masses. I'm aiming to be the outlier, different from your other women."

He released the door handle and flexed his hand. "You don't need two hours to establish that."

She bit her bottom lip. He wanted to bite it, too. "The positives of the micro-relationship outweigh the one negative of not having sex."

"You can't say that when you have no idea what you're giving up."

"I think I'll survive not knowing." Her tone was dry.

He wasn't sure he would.

"When Michael walks into the ball, the micro-relationship poofs into oblivion. I'm back to being Devine and you're Ramos. Our friendship and work relationship stay intact. We play poker together on Friday nights and try to put each other on the mat at the Pit." She took a deep breath and stuck out her hand. "Is that a deal?"

"What do you get out of this?" He gripped her slender hand because he wanted to touch her.

She met his gaze. "You said you like me too much. That you can't stop thinking about me." Her cheeks were pink, but she didn't look away. "I've been thinking about you, too. This is our chance to have a fling in a harmless way. To get this—this... attraction out of our system and still be able to work together." She shook his hand vigorously.

She was giving him what she thought he wanted. On her terms, in a way she could deal with. Only problem was, he didn't want short term any more. Devine, with her sunshine gaze and blunt honesty had slowly finished the job Dr. Hawkins and his own psyche had begun. "I won't pretend the next two hours never happened and I can't guarantee I won't call you Grace ever again."

She frowned and looked at their bobbing hands. "I don't think you're allowed to change the rules of an agreement once we're shaking on it."

He lifted an eyebrow. "Of course you are."

"Then from now on you'll bring me a large mocha cappuccino every morning that we're both scheduled into the office."

He grinned, suddenly happy in a way he didn't remember feeling for a long time. "And you'll ..."

She snatched her hand from his with a laugh. "I don't trust that look. I think we'll call the deal done."

Leo nodded, surprised by the intense satisfaction he felt. "For the next two hours, Grace, you're mine."

He had two hours to convince her to give them a chance at a lifetime.

⟿

A bargain with the Devil, Grace thought as they sat at one of the small tables in the bar, eating hors d'oeuvres. She picked up a carrot stick and munched on it. Her breathing was back to normal now, thank God, and the regular intake of oxygen was helpful in keeping the logical part of her brain functioning. Time to start the get-to-know-you-better portion of the date. Maybe she would discover she really didn't like him. That would be helpful. "I don't know where to start with the questions."

His smile was wry. "I find that hard to believe."

She picked up a spear of something that was probably chicken and took a bite. "Are you implying I usually have a curious mind?"

"Your mind is definitely curious," he agreed, humor in his gaze.

Her lower lip curled in a pout. She'd never tried to pout on purpose, but she'd seen both Tess and Annabelle use the move effectively when being teased by men. "This is how you talk to your dates?"

"Let's get one thing straight, Grace. You're not my usual date." He reached out and gently rubbed her lower lip. "Stop that or I'm going to take a bite."

She sighed. "I don't usually do this sort of thing."

"Date? I noticed that. Why? Men ask you out."

"Hey, I date. Sometimes." Okay, that sounded defensive. "I work long hours and then a lot of my free time is spent with the squad poker games or movies with you." Even more defensive and after all, he went to the same poker games and movies and still managed to date. "What I meant was, I don't usually do the whole flirty pout thing."

"You don't usually flirt?" He looked surprised. "Don't all women flirt?"

"No, all women don't flirt." She frowned at him, offended. "That's a stereotypical statement."

"No, it's not," he said. "Anthropologists have identified flirting behavior in almost every culture. It's an important social interaction. Men do it as well."

"Oh." Great. Now she felt unintelligent and socially inadequate. Maybe it was a good thing this relationship was only two hours long. "I'll have to practice more."

Leo handed her a stuffed mushroom. "Try this one." He watched her take a small bite and chew. "I studied up on male female interactions when I was in therapy."

"You were in therapy?" She took another bite of the mushroom.

"The incident with Dill involved the use of deadly force. Therapy was strongly encouraged."

Grace put down the mushroom, suddenly not hungry. "You're the agent who killed the suspected terrorist."

"That's the pretty way of saying it. In reality, I killed a twenty-two year old kid who had the not-so-great judgment to become involved in a small dope-growing business. " Leo said the words without emotion.

"He also had the not-so-great judgment to be armed and to start shooting when the FBI knocked on his door. Two agents died and one was injured, if I'm remembering correctly. He was no innocent kid."

Leo rubbed the back of his neck and looked down at his plate. "Yeah."

"You got a commendation." Grace watched his eyes squeeze shut briefly.

"The whole thing was fucked from start to finish. Dill totally lost it." His face was expressionless when he looked up at her. "She came on to me when I was assigned to her unit. I had no interest in starting a relationship with her. According to her diary, she thought she loved me. The day after I put in for a transfer, she sent us into an apartment of suspected terrorists without proper intelligence and without back up. Only it turns out it was an apartment full of guys with guns growing weed, not terrorists at all."

Leo was all about emotion. His dark eyes laughed, sympathized, sparked with intelligence. She'd never seen the blank look that was in them now. "You think you're responsible for what happened," she said slowly.

"Dill was angry and not thinking clearly. Her diary said she wanted me to die." His finger touched Grace's lips, silencing the words she wanted to say. "Because of her feelings toward me, Parker died and Stravinsky got injured. Because of me, some kid won't have the chance to learn from his mistakes. Dr. Hawkins is a good therapist and my co-workers were a hundred percent behind me, so intellectually I know that Dill is responsible for her behavior and none of what happened is my fault." He grimaced. "It's hard to put my head in charge on this one."

She didn't even try to argue with that. Guilt was a hard nut to crack. "And so you're steering away from any romantic involvements at work, because if they go bad, they can go really bad."

"That was my logic."

"We've established your head is not in charge on this issue, so your logic is questionable."

"Very good, Devine. If the whole special agent thing doesn't work out for you, maybe you should try law school." He looked faintly amused now. He leaned back and took a bite of a chocolate-covered strawberry.

"Thank you, but I intend to be phenomenally successful as a special agent. And my name is Grace." She wished she'd paid more attention during the psychology sections of training. She had no idea what to say that would be helpful so she opted for her honest opinion. "If you make rules for your life based on the crazy behavior of an unstable person, your rules will be crazy too."

"Tell me what you really think." His tone was dry but there might have been a hint of humor in it.

Since he asked she kept talking. "Most people aren't psychos, Leo, so it doesn't make sense to live your life as if they are." She paused and modified that statement. "Okay, maybe most people have something odd about them, but they're not dangerously damaged like Dill."

He took a petite brownie from her plate. He liked chocolate. "In what way are you odd?"

"I said most people." She took a mini-cheesecake from his in retaliation. She let him change the subject, not sure what else to say about Dill. "I happen to be one of the select few who have absolutely no little quirks in their personality."

"Is that so?" A corner of his lip curved up. "I seem to remember you throwing popcorn at the couple sitting two rows ahead of us during *The Seven Samurai*."

"That wasn't odd. That was justified. The guy was watching a football game on his phone. And you didn't have to flash your ID when he hopped the seats and grabbed my popcorn."

"He was going to dump the bucket over your head. I just wanted to watch the rest of the movie."

His smile made her smile. "So you're really here to see Lewis?"

"The Raleigh office called this morning and wanted to speak to you. They requested help to set up a meet between Kampmueller and the code breakers."

"Seriously? Lewis and the NSA?" She had a hard time wrapping her head around that one. "He'll drive them bonkers in five minutes. He's brilliant, but not government material. He's not into rules and regulations."

Ramos shrugged. "He's already driving the Raleigh office bonkers. He ignores their messages. I said I'd give it a try tonight."

"Why didn't you just call me or text me? I would have talked to Lewis."

"You might still have to. But I didn't have any plans tonight. Driving down was no big deal."

"Really? You expect me to believe you didn't have plans for New Year's Eve?"

He pushed his plate aside and leaned forward, elbows on his knees. "You're right. I'm not being honest. I don't give a damn about Lewis or the NSA. I do have plans for tonight. Big plans. I intend to dance with you."

"You drove four hours to dance with me."

"Yes, I did."

She swallowed. Crap. This fling wasn't going to get him out of her system. If she was honest with herself, she didn't want him out of her system.

Leo lifted his hand and ran his thumb across her cheekbone. He liked to touch.

"You are so soft and yet so damn tough, Grace." His finger traced past her ear, along the line of her jaw, then followed her throat to the hollow of her collarbone. "You take my breath away."

Music started playing in the other room. He stood, took her hand and led her back into the ballroom.

Chapter Nine

LEO HAD MADE the decision to come to Henderson fully aware that he didn't give a damn that Grace worked for the FBI. He'd been telling the truth when he said his head—his intellect—hadn't been taking the lead role in processing the shoot-out in New York. Emotion had been leading him through a crazy guilt dance—two steps forward, one step back, then do-si-do and start again. So in a way, it made perfect sense that it was emotion that pulled him out of that repeating pattern and gave him some perspective. The emotion he felt for Grace had been growing slowly, from attraction to friendship to *this*, without him noticing. What was between them felt strong and clean. She felt strong and clean.

Grace led the way through the ballroom and came to a stop as they reached the edge of the dance area. Leo stopped just behind her, her back almost against his chest, close enough to breathe in her fragrance.

Harry and Jody Devine stood in the middle of the empty dance floor, facing each other. Diamonds of light reflected off a large mirrored ball and swirled across the floor in a slow waltz, as if inviting the couple to join in. Harry leaned down and whispered something in his wife's ear. She laughed and shook her head at him.

Grace's hand tightened in his. "My parents always open the dancing on the last set before midnight. The song is always the same. It's my dad's favorite."

The band began to play the opening notes of the Etta James classic "At Last." Harry Devine took his wife in his arms and pulled her close. His eyes never left her face as he danced her around the floor.

"Your dad is a romantic," Leo commented as he watched the couple. Physically, Grace was a mix of both her parents. She had her father's lean athleticism and her mother's cheekbones and wide mouth.

"He still buys Mom flowers for no reason and whisks her out to dinner when he knows she's had a busy day. You know what I remember from when I was little? Every morning before he left for work, he'd kiss her." Grace turned her head to glance at him, leaning back against his chest. Her body swayed gently to the music. "Not one of those rushed pecks on the lips, but an I-have-all-the-time-in-the-world-to-enjoy-this kind of kiss. Then he'd always say, 'You are my divine Devine.'" Her voice held a hint of wistfulness. "Of course, all of us girls would groan and make gagging noises." She paused and her brow wrinkled. "Or maybe that was just me."

"I guess it's too late to take him out back and give him the Man Talk."

She gave him a light punch on the arm. "This is the song Dad requested the night he asked Mom to marry him."

Leo studied the man who looked with open adoration at his wife. "The Devine women should all come with a 'Romantic Father' warning label."

"You think he set our expectations too high?"

"Hell, yes. Normal males can't compete with that man." Good thing he liked a challenge. "My parents don't have a special song. I don't think they even celebrate their anniversary."

"They don't celebrate their anniversary? My parents plan theirs weeks in advance."

"My father says every day is a celebration of their marriage."

"Nice line," Grace allowed, "but a cop-out."

His mom said the same thing. He searched his memories

for something romantic his overworked father had done. "How about this. Every Mother's Day, Dad would take all five of us kids out for the day. We'd go to the zoo, fishing, or sometimes over to my *abuela*'s. Dad would say this was Mama's one day to do exactly as she pleased."

"Yes, that's definitely romantic," Grace said softly. "What would your mother do on that day?"

Leo grinned. "Boring stuff like taking a bubble bath and reading a book. Once I heard her tell Dad that she sat on the couch for a whole hour and just listened to the silence. I thought we were being mean, leaving her at home all alone."

He released her hand and let his arms circle her slim waist. He leaned down to murmur in her ear. "How does someone show you that you're special, Grace? Do you want wine and roses, or would you prefer a bath and a book?"

"I don't know." She looked at him, then quickly back at the dance floor. "I guess I'd like the wine and the roses set up beside the bath."

He was silent a moment, imagining the scene. He pulled her back, fitting her more closely against his body. "Does a book have to be part of the scenario, or will you accept a replacement?"

She didn't answer.

Other couples had begun to join the Devines on the floor. He lowered his face and felt the silk of her hair against his cheek. Without another word, he turned her to face him.

⌒

Grace stumbled slightly as Leo spun her around, but his firm arms held her upright and against his chest. The heels made her tall enough that her chin was even with his shoulder. She wasn't conscious of the music. She didn't even know if they danced. All she felt was the touch of his body against hers, the strong circle of his arms.

"This is a mistake." His voice was low. His lips moved against her ear.

She shivered. Every nerve in her body was exquisitely attuned to this man. She pushed both hands against his chest, gaining a little distance. "What's a mistake, our thinking we could dance together or our micro-relationship?"

"The micro-fucking-relationship. It won't work."

Okay. Quick mood change. Luckily she was a woman stuck between two sisters, so that didn't bother her in the least. "Of course it will work. Just lose the grumpy mood."

Of course it wouldn't work, but she had no intention of losing him early. Besides, given his rules about relationships, it took a lot of nerve to critique hers. "And it's a micro-*non*-fucking-relationship," she reminded him, just to be bitchy back.

"Did you make your decision about Wolfram's task force yet?" He didn't take her advice to lose the grumpy.

"Yes," she said, and realized that she had. "I'm going to join the task force."

He nodded, face grim. "When will you leave Washington?"

"I'll give notice when I go back. It will take at least a month to close down or transfer all my cases and to pack up the apartment." She was silent for a moment. "I'm going to miss you. Of course, I'll miss Carter and Roberts and Baxter and all the squad." She bit her lip and felt a tight knot in her chest. "But I'll miss you most of all."

"Why do I feel like the Scarecrow about to watch Dorothy click her heels together?"

Luckily, his sarcasm was quite effective at stemming her unwanted emotion. "Maybe because you're missing part of your brain?" The part that was supposed to want her not to leave, that couldn't live without her.

"Joining the task force will be a great career move," he said instead, both ignoring her response and proving her point.

The music must have come to an end. People were shuffling on and off the dance floor. Leo still held her in his arms.

"Yes." She brushed that aside impatiently. "But it's more

than that. Probably like every other American who watched those newscasts, I want to get the Isaac Cult. But unlike most of those Americans, I have the opportunity and the training."

His arms dropped and he stepped back. "You won't give up."

"We're alike in that way." It was the first thing, well, maybe the second thing, that had attracted her to him. He was persistent––a bulldog––when on a case.

"We're alike in another way. I put in for a transfer. I'm looking to go supervisory."

Bodies were moving around them, gyrating to a Lady Gaga song. "It's about time. You're more than ready." Thank God she was leaving as well. The field office would have been hard with him gone.

"The Board will have to approve any promotion."

"Done deal." There was no way he wouldn't get a promotion. The only thing holding Leo back had been Leo. "Next year is going to be a great year for us, isn't it?" She said the words with more determination than belief.

"It will be hard to top this year."

Grace did a quick year-in-review. Maybe he'd had some spectacular cases before she came to Washington in July. She lifted a questioning brow.

He met her eyes. They were full of emotion and life. "This is the year I met you."

He wasn't handing her a line. She heard the sincerity in the words. Damn him. What did he mean, saying things like that? Did he mean he valued their friendship or did he mean something more?

Two large hands dropped on her shoulders, barely registering on her Leo-focused nerve-endings.

"Grace, I made it." Firm lips brushed her ear. "Your New Year's date is here with fifteen minutes to spare."

Michael Wolfram was in the building.

Fifteen minutes to midnight

All things considered, the "break-up" went better than might be expected, given that two alpha males were involved.

For a moment, Leo's face wore a dark, savage look that evoked the image of an ancient Mayan warrior or—if you didn't happen to be influenced by *Ancient Mexico*, a book you were reading only because Leo had mentioned his mother came from Mexico—a terrifying street thug. The look was gone in an eye blink, however, and Leo's easy smile replaced it.

Michael's hands, which had tightened in response to that look, relaxed. "Ramos, why am I not surprised to see you here?"

Leo merely nodded at Michael, then he bent over her hand with a murmured, "An adrenalin rush from start to finish," before he faded away into the ballroom.

Of course, he didn't literally fade away. He stayed quite clearly in view, thanks to her suddenly much-loved heels, which raised her enough to see over Michael's shoulder while they danced.

Leo currently circled the floor with Aunt Helen. Her cane was stuck at an angle in his cummerbund. The band was covering a Frank Sinatra tune, or maybe it was covering Michael Bublé covering Frank Sinatra. Really, did she care? She couldn't think about much else but Leo. He said that she left him breathless. Good friends didn't leave each other breathless.

"You're stepping on my toes." Michael's voice interrupted her attempts to turn him in the right direction so that she could get a better view of Leo and Aunt Helen. The two had a suspicious amount to say to each other.

"I'm sorry. What?" Grace pulled her head back and looked into his amused blue eyes.

"I just said that to get your attention. It's my ego, not my toes, that are taking the beating."

"Michael, I'm so sorry." Grace shook her head hard, hoping to snap out of the Leo haze. All she succeeded in doing was loosening a curl from its mooring. With impatient fingers, she tucked it behind her ear. "I'm glad you're here." And she was. "I've missed you and the rest of the Chicago squad."

"Same here, but you know I have an ulterior motive for making this drive."

"Don't tell me you're here to recruit Lewis as well?"

"Who's Lewis?" Michael's head swung to survey the room, as if searching for a likely FBI candidate.

She scanned the room as well. "*Where's* Lewis is a better question. I haven't seen him all night, which is really unusual." He never missed this ball. She'd have to find her mother and ask where he was. "So if you're not here for Lewis, what's the ulterior motive?"

"I want to continue recruiting you of course."

She gave him her full attention at that, and smiled. How nice to be wanted, if only professionally. She really should tell him that he'd had her at the mention of the Isaac Massacres, but she might enjoy the whole recruitment thing for a while. "Just don't let anyone know that's your real reason for coming. My reputation has really gotten a boost tonight. It's not every woman who has a handsome FBI agent drive almost four hours just to be her New Year's Eve date."

"Then it must be even rarer for a woman to have two handsome FBI agents drive almost four hours to be her New Year's Eve date."

"He didn't come for me."

"Bullshit."

"He's going to break my heart." The words were matter of fact.

"I don't think so." Michael pulled her closer. Grace leaned her head against his shoulder and they swayed to the music. "If he's going to break anything, it will be one of my body parts. He's watching us almost as much as you're watching him."

"I apologize again. Watching Leo stops now. You're my hero tonight. You've broken my dating curse." Leo was watching her?

A low vibration hummed through her body.

"My phone." Michael kept an arm around her as he pulled the phone out of his trouser pocket. He took a look at it and grimaced. "I'm the one who has to apologize now. First I was late to the party and now I have a call that I have to return."

"No problem." Her stomach gave a familiar lurch. "Just make sure you're back by midnight."

He glanced at his phone. "I have ten minutes. This will take five. Where can I find you?"

"I'll be waiting right by the stage. My dad does the countdown from there every year."

They wove through couples toward one of the short flights of steps that flanked each side of the stage. "Stay right here. I promise I'll be back with champagne."

She couldn't stop from reaching out to grip his arm. "Can't you wait until after midnight?" This echoed every other New Year's Eve, with her date leaving at the last moment.

"It's important or I would. Five minutes, I promise." Michael strode off through the crowd toward the lobby, which was quieter.

Grace sighed and leaned her butt back against the stage. Her skirt belled out in front of her. Of course he wouldn't be back by midnight. Even dressed like a princess she couldn't keep a man by her side. She must have pissed off Fate in some previous life and now it was payback time.

But big picture, losing a bet and a New Year's Eve dating curse were minor annoyances. A lifetime without Leo? She was beginning to suspect that would be more painful than she could imagine.

Chapter Ten

Five minutes to Midnight

LEO LED Aunt Helen over to her table at the side of the dance floor, traded "Happy New Year!" greetings with the group of sloshed older women seated there, and headed for the bar across the hall. The room was deserted. Everyone had congregated on the dance floor and roving waiters were busy passing out flutes of champagne.

"Can I get you something?" The bartender looked happy to have a customer.

"I've got a long drive ahead of me. Do you have any bottled water?"

"You're not leaving before the big moment, are you?" The man made no move to go for the water.

"Midnight on New Year's Eve is just sixty seconds in time, special only because we've decided to make it special." Just call him the New Year's Eve Grinch.

"Bet Grace Devine doesn't think so."

"What do you know about Grace?" Leo's muscles tensed and he leaned slightly toward the man. He noted his nametag. *Harry.*

Harry backed up a step, bumping into the bottles at his back. "I saw you with her earlier. And people have been talking. Every year her date deserts her before midnight. It's kind of the town joke." He looked Leo straight in the eye. "Reminds me of rats leaving a sinking ship."

Young Harry had balls. His analogy sucked, however. "First, Grace is not a sinking ship. If anything, I'd call her unsinkable. Second, if that's true, her dates *have* all been rats, me included, but I'm not her date at the moment." He didn't know why he felt compelled to continue this conversation. "Her current rat is dancing with her right now."

The bartender half-turned and reached into the small refrigerator. He pulled out a bottle of water and handed it to Leo. He nodded his head toward the ballroom. "No he's not. And you see all those people gathering on the dance floor? Sure, they're there for the confetti, the balloons, the countdown to midnight. They're also there to see if Grace gets dumped again. I heard more than a couple of side bets going on in here this evening."

"What do you mean, 'No, he's not'?" Leo turned to look at the ballroom. He couldn't believe she'd been dumped in past years. What idiot would walk away from Grace?

"The big blond guy left the room and Grace is up on the stage talking to her dad." The bartender shrugged. "Looks like it's happening again."

Fuck. Where the hell was Wolfram? He looked out over the heads of the glittering crowd. The band was winding down their last number before midnight. People were half-dancing, careful not to spill the champagne they held in one hand. Grace was up on the stage. She looked heart-stoppingly beautiful. She held herself with an almost regal grace. He could imagine men bowing at her feet. He could imagine himself bowing at her feet, and slowly moving his lips up her legs. He could imagine uncovering every inch of her body and finally touching those perfect breasts, the smooth muscles of her stomach, the soft damp center of her.

He took the water Harry held out to him and turned his back on the stage. She was heading to Salt Lake City with Wolfram, the asshole who'd been rubbing his hands up and down her back on the dance floor. The asshole who wasn't an asshole, and who would be working with her every day. The asshole who wasn't an asshole, and who was probably a better man for her than his fucked-up self.

He uncapped the water and took a long swallow. Harry had stopped talking and was turned toward the ballroom, leaning forward on his side of the bar.

Leo walked out of the room, across the empty hall to the edge of the ballroom. Grace was still on the stage. She looked toward the lobby doors and then her gaze moved over the dance floor. She shrugged when someone said something to her and gave a laugh. Then her shoulders firmed, she folded her hands in front of her and she looked straight at him. Her smile was warm and loving and rooted him to the spot. She tilted her head just slightly, waved her hand twice and her smile became a goodbye.

Fuck.

Two minutes to midnight

It was happening again. Grace couldn't believe it. Her date had left her. Only this time, there was no dependable Lewis to kiss. There was no one to kiss. Well, her dad had pulled her up on the stage and offered, but that didn't count. Interestingly enough, even though she felt the eyes of every person on her, could almost hear the whispered speculations, none of it bothered her. Her attention was focused solely on the man standing in the doorway. The man who watched her with brooding intensity but who was willing to let her walk out of his life.

Enough. She blinked and wanted to slap herself. When she had a goal, she went after it. She worked hard, picked herself up when she fell, and kept going. So, okay, with Leo she'd mostly been jogging in place. But faint heart never won the ex-micro-date. Or whatever.

She stepped up to the microphone and gently hipped her father aside. She looked out over the sea of curious faces and for a moment she froze. How did Tess stand up on stage night after night? Her knees were actually shaking. There must be some similar strand of DNA in her body that she could tap. Or maybe not. She cleared her throat and leaned toward the microphone.

"Hello, everybody. Since I know you're all wondering, and some of you—Vance Evans and Brooks Bennett, I'm looking at you—have money on this, it appears as if I may be without a date to kiss at midnight."

The crowd erupted in boos, groans and laughs. Someone yelled, "Where's Lewis?"

"I know most of you—probably all of you—are here with a date tonight, but in case anyone is looking for someone to kiss at midnight, I'm here and available." She frowned when someone let out a loud hoot. "Jimmy Lee, get your mind out of the gutter, I'm talking kissing here." She looked away from the grinning teenager. "There's just one caveat." She paused and sent up a quick prayer. "If you kiss me tonight, you have to be willing to commit to kissing me on future New Year's Eves as well." She didn't look toward the doorway where Leo stood. "I'm getting too old to be going through this every year." The crowd laughed. "So be careful before you head up here. I'm looking for a very special New Year's Eve kiss. I'm looking for the kiss of a lifetime."

Ninety seconds to Midnight

Leo stared at Grace, his heart beating quickly. She stepped off to the side of the microphone, her hands folded in front of her. Waiting. Her parents stood to the left of her, stunned expressions on both their faces. Her mom had a hand on her father's arm. Without Mrs. Devine's intervention, Mr. Devine might have picked his baby girl up and carried her off the stage.

"Gotta love her grit." Harry, the bartender spoke from beside him. "I want to kiss her myself." At Leo's fierce look he held up a hand and grinned. "Just kidding."

If Leo walked up on that stage and kissed Grace, he wouldn't let her go again. She would go to Salt Lake City and he had no idea where he would end up. It was crazy-ass stupid to start a relationship right now.

She wasn't looking toward him at all. She stood tall and glorious on the stage. A proud goddess.

He saw movement in the crowd. His brain shut down and he handed his bottle of water to Harry.

Thirty seconds to Midnight

Crap. About five men were making their way toward the stage, one of them the eighty-year-old widower, Lionel Dexter, the biggest lecher in Vance County. None of the men were Leo.

Maybe she should have texted Annabelle and Tess about her little speech first.

Aunt Helen stuck out her cane as Colonel Dexter passed, and he went down in a slow tumble. Grace sent her a discreet thumbs up. Two teenage boys, drunker than they should be, were ribbing each other as they made their way toward her while two sullen young women yapped in their wake. Grace put her hands on her waist and gave them her best FBI stare. They stopped in their tracks.

That left two men still trying to elbow through the crowd, Charlie Brighton and David Ledbetter, both failed New Year's Eve dates from past years but generally nice guys. Not, however, men she was interested in sharing future New Year's Eves with. She sent her dad a desperate look.

Fifteen seconds to Midnight

Harry Devine step up to the microphone and his voice boomed across the ballroom. "Charlie and Dave, you stop right where you are. You're both fine men, but you had your chance with my Gracie-belle. You don't get another."

Grace breathed a sigh of relief when both men, wearing identical sheepish expressions, stopped moving toward the stage. She concentrated on not looking toward the ballroom doors, but there was no movement on the periphery of her vision. Leo wasn't going to take her challenge. He wasn't willing to give her a commitment.

The air left her lungs in a huge sigh and she felt like a deflated balloon. God knows she wouldn't give up on him. But she might need a few days, or a week or two, or maybe a year to get her self-confidence back.

She listened numbly as her dad started the countdown to midnight.

"*Ten!*"

The crowd shouted along with Harry Devine. Leo worked his way onto the packed dance floor and watched Grace raise her flute, drain it, and look around as if for another.

"*Nine!*"

Leo had to use shoulder and muscle to make it through the crowd that suddenly felt like a wall. Grace's mother handed Grace her flute of champagne. She downed that as well.

"*Eight!*"

Leo caught sight of another man moving quickly through the crowd. "Wolfram." The name came out as a low growl. Several people backed away from him quickly.

"*Seven!*"

Aunt Helen suddenly appeared in front of him, acting as point guard. She analyzed the crowd and shifted to the path of least resistance. Her cane swished at waist height in a large semi-circle in front of her, parting the crowd as effectively as Moses' staff had parted the Red Sea. Leo could only hope God was on his side as well.

"*Six!*"

Leo took a moment to glance at the stage. Grace was watching him, her mouth half-open in surprise. Who the fuck had she expected would take her up on her offer?

"*Five!*"

Wolfram. Had she hoped to bring Wolfram back? He might be the better man, but he couldn't have Grace. Grace was his sunshine, the laughter in his day. She was his, and he'd figure out how to keep her.

"*Four!*"

Aunt Helen stepped aside and there, finally, were the steps of the stage. He took them two at a time. He saw Wolfram bounding up the steps on the other side. Grace stood at center stage, her head swinging back and forth between them.

"*Three!*"

Leo dashed across the stage. Wolfram moved quickly as well, a bottle of champagne in one hand. He reached Grace first, the bastard. He seemed to notice Leo for the first time. He grinned, thrust the champagne at Leo and took Grace's hand.

"*Two!*"

Leo's fingers reflexively tightened around the neck of the bottle as Grace pulled Wolfram toward her. She turned her pelvis and executed the perfect Koshinage hip throw. Wolfram landed with a thud on the wooden floor of the stage. The entire room gasped, and Mr. Devine's next count may have been off by half a second or so.

"*One!*"

Leo set down the champagne bottle. In a single, fluid movement, he gathered Grace against his heart and gave her the kiss of a lifetime.

Midnight

Grace forgot she was on a stage in the ballroom in front of all her friends and family. She forgot she should be worried about Michael, sprawled on the floor. She didn't think of anything but the fact that Leo was holding her like he didn't want to let her go. His lips explored hers with a focused thoroughness that shot fireworks through her body. He lifted his head as the band began to play, and for a moment neither of them had the breath to say anything.

Then a small smile curved his lips and those dimples flashed in his cheeks. "Just so you know," he murmured, "I refuse to have "Auld Lang Syne" be our song for the next fifty years."

After Midnight

Grace dragged Leo off the stage after checking that Michael was fine. The crowd parted for them with laughs and teasing comments. The hallway was empty.

She veered sharply to the right and headed down the hallway until she reached the huge window overlooking the club pool. She turned to face Leo. "I meant what I said up there. You're committed now."

"That works both ways, Devine. You're committed as well. I know it may be difficult when we're both in different cities, but we'll make it work." He studied her face. "It would be in your best interest if we just keep this a friendship."

"Argh." Was the man totally blind? He was intelligent and one of the most savvy FBI agents in the business. How could he be so stupid?

"I didn't know people who weren't pretending to be pirates actually made that sound," Leo said.

"Really? I can't imagine you haven't heard it multiple times." She tried to read the emotion in those deep brown eyes. "I don't want to keep this a friendship."

"Good. Because I was going to say that even though it may be in your best interest, there is no way I'm not taking that dress off you tonight."

Thank you, God. And thank you for the pretty underwear, Annabelle. Still, there were a few things to clear up. "You shut me down that night at the Pub." She took a breath. "I might look different and all girly, but I haven't changed."

"You stopped my heart the first day you walked into the field office. You never needed to change. I did." He frowned. "Or maybe I didn't." He held up a hand. "Wait. Don't make that noise again. I'll explain." He reached for her hand and held it. She moved closer to him because she could, because she had to.

"I've been changing since the day I met you," Leo said. "Katherine Dill shut a part of me down. I know crazy people exist. I've gone after them, cleaned up their messes, locked them away from society. Dill was different. She was one of us. And it scares the hell out of me that I didn't know until too late what she was capable of."

"So, what, you developed a suspicion of women? You had to sleep with as many as you could in order to learn how to trust them again?" She didn't quite succeed in keeping the sarcasm out of her voice.

"No." He ignored it. "The problem was more that I couldn't handle that my judgment was so piss-poor. If I'd seen who she was, understood how she might react, I could have saved Parker, kept Mackenzie from taking five bullets, and saved that kid."

Maybe. "So you had to learn to trust yourself again?"

"In part, and in part I had to learn to live with the fact that I make mistakes. I don't know everything. Sometimes I'm going to walk into a situation and I won't walk out the winner. For a competitive bastard, that's a hard pill to swallow."

She had her own problems getting that one down her throat.

"The competitive bastards are the ones who keep going, no matter what," Michael Wolfram said from behind him. "You combine that with a healthy dose of understanding that shit is going to happen and you've got the ingredients for a hell of a leader."

Michael's hair was tousled and his bow tie slightly askew. He gave Leo a pointed look. "Carter contacted me at the start of the week and told me you were interested in moving into a supervisory role. I got approval today to offer you a position as an assistant team supervisor on the task force I'm forming. I'd like to meet with you in Washington next week to discuss it." Wolfram clapped Leo on the shoulder.

He looked toward Grace. "The Koshinage?"

She nodded.

"Nice execution. Saying 'no' would have worked just as well."

"I'm so sorry. My brain froze and my reflexes took over. I owe you a drink." At his raised eyebrow she amended, "Or three."

"Call it even. I know I've been the date from hell." His smile was crooked. "I don't think you'll mind if I head out. It's starting to snow. I want to get to my hotel and crash before the roads get too bad. I'll call you when I'm back in Washington." He leaned down and kissed her cheek.

"Well," Grace said, watching him leave. "Was that Santa Claus and is this really Christmas? Because I feel like he just gave us a hell of a gift."

Leo wasn't looking anywhere but at her. "You're the gift, Grace. We'd have found a way to make this work, even without Wolfram's offer." His face was serious. She couldn't look away from the desire and love that were clear in his deep brown gaze. "You are strong, courageous and full of warmth and love. I want you by my side for a lifetime, Devine."

He bent down and slowly trailed his tongue from her shoulder to the curve of her neck. She shivered, an odd reaction given the heat rushing through her. "Every inch, Grace," he whispered in her ear. "I'm going to start the new year by licking every inch of you." He raised his head, his expression intent. "In fact, I think that will be our tradition. We'll start every new year that way."

She closed her eyes but felt she was seeing into a future of laughter, love and desire. His hand tilted her chin and she opened her eyes to see his smile.

"Let's go find someplace more private."

She nodded and smiled back, happiness bubbling through her like champagne. "You know, Leo," she said as she took his arm and tried to keep pace with his rapid strides toward the clubhouse entrance. "I'm pretty sure New Year's Eve is about to become my favorite holiday."

Read more about Michael Wolfram's new task force in
Out of the Shadows, available in 2013.

Lewis

Dedicated to every great romance that began on New Year's Eve

The Perfect Kiss

Chapter One

DEAR LORD, *let me* finally *kiss Lewis Kampmueller.*

Darcy Bennett sent the thought out to the Universe, to the Heavens…really, to anyone or anything that would listen and help make her biggest—and oldest—wish come true.

This was her year. She could feel it. It would begin at midnight with the kiss she'd imagined ever since her brother, Brooks, brought Lewis home from school when the boys had been in the third grade. Darcy wasn't even in kindergarten yet, but she knew with absolute certainty that Lewis Kampmueller would one day kiss her and they would live Happily Ever After.

After The Kiss (though usually a practical person by nature, she had always thought of her future with Lewis in capital letters), she and Lewis would spend the rest of the evening and beginning of the new year—Their Year—talking, dancing, laughing, maybe a bit more kissing, and generally falling in love.

He was sure to spout an "I can't believe how much you've changed" or "You're so grown up" or perhaps, dare she hope? maybe even a "What a beauty you've become."

Her friends and parents had told her as much, but Darcy had been the proverbial ugly duckling too long to accept her swan feathers just yet.

But if Lewis gave her even half the look he'd been giving Grace Devine forever, she'd finally believe.

And after all, swans mated for life, didn't they?

Darcy almost pulled out her smartphone to Google that fact for confirmation, but stopped herself. She was already making this into a Cinderella analogy, with the stroke of midnight and all. No need to mix her fairy tale metaphors and add in The Ugly Duckling.

Besides, no gadgets of any kind tonight. Not even a quick text to her girlfriends back in Boston, apprising them of her progress.

She was unplugged, unwired, and ready to finally kiss the man she was going to marry.

⌒

Tonight, when he kissed Grace at midnight, as he had for the past ten years, Lewis would finally tell her how he felt.

No more of the quick peck that she got stuck giving him each year. He'd paid much more to her safety nets to just settle for that, but settle he had. And some of those years, coming up with bribe money had put a serious crimp in his budget.

But he would pay anything—and now had the means to—for just a peck from Grace. He'd take anything from her, and that was the problem.

But no more.

All's fair in love and war. And he'd played by the rules far too long when it came to Grace. But not this year. No, this year at midnight, he was going to take Grace in his arms, give her the kiss they were meant to share—long, slow, deep—look straight into her brown eyes and say, "Grace Devine, I've loved you my whole life. Nobody will ever love you the way I do. And I think it's time we take this beyond friendship."

Lewis would like to say more, would like to propose marriage if he didn't think it would send Grace into shock. Yeah, maybe better to ask for a date first.

He'd been coming back to Henderson for New Year's Eve ever since he first left to attend MIT. He attended the parties even after his parents retired, sold his childhood home, moved to

Arizona and were co-hosts of the party in name only. He flew out and spent Christmas with them but he always made sure to make it home for the party on New Year's Eve.

And his kiss with Grace.

✑—

Darcy gave one final look in the mirror. She'd had her roommate, Susan, spend hours showing her how to curl her long, blonde hair so it looked like she'd just stepped out of a *Real Housewives* episode. She'd spent a fortune at the makeup counter in Macy's, buying anything they had put on her, careful to watch every swipe and swab the girl made to her face so she could replicate it tonight. She'd put her entire bonus check from the most recent video game she'd designed toward her dress.

And it showed. Black, with crystal beading all over it, shimmering with every movement. She absolutely loved it. The low cut neck was more daring than she was used to, and it'd taken Susan's extensive persuasive skills to talk Darcy into it, but she was glad she had.

And the shoes. Oh, the shoes! She'd bought them first, wearing them nightly around the apartment so she could learn to balance on the five inch, shimmery, glass slipper-looking Louboutins.

She twirled in front of the mirror, catching the light. Surely she'd catch Lewis's eye in this—the man was a sucker for shiny objects.

She picked up her phone—one last touch of technology— took a quick snapshot of herself and texted it to Susan, who was probably already on her way to whatever party she was going to in Boston. She didn't wait for a response, but did a final twirl to one of her long curls, grabbed her tiny bag, and walked out the door.

And straight into a human wall.

Lewis propped his tablet up on the dresser, turned to the nearby mirror, and pushed play for the YouTube video on how to tie a perfect bow tie. Annabelle had taught—or tried to teach—him how to do this several times, but apparently those brain cells were put to a different use.

It was a well-done, easy-to-follow video, and he was pleased with the results. He started to move to the bed where the coat of his tux lay, but turned back to his tablet instead. He typed a quick message to the creator of the video, "Interested in doing how-to videos for my company? Email me."

He powered down the tablet, put on his jacket. He checked his phone and saw he'd missed a text from Tess earlier in the day. "Find me a date or you're kissing me at midnight, hot stuff."

Well, if he had to work finding Tess a date into his plans, so be it. Because it wasn't the oldest Devine sister he'd be kissing at midnight.

He put his phone into his pocket and stepped out of the bedroom and into the hallway. He'd gotten halfway down the hall when he remembered his keys, did an about face and ran smack into a tiny, blonde, shiny object.

⟋⟍

Darcy stumbled back on her impossible heels, but managed to use the wall to keep her balance. She looked at Brooks, ready to rip him a new one for scaring her, only to realize that it wasn't her brother in the hallway of her parents' home, but the man for whom she'd spent the last three hours primping.

"Lewis? What are you doing here?"

He looked down at her, his brilliant mind trying to focus on what had just happened. "Who are…Munchkin?"

The old nickname stung, but she quickly regrouped. "Darcy," she corrected.

"Are you okay? Did I hurt you?" He reached out as if to steady her and she leaned toward him, waiting for his touch. But he took that to mean she was balanced and dropped his hand.

"I'm fine," she confirmed. "What are you doing here?"

But he didn't answer; he was too busy looking at her.

Which should be something that made her happy, but his look wasn't one of lust and heat. No, it was analysis. A look she'd seen on his face for years—thinking, putting pieces into place, working out the puzzle.

His head leaned from the left, slowly to the right, as his brown-eyed gaze started at her glorious shoes, up her legs (made oh-so-more stellar by the shoes) to her sparkling dress. He moved past her bust line, then back to it and she felt a moment of triumph that stayed with her as his eyes rose up to her cheekbone-accented, buffed to perfection, face.

"You're not wearing your glasses."

Genius.

"I had Lasik," she replied, then did a tiny shimmer with her hips, drawing his eyes back to her dress.

He pushed his glasses up his nose, a habit she'd shared for far too many years. "Lasik, huh? I'm not a good candidate for it."

"Too bad. It totally helped me."

He tilted his head again, plugging in the lack of glasses, but still coming up without an answer.

"And my hair is different."

He stared at her hairstyle, nodding. "Yes. The hair. The glasses." It looked like it was coming together for him now. "You're so...so..." Darcy waited for it. Grown-up? Striking? "Shiny," he said.

Well, she couldn't argue with that.

"So, Lewis, you didn't answer me? What are you doing here?" Not that she wasn't happy to see him, but she'd planned on a big entrance at the Club as his introduction to the new Darcy—not him slamming her into a wall in her parents' hallway.

"Um..." he took one last look at her, obviously still filing away all the new facts, then looked her in the eye, ready to move on to his next train of thought. "Oh. Why I'm here. Brooks's place can only handle one guest right now, and it made more sense that Duncan crash with him and I stay here. Your parents invited me, of course."

"My parents know you're here? When did you get here?"

"Earlier today. I was over at Brooks's until I needed to get ready. And yes, they know I'm here. Your dad let me in, gave me a key, got me set up in Brooks's room."

"Oh," Darcy replied, trying to figure out why her mother hadn't said anything to her about Lewis being down the hallway. She'd been home for Christmas, but had to work the week in between, arriving back just a few hours ago. Still, she'd seen her mom downstairs when she'd come in.

"It's like old times being in there," Lewis stated, gesturing to Brooks's room. Darcy took the moment to do her own analysis. Designer tux, custom-fitted to his long, lean frame, which no doubt his assistant picked out for him. Lewis never cared about the fit—or label—of his clothes. His deep brown, wavy hair was cut in a spiky style that suited his nervous habit of running his hands through it as he thought—and he was *always* thinking. His glasses were so much better than the huge ones he'd worn through school. Sleek and square, they framed the brown eyes Darcy had fallen in love with so many years ago. His face had thinned out in his twenties. Now it was not quite chiseled, but he certainly didn't have the pudgy cheeks he'd had before.

So, Darcy wasn't the only one to have come out of a cocoon.

It didn't matter to her—she'd loved him as total geek, and now as geek chic.

Suddenly it dawned on her— he was staying two doors down from her! That wasn't anything new, Lewis had slept in Brooks's room hundreds of times.

But never on a night Darcy was bent on seducing him.

Well, okay, she'd wanted to seduce him many times back then, but she'd never actually *done* it. Tonight, she would.

She moved past him, brushing his sleeve with her arm. "I imagine there will be lots of 'seems like old times' moments tonight," she said. Stupid. Why bring up the past? It would only make him think of Grace Devine.

"Yeah, I'm sure," he said, moving to follow her down the stairs.

She tried to do a long, sultry glide down the staircase, but she hadn't practiced stairs in her shoe sessions. There weren't any at the Henderson Country Club and she hadn't planned on Lewis being in her house. Not that she was complaining.

"Although," he continued, "I'm looking to start some new times tonight."

She looked over her shoulder at him, "Me, too," she purred.

"Sore throat, Munchkin?"

She stumbled, but righted herself with the help of the banister that she'd watched Brooks and Lewis slide down a gazillion times.

"You okay?" he asked.

"Yes," she answered, and quickly made her way down to the bottom, not risking looking back—or anywhere else but the stairs—again.

"Little girl, you are a beauty," her father, John, boomed as he and Darcy's mother, Ellen, made their way in from the living room. He wore his tux, which strained a bit at the buttons this year. Her mother looked beautiful in a navy blue gown and the diamond necklace Darcy's father had given her for their twenty-fifth anniversary six years ago. Her hair was just starting to gray at fifty-five and Darcy could only hope to have her genes.

"Thanks, Daddy," she answered, reaching the first floor and letting her father take her hand and twirl her. Twirling in the heels, she'd practiced plenty.

"Is she not the most beautiful girl you've ever seen, Lewis?" her father asked a bit loudly and Darcy wondered if maybe he'd popped the champagne a tad early.

"Oh, John," her mother said, with a swat to his arm.

"Well, she is. Beautiful. My baby. Right, Lewis?"

"Um," Lewis said, then turned to Darcy, looked her over once more. "Yes?"

Yeah, there was a questioning tone in his voice, but she'd still take it.

"Hello, Lewis, honey," her mother stepped forward and gave Lewis a hug and kiss on the cheek. "You look very handsome. How are your parents?"

"They're good. They said to wish you happy holidays."

"One of these years they'll have to come back for the party. It's not fair to you to have to carry the Kampmueller side."

"It's hard to get my dad out of Arizona in the winter."

"Well, hell, it's not like he can't play golf in Henderson year-round," her dad said.

Darcy didn't think her parents would leave North Carolina once they retired. Actually, she couldn't ever see her dad retiring. He loved the banking industry, even with all its recent ups and downs.

"Mrs. Devine pretty much handles it all on her own now, with a little help from my assistant. By the way, thanks again for offering up Brooks's room. It would have been really cramped over at his new place."

"How's it coming along, anyway? He won't even let me take a peek," John Bennett, control freak extraordinaire, commented.

"Can you really blame him?" her mother said with a smile. "We love having you here, Lewis. You know you're always welcome."

"But, really, Lewis, how's it coming over there? Has he got drywall up? Electrical, even?"

"We should probably leave. We don't want to be late," her mother commented.

Darcy noticed Lewis look at his watch. Was he counting down the minutes until he kissed Grace? *Keep counting, bud, cuz it's going to be a different set of lips this year.*

She still hadn't figured that part out, but if Lewis could devise a way to rig whatever contest the Devine sisters had going every year, then Darcy could figure out a way to rig it in her favor.

She did design games for a living, after all.

"So, Lewis, you'll take Darcy with you?"

"Um…but…"

"Great. See you at the Club," her father said and opened the door for his wife and exited the house. But not before she saw the look her parents exchanged with each other.

Those sneaky…absolutely awesome parents. Must be where she got her love of games.

"Let me just grab my wrap," she said and quickly found the organza shawl which was much too sheer for the end of December, even in North Carolina. But no way was she going to cover up this dress. She handed it to Lewis who held it up for her to step into. His brain didn't retain a lot of the social niceties, but he'd been raised by a former deb, and some things were just instilled in a Southern boy.

"Thank you," she said as he placed it upon her shoulders and she took up the ends.

"It doesn't seem like much protection," he said as he held the door open for her.

I hope not, she thought as they made their way to the car.

Chapter Two

HOW DID HE get roped into bringing Munchkin along with him? Lewis started his car and made his way around the circular drive. In a way, it felt familiar having Darcy tag along. But it had always been Brooks and him telling her to go home or to leave them alone. And when they were older, and were able to drive, she'd always found a way to finagle a ride from them, even though she'd always been relegated to the back seat.

But here she was, in the front seat. And she wasn't a little girl anymore, that was for sure. It had given him pause, placing her in the hallway. He knew it had to be Darcy. What other girl would be in the Bennett's hallway? In fact, he'd quickly computed the statistics that a random woman had found her way into their home. But then, if you added in things like having the same coloring as Darcy and being approximately the same age (though that had fooled Lewis for a moment because for some reason, he always seemed to think of Darcy as fifteen), the odds just became too great.

But it wasn't any Darcy he'd seen before.

"Did you come home for the party last year?" he asked, trying to conclude why he'd been stumped.

"Yes. Why?"

He turned out of the Bennetts' neighborhood—his old neighborhood—and started through town. "I just couldn't remember."

"We danced together," she said.

"Did we?"

"Twice."

"Hmm." Nope, it wasn't coming to him. Nothing. He only remembered dancing with Grace. "So, how's Beantown, Munchkin?"

"Darcy. It's great. You should have stayed, it's a great place to live."

He nodded. "Yeah, I know. But it made sense to make the move. For the company."

"Well, New York's just a train ride away. I go down all the time."

"Do you?"

She didn't answer right away. "Well, not *all* the time. But I've gone down quite a bit."

"Hmmm," he said while his mind turned to a new app idea. Wouldn't be cool if you could—

"You just missed the turn to the Club," he heard from afar.

"Hmmm?"

"Lewis? You just missed the turn."

He came out of coding in his head to realize that, yep, he'd gone a half-mile past the turnoff to the Club. So many times he'd be walking through Manhattan and realize he'd gone five blocks past his office. *That's* the app he needed—a warning on his watch or something for when he walked past his building. Something like a Garmin, but tiny and wearable.

"Unless you'd like to go somewhere else…" Darcy said beside him, jolting him out of his app nap.

He looked over at her as he pulled the car to the side of the road to turn around. "What? Where else would I want to go?"

She was looking at him like he should know something. He got that look a lot from women. She shook her head (again, something he got a lot) and turned her head toward her window. "Nothing. Never mind."

The parking lot at the Club was filling up fast, even though the party was just beginning. You didn't arrive fashionably late for this event. You sucked every minute out of this night.

What if there was an app where you could rate the party you were at and your entire social network could see it, rate theirs, and you could all move to the best one? As he parked the car, he reached for his digital recorder to get the idea down, then paused.

You could kind of do that already on Facebook. Damn Zuckerberg. (This was a sentiment Lewis thought daily.)

"Are you ready?" Darcy asked.

He looked at the Club, lit up with not only from the inside, but also the tasteful holiday lighting along the outside of the building. Grace was in there. His future started now.

"I'm ready," he answered and got out of the car.

ᴐ

Darcy watched as Lewis rounded the car to open her door. She knew what he was thinking. She always knew what he was thinking—which wasn't easy with a mind like his. He was thinking about Grace and their kiss. Maybe even something along the lines of it going differently this year.

Oh, it was going to go differently, if she had anything to do with it. She just hadn't worked out the logistics of it yet. But she'd designed many games, and you always started with the goal and worked backward.

But was Lewis kissing *her* at midnight the goal, or just him *not* kissing Grace?

"Coming?" he asked as he held out his hand for her.

She took his hand and felt a tiny spark as his cool, smooth hand enveloped her small, warm one. She looked up at him to see if he felt what she did and saw him stare at their joined hands. Will his head turn? That would mean he was trying to figure something out. *Turn. Turn.* And then, ever so slowly, and ever so subtly, his head tilted as he rotated their hands just a fraction.

She pressed her palm deeper into his, loving how big and

protective his felt, and watched as his brow furrowed just the tiniest bit. She stepped out of the car, and was greeted with a blast of cool air, from more than Lewis letting go of her hand as soon as she was standing.

"Wow. It must have dropped ten degrees in the time it took to drive over."

Lewis looked up at the dark sky. "No stars. Must be heavy cloud cover. Could be a storm."

Great. No way was she going to let these perfectly executed curls get caught in the rain, even though she'd pictured a stolen moment with Lewis on the terrace. Guess she'd just have to find an alternate private nook, indoors.

Lewis started through the parking lot and Darcy hurried to catch up to him. She wanted to enter with him, and let people think what they would. "Lewis," she called. "Slow down. These shoes are really hard to run in."

He stopped and waited for her, noticing her shoes. "Wow," he said and she felt total justification in the money spent. "Those are going to be killing you by the end of the night." And then, total frustration.

"I know," she grudgingly admitted. "But I like how they make my legs look." He looked at her legs and she struck a pose, flexing her calf and shifting so the slit up the side of her dress fell open.

"Hmmm," he said and turned to hold the entrance door for her. She went through and nodded to the girls set up at the coat check station. She handed them her wrap, took the ticket they gave her, put it in her tiny clutch (also beaded!) and hurried down the hallway to catch up to Lewis, who had no coat to check.

"Lewis, wait," she called and he turned, looking as if he'd forgotten she was with him. Not that she was *with* him, but, still. He stood at the entrance doors to the party and did as she commanded—waited. One thing about Lewis: his self-awareness about being so absent-minded had made him good at taking orders.

"Lewis, stay," she added, not wanting him to go through the doors and make a mad dash, at least attention-wise, to wherever Grace may be. Maybe she'd get lucky and Grace wouldn't be there yet, and Darcy would have a few more minutes of Lewis's attention, such as it was.

When she reached him, she took a deep breath, preparing to enter the room where she'd spend the first night of the Rest of Her Life. He held the door for her and she walked into the already crowded room.

"Wow," she said, taking in all the gorgeous gowns and dazzling tuxes.

"Wow," Lewis said and Darcy didn't need to follow his gaze, but she did anyway.

There stood Grace Devine, looking like she never had before, in a beautiful gown that Darcy suspected belonged to Annabelle, talking with a handsome man Darcy had never seen.

And just like that, all the work Darcy had done in the last year in preparation for this night—the Lasik, growing out her hair, the highlights, the ridiculous amount of money she'd spent on her dress and shoes—didn't seem nearly enough to compete with the way Lewis looked at Grace Devine.

Something inside Darcy snapped. And then, something outside her did, and she felt herself falling off her glass slippers. Her last thought before she hit the ground was of turning into a pumpkin.

Chapter Three

OUT OF THE corner of his eye, Lewis saw Darcy going down. He reached for her, but was too late. She lay huddled, face down, on the floor, her shiny dress askew, the slit up the side showing a good amount of leg. Not just leg, but thigh in particular. Toned, creamy thigh that stood in stark contrast to the black, beaded dress.

He knelt down beside her, gently laying a hand on her shoulder. "Munchkin? Are you okay?"

"Darcy. I'm fine. I think I did something to my ankle."

"Can you sit up so we can take a look at it?"

"I can…but I don't want to," she said so softly he almost didn't hear her over the party noise, which had gotten much quieter.

"Does it hurt that much?"

"No. I…is everyone staring?"

Lewis looked up to see that, indeed, people in the room were staring, and several people had quickly moved toward them to offer help. He held up a hand as if to ward them off, which worked on everyone except the Bennetts and the man who had been standing by Grace.

Grace. Who looked beautiful, of course, but not like any Grace he'd ever seen before. First Munchkin with all the changes so that he'd barely recognized her, and now Grace. He wasn't so sure he liked this much change in one night.

Change threw him.

As the Bennetts neared them, he patted Darcy, knowing his touch was most likely ineffectual. "No, nobody noticed. The party's in full swing, nobody was even looking this way."

"Liar," she said, but she did begin to move, to right herself. Sadly, the slit in her dress fell back into place. She didn't look up, though. She hid behind the mass of honey gold hair that was hanging in her face. Had her hair always been that…that… massive?

"Darcy? Honey, are you all right?" The Bennetts had reached them now, their concern showing in their faces.

"Baby girl?" Mr. Bennett said as he knelt down.

"I'm okay, Daddy. Just humiliated."

"She thinks she might have done something to her ankle," Lewis told John.

"Let me take a look at it," said the man who'd been standing by Grace, and was now reaching for Darcy's ankle.

Some irrational emotion overtook Lewis, and he swatted the man's hand away. "Don't touch her," he nearly growled. Odd. He never growled. Or had irrational emotions for that matter. "It might be broken," he added, as if to justify himself.

The man studied Lewis for a moment, a moment that lasted a little too long for Lewis's liking. Who was this guy? He was in a tux, was part of the party, but seemed…different somehow.

"I've had some experience with these types of things," the man said and reached for Darcy's leg, slowly this time, his eyes on Lewis. His hands hovered just above her tiny ankle, and he looked at her. "May I?"

Lewis watched as Darcy looked up, her hair falling back off her face, parting like golden curtains. Her eyes grew wider as she took in the man, but she only nodded her assent. Like the guy left her speechless or something.

Lewis studied the man as he tenderly prodded Darcy's ankle, causing a sharp intake of breath from her. "Careful," Lewis warned.

The man shot Lewis a look that seemed like…amusement?

But surely he wouldn't be amused by Darcy's pain. So he was amused by Lewis?

"Just who are you, anyway?"

The man took his hands away from Darcy's ankle—finally!—and offered one for Lewis to shake. "Leo Ramos. Nice to meet you, Mr. Kampmueller."

"How do you know who I am?" Lewis asked, not trying to hide the suspicion in his voice. Something was off about this guy—he was too...too...just too much.

"You're the reason I'm here."

"Me too," he thought he heard Darcy whisper.

"What?" he asked them both.

"Nothing. Damn, this hurts," Darcy answered as she tried to turn her ankle, causing another intake of breath—different from when Leo Ramos touched her.

"It doesn't appear to be broken," Ramos said to Darcy, ignoring Lewis's question. "Probably just a pretty nasty sprain, but you should have it looked at."

Lewis did look at it—her ankle—and could see it already starting to swell. Darcy started to rise and Lewis took one of her arms as Ramos took the other. "Her father can help her," Lewis said, but only received that smirk again.

"Can you put any weight on it?" Ramos asked Darcy, who tried, but winced painfully, then tried to hide it.

Just like she used to when they were kids and she'd hurt herself doing something stupid that Brooks and he were doing. Trying to keep up with them. Not showing them she was in pain.

"Oh, honey," Ellen Bennett said. "You really need to go to the emergency room." As Darcy gasped and started furiously shaking her head—causing that massive hair to shimmer—her mother quickly added, "To make sure it's not broken. I'm sorry, honey, you really have to go."

Were those...tears? He'd never seen Darcy close to anything like tears. "I don't want to go," she whispered.

"I know, honey, but we really need to make sure it's not

something more than a sprain. At the very least, we need to get that ankle elevated and some ice on it."

"Maybe I could just get some ice from the kitchen and sit down for a minute to rest it? I'll be fine if I just stay off of it for a little while."

Any fool could see that wasn't going to happen. But she gave it a shot, trying to walk, only to crumple again, this time into Ramos' arms. Damn, he needed to be quicker at this damsel in distress thing.

But that was just it. Darcy had never been much for distress. Or being a damsel, for that matter.

"I don't think she should even try to walk," Ellen said.

"I'll carry her to the car," John said and moved toward Darcy and Ramos.

"No, John, your back."

Ramos made a movement, like he was going to lift Darcy, and that growling emotion roared inside Lewis. "I've got her," he said, extricating Darcy from Ramos' arms, then lifting her into his own. Even with all that beading on her dress, she was still light as a feather. She always was a string bean.

But it wasn't a string bean he held in his arms. Nope, there were definite curves and they were nuzzled tightly against his chest. And lower.

He was just about to tell John he'd carry Darcy to their car so John and Ellen could take her to the hospital, when Ellen said, "Thank you so much, Lewis. I know she's in good hands with you."

Darcy, John and Lewis all gave Ellen a confused look, which she seemed not to notice. "Darcy, honey, we'll see you later. Text us if it's anything more serious than a sprain." Then she grabbed on to her husband's arm and dragged him away from their injured daughter. Odd.

"Mom?" Darcy called after them. But they must not have heard because they kept on going, only to be swallowed up by the crowd, who'd stopped staring at their small group.

Darcy looked up at him, her blue eyes full of sadness. Had her eyes always been that blue? Or were they just so much more noticeable now without her ever-present glasses?

"Lewis, you don't have to do this. Leave the party, I mean."

Well no, he didn't, and he had no intention of it. He'd find Brooks and make him take his sister to the emergency room. He wasn't an unfeeling monster, but Darcy was basically fine, Brooks was her brother, and Lewis...Lewis needed to see Grace in that dress again.

He was just about to ask somebody passing by to find Brooks for him when Ramos—he'd forgotten about that guy—opened his mouth.

"Mr. Kampmueller, about the reason I'm here."

"Yes?"

"I'm with the FBI, here on behalf of the NSA, and I—"

Oh, shit. "Can't you see this girl's in pain? This is hardly the time—"

"I'm okay, Lewis. What would the FBI—"

"Darcy, we need to get you to the hospital right away. You could have broken your ankle. Or triggered a blood clot or something." He turned, Darcy still in his arms, still very curvy in all the right places, and made for the exit.

"I don't think blood clots work like that," Darcy was saying as Ramos called after them, "Mr. Kampmueller, I'd really like to speak with you."

"Later," he called over his shoulder to the man. Agent. They were called agents in the FBI. At least Grace was. "I'll be back as soon as I get Darcy looked at and then settled at home."

"You're coming back?" both Ramos and Darcy said together.

"Yes. I'm coming back," he answered them both and sped out of the main room, down the hallway, toward the coat check area.

"Oh, let me find my slip," Darcy said as she opened her tiny pursey-thing. Her body shifted at the movement, and Lewis hiked her up, getting a better grip. A much better grip, right across her thighs—those creamy, toned thighs—and causing her to press tighter against him. In all the right places.

Damn. He should find Tess. Let her know what had happened and that he'd definitely be back in time to enact Plan B.

"What's wrong?" Darcy asked at his abrupt about-face.

"I just need to—" Ramos was down the hall, watching them. "Nothing. Nothing. It can wait." He did another turn and headed through the doors to the outside.

"But my wrap," Darcy protested.

"We'll get it later," Lewis told her. "It's not like it'd give you any warmth anyway."

"Wow. It has really turned cold. It's even colder than when we came in." She rubbed her arms together, causing a delectable amount of cleavage to peer out of the neckline of her dress. He debated putting her down to give her his coat, but figured it'd be quicker to get her inside his car. He half walked, half jogged, to the vehicle.

"I need to set you down to get my keys," he told her as he moved to lower her. She leaned against the door, but kept her other hand on his chest for balance, her bad leg lifted behind her like a flamingo. That pesky slit in her dress fell from her lifted leg and Lewis desperately wished the parking lot had better lighting.

He fumbled for his car keys, opened the car, helped Darcy into the seat and then took off his jacket and laid it across her, blanket-like. He moved to the other side of the car, got behind the wheel and pulled out of his parking space.

He looked back at the building, sparkling with lights, the party now in full swing. Then he looked at Darcy. How long could this take, anyway? He'd get Darcy checked out, get her settled at home, then be back well before midnight and his kiss with Grace.

Chapter Four

WELL, SHE'D wanted to get Lewis alone. But she could do without the unbelievable pain in her ankle. And Lewis's obvious rush to get rid of her and back to the party. Though, bless him, he was trying to hide it from her.

"Isn't there some way you can elevate it?" he asked as they drove from the Club to the hospital. "If I'd been thinking, I'd have put you in the back seat, so you could've had it up."

His brow furrowed and she knew he was doing the mental "stupid, stupid, stupid" that he did when he realized he could have thought of a better way. It was that look which made her first fall for Lewis. Or maybe it was the head tilt while he was thinking.

"I'll try," she said and raised her leg to rest her heel on the top of the dashboard. The slit in her dress fell all the way open. She tried a couple of times to pull the bottom of her hem back up and tuck it around her foot, but it kept slipping, and damn her ankle hurt. She let it fall. "There. Elevated."

He looked over at her, and it was hard to tell by the dashboard lights, but she didn't think he looked all that long at her foot. Her leg, he looked plenty.

Okay, Darce, it wasn't how you might have wanted it, but you have the man of your dreams alone on New Year's Eve. You better not waste this opportunity.

She bent forward and gently touched her ankle. Then, ever so slowly, she ran her hand up her calf to her thigh. She didn't look at Lewis, but she could tell by the slight swerving of the car that he'd noticed.

So, maybe he *could* think of her as more than a sister.

He cleared his throat. "Good. Yes. Keep it like that until we get to the hospital." He cleared his throat again. "Just like that."

Oh, there was no way she was going to put her foot down.

Unfortunately—or maybe fortunately, since she really was in a lot of pain—the hospital was on the same side of town as the Club and the ride didn't last for long. As they pulled into the drive, Lewis brought the car to a stop.

"What are you thinking?" she asked, seeing the tilt of his head.

"If I should drop you at the entrance, then go park. Or, if I should park and carry you in."

"Well…" She did like being in his arms.

"If I drop you off, what? They'll have somebody there to hold you up? Put you in a wheelchair or something? But what if they don't? What? You're going to do your flamingo dance while I find a parking spot? But if I park first, the—"

"Lewis, park," she said and he turned into the parking lot and tried to find a spot. When he started doing "what ifs", he could go on for hours. Normally she loved how his mind worked and could follow right along with him—a fact which scared her in its own way—but her ankle was now twice its normal size.

And she really did like being in his arms.

She could hear the wind howling as he pulled into a spot and cut the engine. She wished she'd opted for being dropped off, flamingo dance and all. Well, crap. The wind was going to totally kill her killer hair.

She handed Lewis his jacket, but he shook his head. "You keep it. Wrap yourself tight, it's really cold out now."

She started to burrow deeper into his jacket, loving that it smelled just like Lewis.

"Wait. Let me," he said and took the jacket from her. "Bend down a little." She followed his instructions and was encased in darkness as he draped the coat over her head and around her arms. She felt him slide his hands under her butt and knees. His hands stilled for a moment, and she was certain she felt the tiniest of squeezes. Then, ever so gently, she was being lifted into his arms.

She was bummed she couldn't look up into his face as he carried her across the lot, but very happy he'd thought to protect her hair.

And so unlike Lewis to have realized not getting her hair wrecked by the wind would matter to her.

The wind whipped against them and he picked up his pace. She heard the whoosh of doors opening and then blessed heat as they entered the emergency room. Two sets of footsteps approached.

"What've we got? Burn victim? Car crash?" A young, male voice said, with almost with joyful anticipation.

Darcy uncovered herself just as Lewis said, "Sprained ankle." Yep, it was definite disappointment in the guy's eyes.

"Put her over there. We'll get to you." He turned and walked away, his white coat—that kid was old enough to be a doctor?—flapping against his legs.

"Come on, honey, follow me," a nurse who'd been standing with the retreating doctor said to them as she led the way to a row of plastic chairs and a registration desk area. She was short, squat and black, with her hair cropped close to her head. Of indeterminate age, she looked like she had just stepped out of Central Casting for any medical show as the tough, no-nonsense, seen-it-all, take-no-crap nurse.

Darcy was relieved. Those nurses were the ones who really ran the show, at least on TV. She'd be in good hands with this one.

"Y'all take a seat and I'll bring you your paperwork." The nurse motioned to the row of empty chairs and moved on to the desk area. "It shouldn't take too long to get to you, it's pretty quiet right now. The real craziness won't be 'til later." She looked at Darcy and shook her head. "Lord, we'll see some idiots tonight, that's for sure."

"Really?"

"Mmm-hmm," she answered as she gathered up forms on a clipboard from behind the desk. "New Year's Eve is one of the busiest nights in an ER. Even in a town the size of Henderson." She looked up at them. "Boy, sit that girl down. She can't be filling out paperwork wrapped up in your arms." She mumbled something under her breath that Darcy thought was something like "Not that they're not fine arms," but Lewis didn't hear her. He was looking at the rows of empty chairs, his head tilted.

"Lewis, sit," Darcy said, and he did, with her settling in his lap. And what a lovely lap it was, his thighs firm and strong beneath her. She kept one arm looped around his shoulder, her meager—but highlighted in the magic dress—breasts pressed to his chest.

She looked up at him and froze. It was Lewis, of course, her Lewis, but with a look on his face she'd never seen before. And she knew all his looks.

"You're all...windblown," she said. Her voice, unsure at his look, came out as a whisper.

"You're all...all..."

"Yes?"

"Soft. And warm," he said, then shifted in the hard plastic chair, causing Darcy to settle deeper into him.

"Here, take your jacket back," she started to remove the warm tent, but he squeezed her, stopping her movement. And her breath.

"No, you keep it. Stay warm. You could be going into shock or something."

She was in Lewis's arms, pressed against his strong body, his white dress shirt crisp against his wiry but definitely muscular frame. "Shock. Yes, you're right," she replied.

He started to loosen his hold on her, and she looped her arm tighter around his neck to help him move her to her own chair. "It's okay," he soothed. "I've got you." He cradled her closer.

She was never one to play the helpless female card. She didn't even know what that card looked like, but she burrowed even tighter into him. "Okay." She brushed her hand against his collar feeling both the cotton of his shirt and his smooth, glossy hair.

The nurse came back to them brandishing a clipboard filled with forms. "Don't suppose you got an insurance card in that itty bitty purse of yours?"

Darcy held up the beaded bag she'd completely forgotten about, its cord thankfully wrapped around her wrist or who knows where it would have ended up when she fell. "Lipstick, perfume and hairspray."

"Hmmph. Well, at least you've got the important stuff covered," she said, but there was no censure in her voice. In fact, she almost cracked a smile.

"I do have insurance. I know the company and all that, but not, like, the member number or anything," Darcy told her.

"Fill out what you can. We'll get the rest squared away later."

"Thanks…"

"Georgie."

"Georgie. I'm Darcy, this is Lewis."

"Nice to meet y'all. Now fill out those forms," she nodded at the clipboard then went back to the desk area.

Darcy hated to admit it, but she couldn't use her right hand to fill out the forms while it was still looped around Lewis's neck. "I guess you should put me in a chair of my own," she reluctantly said.

"Right. Sure," he answered, then carefully stood and gently swung her around to sit in the chair that had been next to theirs. "Can you keep it up?" he asked, looking at her ankle then the hard chairs, which were separated by a metal bar. The formed plastic was obviously made for people to face forward. She tried turning to her side so she could put her bum ankle up on the seat next to her, but the hard ridge dug into her butt.

"That's not going to work. It'll be okay for the time it'll take before they can see me."

Lewis went down on one knee before her. How many times

had she imagined that in her life...minus the overwhelming stench of antiseptic, of course. "I don't know, Munchkin, it's really huge."

"Darcy. Is it really ugly looking?" she asked, hoping he could be un-Lewis like for just one moment.

"Yes. God, it's hideous. Swollen twice its size and—what? What's so funny?"

"Oh, Lewis...nothing." She shook her head and looked at him. She couldn't not touch him, her funny, brilliant, socially clueless, Lewis. Her hand brushed his hair away from his face. Expensive cut or no, his locks always had a mind of their own. Her hand lingered, sliding down his cheek. She finally pulled her hand away and watched as his head tilted.

Good. Let him think about that.

Chapter Five

THAT WAS ODD. Munchkin touching him that way. Lewis filed it
away, knowing he could easily be pulled into a vortex when trying
to figure out what a woman was saying or doing or meaning.
Basically, any kind of communication with a woman that wasn't
computer coding related could throw him.

It wasn't like he was a virgin or anything. He'd even had a
couple of semi-girlfriends along the way. But he'd always felt as if
he were underwater when they were sending signals. He could tell
they were communicating with him, but the message was muted
and unintelligible.

Granted, he didn't try very hard with any of them, immersed
as he was in getting his company to the level it had become. And
knowing that in the end, none of them were Grace Devine.

He'd never felt anything like that with Darcy before. Had
never needed to decipher her meaning. But she'd never gently
stroked his cheek before either.

Oh, wait. Yes, she had, that one time when he and Brooks
had gotten really scraped up scaling a chain link fence they had no
business climbing. She'd stroked his cheek then as Ellen Bennett
sprayed Bactine on his scrapes. She'd brushed his hair out of his
eyes, too. So, could he deduce that it was her Florence Nightingale
mode when she touched him like that?

But no, she was the one hurt now, not him.

Right. Her ankle. He looked around for something that

Darcy could rest her leg on while sitting in the hard-as-hell chair. Everything was bolted down. What kind of people would steal chairs and tables from a hospital emergency room? He didn't really want to know.

He lifted her leg and rested it on his knee. "This will have to do for now."

"Um…but…"

"It's okay. Just fill out your forms." She nodded and took the pen that was attached by chain to the clipboard (another thing fastened down!) and started to write. Her hair fell forward and she tucked the right side behind her ear, something she'd been doing ever since Lewis had known her. Even when she wore her hair in a ponytail, as she had for most of their lives, strands would inevitably come loose and she'd push them behind her ear. It was a movement as familiar to Lewis as his own name and he felt a rush of…nostalgia? Tenderness? Something that made him feel instead of think.

How unusual.

He stopped staring at her hair and studied her face, which now sported another look that conjured up more emotions in him that he didn't understand. She was biting her lower lip, something she always did when concentrating. He'd seen that look a thousand times, but he'd never really noticed her lips before. Never noticed how plump and full they were. How when she bit the lower lip it became even redder.

And tempting.

He nearly fell over with that crazy thought. He righted himself just in time. Darcy glanced up at him, but he looked away and she returned to her forms. His eyes were just about to stray back to her mouth when the whoosh of the outside doors caught his attention. In stumbled four college-age kids, two boys and two girls, arm in arm, seemingly holding each other up.

Lewis quickly looked them over, trying to figure out which one was hurt. No blood on any of them, no discernible limp, no—

"Bluuuurgh," one of the boys bellowed as he vomited all over himself and the floor. Darcy's head popped up, taking in the group just as one of the girls followed suit and blew chunks, out-spewing her pal by a good three feet of splatter.

"Oh God," Darcy whispered and gagged.

"Don't look. Keep your head down," Lewis told her and she followed his suggestion, but her shoulders lurched when the third kid erupted.

Nurse Georgie was out from behind the desk area, a bucket in one hand, a large pink plastic container in the other, moving much more quickly than Lewis would have thought her able. "Dear Lord, please tell me none of you drove here," she said as she put the bucket down in front of the fourth one just in time.

"We're not drunk," said the first boy who had puked. "It must be food…." He couldn't finish, but Georgie had shoved the bedpan into his hands so at least when he hurled this time, it wasn't all over the floor.

She turned back to Lewis and Darcy. "Take her into room number three. I'll be with you when I get some help with these four."

Lewis was about to ask questions when another one of the kids erupted, so he swept Darcy into his arms—clipboard, jacket and all—skirted the group of kids as widely as he could, and moved down the hallway to the well-marked rooms. Darcy opened the door to Room Three for him and they stepped in. He quickly shut the door behind them with his foot. You could still hear the horrible retching, but not quite so loudly. And at least they didn't have to see—or smell—it anymore.

He placed her on the examination table, which was more of a gurney with wheels and its side rails in the down position. He turned and studied the door. It was wider than most, so that you could easily wheel out the bed. This set-up was better than most emergency rooms he'd seen on TV where there were only the thin curtains that separated patients. He turned back to Darcy, who seemed to still be holding back an eruption of her own. "Munchkin? You all right? That was pretty gross out there. I mean, my God, who'd have thought those kids could even hold that—"

"Stop," she said firmly. And he did. "I think I'm a sympathy spewer. Whenever I see it, I just…" Her shoulders, exposed and creamy pale next to the black of her dress, lurched forward and Lewis quickly found the wastebasket and brought it to her. She pulled back from the brink and waved the basket away. "I think I'm okay. At least I can't see it anymore." As if on cue, another loud gagging sound came from the outer area. "Dear God, why did I leave my phone at home? At least I could have put some music on, and my earbuds in."

Lewis pulled out his phone, turned the volume as high as possible, and put the music rotation on shuffle. He set it down next Darcy's hip brushing the full curve as he did. "No earbuds, but it should help."

She patted his hand. "Thanks, Lewis. Thank you for everything."

"No problem," he said. And really, it wasn't. He still had plenty of time before midnight.

"So, Lewis…"

"Yes?"

"What did that gorgeous man from the FBI want with you?"

He stiffened, not sure it was from the reminder of the FBI, or from Darcy thinking the man who had been with Grace was gorgeous.

"Um…well…I'm not entirely sure. It could be…"

"Lewis, spill."

And he did. "The NSA…" At her blank look, he clarified. "They're the guys who create and break code."

"Like, computer code, or secret code?"

"Both. But mostly secret code. The thing is, secret codes can be embedded into computer codes, gaming codes in particular. They've been trying to interview me. One appointment I completely forgot about."

Darcy shrugged, not surprised. She knew him pretty well.

"The other appointment? Well, we'd just acquired three new games through a company we hadn't dealt with before. We usually do pretty thorough checks on the designers, basically looking for infringements on other designs, that type of thing. We don't usually buy from outside sources because we have so many great designers on our own staff. But these games were so great, we wanted them." Darcy sat up a bit straighter at that and he wondered if her ankle had begun to hurt more. "You okay?" he asked.

Nodding, she replied, "Go on. The games were so good, you just had to have them…"

"Right. They all passed our usual code checks. We were just about to do clearance on the designers, when we heard PlayStation was sniffing around, so we bought them. Fast."

"So, you never knew who actually designed them, just the development company they worked for."

"Right. And not too long after that sale, I got a call from the NSA wanting to set up a meeting."

"That could just be coincidence." She shifted on the bed. Assuming she was in pain, he reached behind her, grabbed a pillow, gently lifted her ballooned ankle, and slid the pillow underneath. "There's probably nothing in those games that would set off the NSA."

"Yeah, it could be. But the timing is suspect."

"I wouldn't worry about it. Just meet with them. They probably want to just pick your brain."

He sighed. He'd thought of that, of course. But for some reason, the buying of games before he'd thoroughly checked them—and their designers—out seemed a little easier to face than the idea of being some guinea pig for a government agency.

"Yeah. I know. Doesn't look like I'm going to be able to avoid it with this guy Ramos in town. Still, I'd like to put them off a little longer. At least until I can do the due diligence I should have done with those games in the first place. It was just sloppy, and if I hadn't been so eager to beat a competitor, none of this would be happening."

"It's not the games. At least not the three new ones you bought."

He looked at her, his head tilted. "Huh?"

"What was the name of the development company you bought the games from?"

"Pegasus. They're fairly new, and I don't think they have that many designers, but they've developed a few awesome—" Darcy had turned her clipboard around and nudged it into his gut. "What?"

"Look under 'Employer'," she said, nudging the board at him again.

He pushed his glasses up his nose, took the clipboard from her and scanned the form. "Pegasus? Not the same Pegasus?" She nodded, her shimmery hair swinging. His mind followed the movement for a moment until Darcy softly but firmly said, "Lewis, focus," which brought him back to the form. "Under position it says video game designer." She nodded again.

"I knew you'd majored in Graphic Design, but…"

"With an IT degree, too. I've been designing for the last four years."

Brooks had never mentioned that fact to him. Or had he and Lewis just never processed it? Likely it was the latter. A thought came to him. "Those three games we bought? They weren't yours, were they?"

Darcy nodded, a smile widening across her face. "You're looking at what my bonus on 'The Geek Shall Inherit the Mirth' bought me." She did a little "ta-da" movement with her hand down her sparkly dress and to her see-through shoes. Well, shoe. "Oh crap, I lost my other shoe when I fell!"

"I don't know what Pegasus' bonus structure is, but given what we paid for that game, I'm guessing that was a pretty nice bonus check."

"Exactly," she said, but her tone had turned from triumphant to dismal as she stared at her shoe-less right foot.

"And you spent it on a dress and shoes?"

"Not just any dress and shoes. A Dolce & Gabbana gown and Louboutin shoes."

"I…what…"

"Never mind. Fat lot of good either of them did me. Stuck in here all night." She waved her arm around the small room.

"You could wear the dress to next year's party." The look she gave him made him realize he'd once again stepped into it. "Or not."

"No," she sighed. "But maybe somewhere in Boston, though I don't get many invitations to formal events." She wiggled her good foot, still ensconced in the impossibly high heel. "But I'll never get to wear these again."

She let out another sigh, and Lewis thought this sigh could turn bad. Like, to tears or something. He had to do something to take her mind off her dumb, and crazy-expensive, shoes. "So, Munchkin, is—"

"Darcy," she interrupted. "I'm not a Munchkin anymore, Lewis. I'm a woman now, well into my twenties. I will always be small, okay? But petite. Not a Munchkin." There was a definite tone in her voice.

Ohhhhkaaay. Lewis didn't understand women's moods—didn't understand other people's moods much at all—but he knew this could get ugly real quickly. "I loved your games, Darcy. The minute I saw them I told my guys to do whatever it took to acquire them for KampsApps' gaming division."

That perked her up a little. At least she stopped staring at her foot where the missing shoe would have been. "Really? I didn't know that. I wasn't in on any of those discussions. Designers at Pegasus never are."

"Really. Especially Mirth. The minute I saw the prototype demo, it was…I don't know…it's totally original, of course, and hilarious, but something about it just seemed…hmm…familiar, somehow. It was weird. But I had to have it."

Chapter Six

IT SEEMED familiar to him because Lewis was the model for the protagonist of the game. Darcy had designed that one as a labor of love. The hero, a geek with incredible brilliance but no social skills, must evade the pitfalls of everyday social life before he can obtain the love of the heroine. Who, suspiciously, looked a bit like Darcy.

When she was told KampsApps was trying to buy it and two of her other games, she assumed they'd known who had designed it. But Pegasus, leery of having their employees stolen, kept a tight lid on proprietary information. And each one had to sign a confidentiality agreement about what they'd designed. So it seemed that it was a giant coincidence that Lewis's company had bought her game.

Which, of course, she took as a Sign. That's when she'd started planning for this night. The one that now was being spent in a hospital ER with college kids puking en masse mere feet away from her.

She couldn't believe that nobody on his staff had told Lewis he looked exactly like Poindexter, the hero of Mirth. Was she the only one who saw it because she'd designed it?

"Well, it's no Call of Duty…" she acknowledged. Nor, in her mind, was it supposed to compete with that audience.

"That's the beauty of it. It's simple, reality-based and funny. It goes more for the Facebook crowd than the hardcore gamers.

People who never thought of themselves as video game players, but are beyond Angry Birds and Words with Friends. It's a niche we think is ready to explode."

He continued, clearly in his element. "The apps we design around these games make them more compatible for tablets and phones. Yeah, sure, you designed them to play on a home gaming system, but Kamps can make them accessible to people who don't want to spend the time and money on all that hardware."

"That's great. But Lewis, let me assure you, there's nothing in any of those games that the NSA would be interested in. I know that code inside and out…there's nothing there."

His head tilted for just a second, his chestnut hair flopping slightly, but he was already nodding and straightening it. "I guess I knew that. And I guess I was just hoping maybe that was the reason. But I think deep down, I knew that wasn't it."

"So?"

"You were right. They just want to pick my brain on coding. Probably the secret kind."

"Holy crap, Lewis. You're like out of *A Beautiful Mind* or something."

"Nah." He shrugged it off, but Darcy knew—had always known—Lewis had so much more in reserve in that head of his, even with all he had already accomplished. "I guess I need to just suck it up and meet with them."

"Yes, you do. Maybe it's some National Security thing that you could really help out with."

"Maybe. I'll call them after the holiday."

"Aren't you going back to the party? You could just find that guy who…" She trailed off, not wanting to mention Grace. No need to swing that shiny pendulum in front of his mind.

"I wonder why they just didn't have Grace contact me? Why this other guy?"

So much for not sending him down the road of Grace Devine. "Maybe they asked her and she said no?"

His brows furrowed, he pushed his glasses up. It wasn't a

head tilt this time. Not thinking, no. Confused. "Why would she say no? Why would she not want to meet with me?"

It was seldom that Lewis seemed vulnerable. This was an opening, and Darcy recognized it. She could say something along the lines of "Maybe she just didn't think there was much of a reason for her to do it. After all, it's not like you mean anything to her. She has no special relationship with you beyond being childhood neighbors." But that would hurt him. And she could never knowingly hurt Lewis.

"Maybe...I don't know...she felt she couldn't be objective interviewing you. That there's too much history?"

He jumped at it. "Right. Yes. Of course." But he wasn't totally sold, she could tell. She wanted to say something more, to soothe him somehow, but Nurse Georgie made her entrance.

"Sorry about that, kids. Lord, what a mess." She motioned for Darcy's forms.

"Are they going to be okay?" Darcy asked as she handed Georgie the clipboard.

"Those four? They'll be fine. We're pumping them up with fluids and keeping a watch on them. Not much else we can do for them. It's all coming out on its own, anyway. From pretty near every orifice. But, if you'd planned on going to the Sushi Garden for a late night dinner tonight, I'd suggest you skip it."

"Yes, ma'am," Lewis said. Darcy thought she would never eat sushi again after what she'd just seen, and continued to hear.

Georgie read through Darcy's forms, then cocked a brow at her. "Darcy Bennett? I guess somebody was a *Pride and Prejudice* fan."

"My mom," Darcy answered the familiar question.

"Actually, she was going to name her Elizabeth, to be a purist, but her dad put his foot down and they compromised on Darcy," Lewis said.

Which was news to Darcy. "What?"

"Yeah. You didn't know that?"

"No. How did you?"

He shrugged. "I don't know. I guess I asked your mom about it once."

"You asked my mom about my name? When?"

The head tilt again. "I think after my freshman year at MIT. When I'd read it. I hadn't put it together before then."

Well. That left her speechless.

"It's not quite so obvious, but some people would get it. Kind of like Darcy herself."

Darcy stared at Lewis, flabbergasted by his…insight. He was looking at Georgie who was nodding along as she finished going through the forms. "We can put a call into your company for the insurance member number."

"I can run my card over tomorrow if that would help."

"Honey, by the looks of that ankle, you aren't going to be running anywhere tomorrow, or for at least a couple of days. My guess is the doctor will want X-rays, but looks to me like a really bad sprain. I'm thinking we'll wrap it and you'll need to ice it for a while. Maybe you'll get lucky and he'll give you a script for pain meds. Lord knows you deserve a little la-la after spending New Year's Eve in the ER. And looking so pretty and all." She touched Darcy's shoe on her good foot. "Are those Louboutins?"

"Yes."

"Those are some beautiful shoes. Almost worth not being able to walk in."

"I lost the one I fell off of."

Georgie got it. Her eyes went wide with compassion. "Oh, honey, *no*."

Darcy nodded, feeling the tears well up again. "I know. I can't believe it, either."

"It's just a shoe," Lewis said, but quickly ducked his head when he saw the looks she and Georgie shot him.

The nurse rummaged around in one of the trays that held equipment and came up with a pack of some sort. She put pressure on it until there was a small pop. She then put the pack over Darcy's ankle. "A little late for the ice now, but with those four out there…"

"It's okay," Darcy said, adjusting the pack on her ankle, the cold already seeping in. "They were in worse shape. And I appreciate you putting us in here."

"Normally we'd put you in one of the open units so we could keep an eye on you, but the sounds that were coming out of those kids? You looked like you were going to need your own bucket any minute."

Darcy nodded. "You're right, I was."

"Okay, keep that ice on there, I'll have the doctor come check you out as soon as he's able. Though it might take a little time— we just got a car accident in. Nothing dire, but some bleeding that will need to be stitched up," she said. She looked at her watch, wrote down in her chart the time she applied the ice to Darcy's foot, then left them alone.

Lewis looked at his watch and Darcy knew the decent thing to do would be to tell him to go back to the party. She was going to be stuck here for a while, but was basically fine (and not puking up her guts!). She could call for her parents to swing by and pick her up on their way home, or even take a taxi.

Instead, she said, "So, Lewis, besides my games, what else is Kamps looking at right now?"

That was all it took to launch Lewis into a twenty-minute dissertation on games, apps, expansion, and development. Which Darcy found fascinating, thus proving to herself that they truly were soulmates. Not that *she* needed proof.

"And, well, the last thing that we're kind of excited about is…No. Never mind, I've talked long enough as it is."

Odd. He looked almost embarrassed. Lewis embarrassed by something he was working on?

"Tell me," she prodded.

He waved a hand in dismissal. "Nah, never mind."

He was standing by the edge of the bed and she nudged his hip with her knee. "Come on, Lewis, tell me."

He shook his head again. "I don't think it's anything –"

"Lewis, spill."

"It's a kissing app."

She was thinking it was going to be something top secret, maybe the reason the NSA wanted to talk to him. But…a kissing app? This could be interesting.

"Explain it to me," she asked in her best designer-to-designer voice. As if she had no personal interest in Lewis and kissing. "Talk to me about kissing, Lewis."

Chapter Seven

NORMALLY LEWIS wouldn't talk about an app that was still in development. Especially not with a fellow designer who wasn't on his payroll. But this was Munchkin, she seemed genuinely interested, and they had time to kill before the doctor would come to examine her ankle.

Much as Lewis would like to get back to the party—there was still time until midnight, but not a lot of room to maneuver his Plan B—he really should stay until Darcy was checked out by the doctor. That way he could give John and Ellen an update when he saw them. Maybe he'd even have time to take Darcy home and get her settled before he absolutely had to get back to the Club for midnight.

Plus, it was just a fun little app—nothing that would change the world—and he'd like to get her take on it.

He took his phone from where it sat beside her hip, still playing music, and started touching and sliding his way to his new baby.

"It's already available?"

"No, it's just a prototype, but I have most of the stuff we're working on stored here," he lifted the phone to her. "And my tablet. And my laptop. I basically don't set foot outside the office door without everything in about three places."

"Still misplacing things, a lot?"

"Like you wouldn't believe."

"What's it called?"

He had it called up now, but they were still throwing around name ideas and he didn't want Darcy to see the working title card. "Um, we're still working on that." She was reaching for his phone, but he held it away, waiting for it to load. That was one of the bugs they were working on—the thing took forever to load. "The idea is you load a picture on it, either sending it to your email or something, or even taking a picture of someone right from your phone or tablet. Or, there are some pre-loaded. It starts with a shot of their full face." Which was now up on Lewis phone, but he still held it out of Darcy's sight. "Then, when you're ready, you touch the lips, and it zooms in so all you see is their mouth." He did just that to his phone so that only lips, though definitely female ones, showed on his screen now. He turned it to Darcy, handing it over. And you…you know…"

"Make out with your phone?"

"Basically, yes."

She stared at the lips on the screen, then at him. "And you think people will do that? Put their mouth on the phone that they've been touching all day?"

"More likely a tablet. That way when you started, the face would be more lifelike in size."

"Still. All those germs. You've had your phone in your pocket, or your tablet in its case, or out in the open…"

"I think the market that we're gearing this to don't care about stuff like that."

"And who's the demographic?"

He shrugged. "The same guys who twenty years ago would have bought inflatable dolls. This is kind of a high tech version."

"Um, but Lewis, those dolls had, you know."

"Well, obviously, this is a little more innocent. Like I said, it was just meant to be a fun, little throw-away app. We'd give it away." He reached for the phone, but she held her arm away from him. He would have had to stretch across the table—her whole body—to get it. Which actually didn't sound like a bad idea.

"Don't be mad," she said, reading him pretty well.

"I'm not mad." Defensive, more like.

"Defensive, then. I'm sorry, but you probably have only guys working on this, and you should have a woman's point of view."

She was right. He hadn't thought about it that way. "Okay. You're right. So, you wouldn't use it. I get it. It will solely be for guys. Maybe we won't even pre-load pictures of men on it."

"What about for gay men?"

He nodded his head. She was good at this. But then, the designer of Mirth would be. That new fact still blew him away. "Right, again. We'll keep the pics of men on it."

"And is there a goal? A way to score points? Or are you just… kissing your phone?"

"You're not kissing your phone. You're kissing your ideal mate. The person you want to be kissing more than anything, but for whatever reason, you aren't. So, this is the next best thing."

She was turning the phone, seeing the lips move from portrait to landscape view. He hoped they'd remembered to…yes, the lips stayed in place, it didn't zoom back out to show the whole face.

"And yes, there's a scoring system. We did a weighted algorithm on the components of the perfect kiss, and you score more points as you achieve better proficiency at those components. Due to the…ah…nature of the game, you'd probably just be trying to beat your own best score. I can't imagine you'd play against someone else."

"No, I can't imagine that." Her brow furrowed, and she bit her lower lip, obviously thinking, and Lewis found himself torn between wanting to hear what gem she was stewing on, and wanting her to keep biting that lip.

Or maybe biting his?

He stepped back, away from the table. Whoa. Where had that come from? This was Munchkin, who'd followed Brooks and him around since they were kids.

But that was just it. Munchkin wasn't a Munchkin anymore. She'd said it herself, and those curves and that softness he'd held in his arms confirmed it.

"Unless..." she said, which pulled him out of his lust-filled thoughts for his best friend's sister.

"Unless?"

"I don't think guys would play against each other, no. You're right on that. But, have you thought about marketing it to tweens?"

"What's a tween?"

"In this case, girls around eleven or twelve."

"Girls? Young girls?"

She nodded, twisted the phone in her hand. "Say you pre-loaded a bunch of hot celebrity photos on here. And you—oh my God."

"What?"

"What group of fifth grade girls wouldn't fight over trying to get the highest score of kissing, say, Justin Bieber?"

"Seriously?"

"Oh, Lewis, totally seriously." The smile on her face was something to behold. He imagined it was the same smile she'd worn when she'd first thought up the concept of Mirth.

"We already looked into pre-loading celebrity photos. More along the lines of Angelina Jolie and Scarlett Johansson, though, not Bieber. Can't legally do it. We were going to hire models for the photos. And buy stock photos."

"But you have an option to upload your own photos, right?"

"Of course."

"So, you make it easy. Make a link to the Google Images search engine. They type in Justin Bieber, find the image they want and tap a button to make it part of...part of..."

"Like I said, no title yet, it's—"

"The Perfect Kiss."

"What?"

"The Perfect Kiss. That's what you should call it."

He didn't like it. Way too girly.

"Yes, it's girly," she said, reading his mind. "But Lewis, I really think that's your market. Young girls who have crushes. It's sweet and innocent and non-threatening. It's like horses being girls' first loves."

"You lost me."

She waved her hand, dismissing him, clearly in her own zone. "I had pictures of boy bands all over my walls in middle school. I used to kiss one particular boy goodnight every night. Imagine if I'd had him on my phone and could try to beat my best score of kissing him goodnight. My parents would have had to drag the thing out of my hands."

She went on, "Of course, girls may be more advanced now, so this would be geared a tiny bit younger. And you'll want to put a message on about wiping off your tablet, or phone, between users. Maybe a stop in play when you go to a new user with a "Did you clean your device?" prompt. Where you have to answer yes to move on. But word it better than that. You don't want to break the mood with a bunch of techno-speak." She was pointing at him like he was an old-fashioned stenographer taking dictation, and she was a cigar-chomping boss yelling, "Did ya get that?"

And his hands may have been empty, but oh, he got it. He may walk by his front door all the time, but he *never* forgot a detail about one of his creations.

Which was quickly turning into one of Darcy's creations.

And he was totally cool with that. The business was full of collaborations. Some went really well. Lewis's company was proof of that. And some landed you in court with movies made about it.

"So tell me about the algorithm. How do you score points? How do you achieve—drum roll, please—the Perfect Kiss?"

Okay, the name was starting to grow on him. "Well, there are certain parts of kissing that obviously can't be measured with an inanimate object, like…um…moisture."

She grimaced. "You mean, like if you're a wet, sloppy kisser."

"Right. Can't measure that."

"No, I suppose not. Too bad, because if you using it as a learning tool, that's the one thing you'd want to instruct on."

Was it? Well, yeah, of course it would be. Suddenly his mind was full of thoughts of his own kissing. The kernel of idea for this app had come from doing some preliminary reading on good kissing, years ago, right before a different New Year's Eve and his kiss with Grace. She hadn't swooned and fallen into his arms after that one like he'd hoped.

Was it because he was a wet, sloppy kisser? He'd never had any complaints from any of the girls he'd dated. But then, would you tell that to someone?

"So, if not wetness, what do you measure?" she asked.

"What?" he asked. She held up the phone. "Oh, right. Well, amount of pressure was another thing we thought was important—"

"Of course."

"But that can't be gauged from a device."

"Right…" She was leading him now, hungry for every word.

"But you *can* measure length of pressure." She processed that, looked at the phone, nodded her head. Her golden hair shimmered, even under the God-awful hospital fluorescent lights. "And…movement."

Her eyes grew wide and damned if she didn't lick her lips. And damned if her eyes didn't drop to his mouth.

And damned if he didn't start sporting wood. He moved closer to the examining table, right next to it in fact, putting his offending area out of her eye-line. And himself closer to her body. Which included that mouth. Hers, not the one on his phone.

"So, more points for more movement? That doesn't seem right. You could just rub your mouth up and down the screen and be high scorer, but that's not good kissing. But you would have thought of that."

He knew she continued on, but Lewis heard nothing past "you could rub your mouth up and down." He pressed into the side of the table.

Holy crap, get a handle on it. You're in a hospital!

"So what was the measurement?"

"What?"

"How did you decide what types of movement would score higher?"

"Research?"

She giggled at that. "I can just imagine those design update meetings. 'Well, Mr. Kampmueller, we're nearly there. But I'm taking Susie out one more time tonight to make sure the algorithm is in place'."

"They don't call me Mr. Kampmueller."

Now she outright laughed. Then she looked at him, shook her head and said, "Oh, Lewis."

The way she said his name. Not with good-natured exasperation like he got with most people, when they shook their heads at him in disbelief. No, it was breathy, and full of warmth, and…knowing.

"But yeah, there was personal experience, both good and bad, that played a part. Discussion of course. We watched…um…movies."

"Porn."

"No, not porn. Well, not *always* porn. We found a list online of the one hundred best movie kisses and we divvied them up and watched those."

"So, what was the final consensus on movement and length of pressure? What did you build into the scoring algorithm?"

"It's kind of hard to explain. First we…" he stopped. She was watching him, and then she licked her lips and nodded for him to continue.

All logic flew out the window of the windowless examination room, and he leaned forward and said, "It'd be easier just to show you."

And then he kissed her.

Chapter Eight

LEWIS KISSING her took Darcy off-guard enough that she barely had time to close her mouth from the round "O" of shock as his mouth descended on hers.

His lips met hers and it quickly became clear that Lewis had mastered his own game. His lips were strong on hers, then gentled. They moved just the slightest bit, waiting for her to catch up. And when she did, when she met his movement, his rhythm, he growled just a little bit in the back of his throat, causing her to gasp. Causing *him* to pull away.

"Sorry. I just thought…but it was stupid. Darcy, I'm really—"

"You're overthinking it."

"I overthink everything."

"I know, but not this. Not now. Shut down that million dollar brain of yours and just feel how good the kiss is."

"But, I'm wondering if the pressure is enough. I mean, I kind of stopped paying attention to the pressure."

"That's good."

"Is it? Because another thing I read about—"

She grabbed his crisp, white shirt and pulled him back to her. "Lewis, kiss."

And he did.

This time all her thoughts of algorithms and high scores and marketing demographics were gone. Nothing mattered except kissing Lewis.

Finally kissing Lewis Kampmueller.

She let the phone slide to her lap so she could wrap her arms around his neck and pull him closer. He didn't need much encouragement, quickly putting his arms around her and crushing her to his body. The heat rolled off him in waves and she pressed closer.

"Darcy," he whispered her name as they gasped for breath. Before she could answer, his lips were on hers again, the pressure exquisite, the moistness just perfect, the movement…oh God, the movement. Definite high-score material.

She'd dreamed about this moment her whole life. And though none had involved her leg being propped up and iced, it far exceeded her wildest expectations.

He buried his hands into her hair, and she couldn't have cared less that it would mess up her curls. He held her head in place, deepening the kiss, tilting her head just a tiny bit…there, oh, that was nice. He'd rack up more points for that move.

She leaned back from her sitting position on the table at the exact moment that he pressed more deeply into her, and as she lay down, he followed her, moving half his body on top of hers.

But she wanted…needed…all of him. "Get on the table with me," she half whispered, half moaned in his ear as he nibbled her neck. She hadn't used her command tone, but he acted as if she had, nearly launching himself on top of her as he scrambled onto the table.

She thanked Misters Dolce and Gabbana for the foresight to put a high slit in this glorious dress, which allowed her to widen her legs and cradle Lewis.

And, oh, wow, was there ever a lot of him to cradle. She could feel the hot, hard length of him against her and she slid her hands down his lean back to his butt, urging him to move. Which he did, to her everlasting gratitude.

One of his hands slid down her body, pausing and squeezing in all the right places, sliding his jacket out of the way, and finally resting on her hip. Then lower, lower still until she felt the warmth of his hand on her bare thigh.

And all along he never broke the kiss. The glorious, just right, pitch-perfect kiss of her dreams. Their tongues tangled, he sucked on her bottom lip, she nipped his top one. God, she could kiss this man forever.

His hand slid around to the back of her thigh and gently pulled her leg open wider just as he did a small thrust with his hips. "Oh, God, Lewis," she moaned and he pulled his face away from hers and looked down at her. His brown eyes were warm and tender as he watched hers, even if his glasses were on the verge of fogging up. He scanned her face, as if seeing it for the first time.

Seeing *her* for the first time.

"Don't stop," she whispered, moving her hands from his butt, up that wonderful back and into his hair, pulling him back down to her. But he resisted, and then, oh dear God no, his head started to tilt. "Don't think, Lewis, just keep kissing me," she said and raised her head off the table, her mouth seeking his once more. She kissed him soundly, lowered her head back to the table, and said what she'd wanted to say for years and years and years. "Don't *ever* stop kissing me."

She saw him swallow, almost gulp. Aw, crap, she'd scared him away. But then his gaze dropped to her mouth. She bit her lower lip, waiting for what seemed like an eternity. Waiting for Lewis to get it. To finally understand that it was supposed to be *them*.

And then a small smile crept across his handsome face and she knew he'd found the winning formula.

He leaned to kiss her again just as the door swung open. The kid-doc entered the room, saw Lewis on top of Darcy, snorted his indignation and said, "Are you kidding me?"

⌒

Lewis leapt off Darcy, managing to grab his jacket and hold it in front of himself all as the doctor watched. He quirked a brow, looking pointedly at Lewis's hard on, which he tried valiantly to cover with the jacket. "Nice recovery," the doctor all but sneered at him.

He didn't really blame the doctor. To be stuck in an ER on New Year's Eve—and not be kissing Darcy—would suck. Having to attend to vomiting college kids and whatever else had come in since they'd been in the private room…not fun. Not fun at all.

He turned away from the doctor and Darcy, untucking his shirt and sliding on his tux jacket, trying to hide the damage.

"Okay, sorry it took so long, but be grateful that yours is the type of injury that could wait," he heard the doctor say to Darcy.

"I am," Darcy replied.

"Let's take a look."

Lewis kept his back to the two of them, waiting till the throbbing of his dick subsided. The doctor asked questions, Darcy answered, and Lewis pretended to be engrossed by a poster on the wall about STDs.

"I think we should do X-rays to be safe, but it looks like a bad sprain."

"That's what the nurse thought," Darcy said.

"Well, then it's probably true," the doctor replied. Lewis thought there was a touch of resentment in the young doctor's answer. Probably didn't like having a nurse who knew more than he did. If the kid were smart, he'd learn to embrace and use Georgie's experience. It had been the most important business lesson Lewis had learned.

He heard Darcy gasp, took a look down at himself, deemed himself decent and whirled around to see what kind of pain the incompetent kid had caused his Darcy.

But the doctor was writing something on her chart, not even touching her. He met Darcy's eyes, but she quickly looked away. Probably still embarrassed about the doc catching them nearly in the act. They'd been close, so close, to shedding their party duds and getting down to more skin than just that awesome slit in her dress allowed. That thigh of hers was as soft to the touch as he'd imagined it would be. He couldn't wait to get his hands on the rest of her.

"I'll have a tech come for you to take you to X-ray. Shouldn't be too long."

"Okay, thanks," she said, but still wouldn't look at Lewis. He moved to her side, to take her hand, to just touch her again—but she leaned away from his touch. "Doctor, there's no reason Lewis has to stay, is there? There's nothing he can really do, right? And it's still going to be a while?"

"Well, like I said, the tech shouldn't be too long. And I'll try to look at the image as quickly as I can, but yeah, you're looking at another couple of hours, probably. And no, technically we don't need your boyfriend for anything. You—"

"He's not my boyfriend," Darcy said quietly.

Lewis didn't say a word. He was too stunned about the series of events. His body was still humming and all he wanted to do was get this doctor out of the room so he could keep on kissing Darcy and she seemed to be intent on getting rid of him.

Or was she just trying to be nice?

"Lewis, I want you to leave," she said looking him full on for the first time since they'd been interrupted.

"But, I want to…no, Darce, I want to stay with you."

"You don't need to. The doctor just said so."

The doctor held up his hands in a surrender motion, said, "I'm out of here. I'll get the tech to you as soon as I can," and left the room.

"Who cares what he says. I think I should stay."

"Lewis, go." It was her command voice, and he stood, helpless—not knowing what had just happened. This must be one of those times when he couldn't read the situation. It happened to him all the time. But never when he was with Darcy.

Had he read the situation wrong? Was the kissing all on his side?

"The night is still relatively young. Go back to the party. Tell my parents I'm fine and that I'll meet them at home."

"How will you get home?"

"I'll call a cab."

"A cab? On New Year's Eve? And what, hobble up the walk and into your house on your own? Because you know no cab driver is going to carry you."

"I'm sure I'll have crutches by then."

"You're going to use crutches in that dress?"

She let out a sigh of exasperation. *That* cue he could recognize just fine, hearing it often enough. "Fine. Find my parents at the party and ask them to swing by here to pick me up on their way home. They never stay much past midnight anyway. The timing will be per…just right."

"I really don't feel right—"

"Lewis, you can still find Grace. You can have your kiss with her. God knows you're more than ready."

She knew about Grace? And the kiss? How much exactly?

She sighed. "I know it all. How you and Tess conspire every year to make sure Grace loses that stupid bet."

"You know all that? How?"

"I figured it out years ago."

Had she? Had Grace? He wanted to ask, but Darcy spoke first. "It's okay, Lewis. I want you to go. I want you to be with the one you want to be with. That's what New Year's Eve should be." She turned away, adjusting the ice pack on her ankle. "Lewis, go."

And he did.

Chapter Nine

SO, HE'D MADE his choice, Darcy thought, half an hour after Lewis had left. She'd waited hopefully for a few minutes, thinking he might come back. But no. He was on his way to Grace. To the kiss he'd designed a damn app around.

When the doctor came in, Darcy had been embarrassed, but had also been flying high, knowing that what she and Lewis had just shared was a real connection. Not some schoolgirl fantasy of hers, or a kiss claimed through deceit—as was his annual kiss with Grace.

She'd never been more certain in her life that she and Lewis truly had a future together. Until the doctor examined her and she realized Lewis's phone was still in her lap. She started to give it to him—his back still to her. But when she touched the screen, the picture of the lips zoomed out to show the entire face of...no big surprise...Grace Devine.

Okay, she could handle that. Though the thought of Lewis testing the app on Grace's picture fueled a fire in her, she really couldn't blame him. *She* had designed the lead in Mirth to look, sound and act like Lewis. Then she touched the game to escape and saw the working title card.

"A Kiss of Grace."

And it was just like a few hours earlier when she'd watched Lewis see Grace in her beautiful gown—something inside her snapped. She wanted Lewis desperately, but not if he still wanted

Grace.

Set a caged bird free and if it returns...oh whatever the hell that saying was, Darcy knew she had to do it.

So, she set Lewis free to fly. Being the stand-up guy he was, he didn't want to leave her stranded at a hospital, but she'd convinced him she didn't need him.

She wasn't sure if she'd done a great job, or if it was easy for him to believe, but he left. The memory of their kiss, of their bodies fitting together so perfectly, stayed with her. And she hoped maybe Lewis would return to her after all.

Lewis tucked his shirt back into his pants as he made his way into the Club. It was just before midnight. If he hurried, he'd get there just before the craziness. When he'd pulled his phone out to show Darcy the kissing game, he'd noticed texts from Tess, but didn't bother reading or responding to them. The point seemed moot at the time, as it looked like he'd be in the hospital at midnight, not in any position to help out Tess.

Now he fumbled in his pocket for the phone as he approached the Club. He patted his pockets, but came up empty. He must have left it at the hospital. Was Darcy hanging on to it when they'd started kissing? Honestly, he lost his phone all the time when he was on top of things. But to be able to keep his wits—and possessions—about him during and after that kiss? Not remotely possible.

He entered the building where all his friends still were. And some people not so much his friends. He remembered the co-worker of Grace's. Ramos. Was he still here? Would he be Grace's first kiss of the new year? The thought of that would have seriously pissed him off just a few hours ago. Now, Lewis found he couldn't work up any anger over the idea.

Maybe Grace really liked the guy. Maybe they'd make a good match. They could clean their guns together in front of the fireplace.

He walked by the coat check girls, thinking that he should get Darcy's shawl thingy to bring home to her. Or maybe he'd just tell Ellen and John that it was still with the coats, because he wasn't sure if Darcy would even want to see him around the house later. Or tomorrow.

Man, if she was pissed at him, and regretted their kiss—and he wasn't sure about either of those things, unable to read those last few minutes in the examination room—being a guest at the Bennett house was going to be pretty awkward.

The unfinished floor of Brooks's place was sounding better and better.

But maybe if he could…just maybe

When he entered the main ballroom, he stopped. It was too quiet, something was off. He realized everyone was looking at the stage where Grace stood, looking proud, and yet a little bit nervous.

Grace, nervous? That didn't seem right. He took a step back, and then another, and then another until he was standing back in the hallway. He could hear Grace's voice, but not her words.

He turned around, and ran smack into Brooks.

"Dude, what are you doing here?" Brooks asked him.

"I'm…I'm…." This was crazy. What was he doing here? It was a dumb, futile idea. He'd never be able to…. "I'm going back," he finally finished his sentence, and looked at Brooks fully. "I'm going back to Darcy. Right now." He'd simply ask her why she'd kicked him out. He could do that, couldn't he?

"Um. Okay. Good. She's okay, right? Mom said Darcy would text if it was serious. That's not why you're here, is it?"

"No. She's fine. Just a sprain. Bad sprain. But it doesn't look like anything's broken. They're doing an X-ray just to be safe, and she's waiting on that."

Brooks let out a sigh of relief. "So…?"

"I just…." How could he tell Brooks why he was really at the Country Club? It sounded idiotic in his head, he could only imagine what Brooks would say, so he decided to fudge the truth a bit. "I, um, wanted to let John and Ellen know. And that I'd be bringing Darcy home from the hospital."

"Hey, Lewis, there's these new things called cell phones that allow you to call, or just text people, and tell them things so you don't have to drive all over town."

"Very funny. I—"

"Listen, buddy, I'd love to find out what the hell is going on with you, but if Darcy's okay, I was actually on my way out."

"But it's not even midnight yet. You can stick around for a couple of minutes can't you?"

"Nope. Can't do it, not even to steal a kiss from somebody. I just got a call that there's an ice storm headed our way. Could be really dangerous driving. Add that to the usual drunk drivers on New Year's Eve, and it could be a bad night."

"You got called in?"

His friend nodded. "Me. Vance. All of us did. Anybody who was off duty."

"Aw man, that sucks."

Brooks just shrugged. "That's the job. We can't all be CEO of our own company."

"Ha, ha."

"I've got to go. Tell Darce I'll stop by the house tomorrow and see how she's doing," Brooks said and hustled down the hall and out the front entrance. Lewis followed close behind him. Then stopped.

Crap.

He had to look. He had to try. He sighed, ran his fingers through his hair, turned around and started heading back toward the main room. A man who was dressed like a waiter or bartender neared him and asked if he needed help.

"No, I'm just looking for...." But he couldn't explain it to this stranger any more than he could to Brooks.

"It's not in there," the youngish man said. Odd that he said "it" and not "they." One would assume he'd be looking for a person. And how did he know who or what Lewis was looking for, anyway?

"You should look in the other direction," the man added as he walked past Lewis.

Confused, Lewis turned and watched as the man strolled down the hallway and around a corner. Lewis turned back toward the main room just as Tess walked out.

"You're here," she said. She looked at him strangely, but it'd been a very weird night already, so Lewis didn't even try to understand her look.

"Yeah," he answered. Could she help him with his quest? Or would she be pissed about him not answering her texts and tell him to piss off? "Uh…"

"Just in time. I should have known you wouldn't miss it," Tess said. She glanced behind her, back into the ballroom, but Lewis was still in the hallway and not able to see what she was looking at. "It's two minutes till midnight. I think you should kiss me tonight."

Seriously? Tess wanted him to kiss her? After all the years they plotted together so she *wouldn't* have to kiss him. Which had been fine with him, because then he got to kiss Grace. He glanced around the hallway, tried to see into the ballroom. If he had to kiss Tess, at least it'd be out here and nobody would see. Grace wouldn't see.

And Darcy wouldn't find out.

"Uh," he said, stalling for time, still searching the hallway with his eyes.

"One minute," came the call from the ballroom.

"I—" he started, not really sure what to say. Just a quick peck and then he could get on with what he'd really come here for.

Tess stepped toward him, putting her hands on his upper arms. She looked kind of surprised to grab onto something solid, like she thought maybe he really was just a brain in an empty suit. There was resignation in her voice—resignation Lewis shared—when she said, "Let's just kiss each other and be done—"

"Why break your streak now, Tess?" said Johnny Wilder who'd stepped out of the ballroom behind her. At the sound of his voice, Tess swung away from Lewis. "After all, it's been ten years. You've never lost the bet yet," Johnny added, his eyes never leaving Tess.

And from the way Johnny was looking at Tess, Lewis knew she wouldn't be losing it tonight, either.

"Ten," came the cry from the ballroom.

"Oh, hi Johnny," Lewis said in greeting. Not really surprised at the scene that was unfolding in front of him. So, Johnny finally was playing his cards. Good for him.

"Nine," from the next room.

Yeah, they were so not going to notice if he just slipped away. He could go into the ballroom and try to finish this. Or he could call the whole stupid idea off.

Tess and Wilder continued talking as Lewis turned and started toward the doors but did a detour to the coat check area. He'd at least get her shawl. The girls that had been manning the area were nowhere to be found. They'd probably stepped out from behind the booth and snuck into the party, it being so close to midnight.

"Eight."

Lewis looked around to see if anybody was available to help, but there was nobody.

"Seven."

But he could see the corner of Darcy's filmy wrap on a table behind the counter.

"Six."

He scooted around the counter and moved a couple of fur stoles on the table out of the way.

"Five."

He grabbed Darcy's shawl.

"Four."

Started back.

"Three."

Saw something shiny on the floor out of the corner of his eye just as he stepped on it.

"Two."

And went down like Darcy had done hours earlier.

"One."

Collapsing to the floor in agonizing pain.

"Happy New Year!"

Chapter Ten

"ARE YOU SURE there's nothing else we can get you, honey?" Darcy's mother asked her the next morning.

"No, I'm fine, Mom, thanks."

"Okay, well, we won't be long. There are just a few items we forgot and need to pick up for later."

Odd. Her mother was the consummate hostess, and they'd always hosted a bowl game watching party on New Year's Day. Never could she remember her mother not having exactly everything she needed. Maybe she would send Darcy's dad out for ice as game time drew near, but that was it. "You're both going out?"

"Yes," her mother said, looking pointedly at her father. "Both of us."

"I'm good here," she assured her parents. Her father had helped her down the stairs and into the big, overstuffed chair, gotten her wrapped ankle settled on the ottoman, propped her crutches next to the chair, and given her the remote. She pulled her cell out of the pocket of her hoodie, putting it on the table next to her. Her mother had already placed a glass of water and Darcy's pain pills on the table as well as a couple of pieces of toast, heavy with peanut butter, just like she loved.

"Text us if you think of anything we could pick up for you," her mother said and hurried her father out the front door.

Darcy pulled the throw off the back of the chair behind her

and threw it over her yoga pants-clad legs. She picked up the remote, turned on the television and surfed until she found the Rose Parade, a New Year's tradition for her. The games would come later, and that's what drew the party crowd, but she was a die-hard parade fan.

She reached for the pain killers, but figured she should eat the toast first so she picked up the plate and laid it in her lap. The pain wasn't unbearable, but the pills she'd taken last night when her parents delivered her home had given her a nice warm glow. It helped to take her mind off the fact that Lewis hadn't come back for her.

She was too proud to ask her parents about it, but the very fact that they'd shown up at the hospital and Lewis hadn't was all she'd needed to know. She desperately wanted to know if they'd seen him kissing Grace, but had kept mum. She did, however, nearly rip the prescription for pain meds out of kid-doc's hand when he assured her the ankle was not broken, just sprained as everyone had suspected.

So, she'd slept like the dead in her drug-induced haze, never hearing whether Lewis had walked down the hall. Not knowing if he even made it home last night. She had hobbled her way over to her bedroom window this morning when she woke and could form a coherent thought. Lewis's car wasn't in the driveway.

He hadn't come home. Had he spent the night with Grace?

And apparently there'd been some kind of freak winter storm. Patches of melting ice were all over the yard and driveway.

She finished off the toast, put the plate back on the table, and eyed the bottle of pills. She moved her ankle, turning it slightly. It hurt. And yeah, she deserved to get some—what did Georgie call it?—la-la.

Just as she was reaching for the anti-thoughts-of-Lewis pills, she heard a large thump coming from the staircase. She craned her neck, but couldn't see out into the hallway from where she sat. And another thump. A few seconds later, another. They came in a rhythm, about fifteen seconds apart.

"Mom?" she called. "Dad?" But she'd heard them go out the front door and heard the car pull out of the driveway. "Brooks?"

The thumping stopped, and Darcy reached for her phone, ready to dial 911 if needed. A different, quieter thump came now. One that Darcy recognized because she'd made the same noise herself just a while ago.

Lewis, wielding crutches, entered the living room, his leg in a cast from ankle to just below his knee. He wore sweatpants that were cut off on his bad leg, a wrinkled tee shirt, and had what looked to be a grey sweatshirt tucked between his arm and his body. His hair was at all angles.

"What happened?" she gasped. "Are you all right?"

"I tripped and fell," he answered, swinging his way into the living room, sitting in a chair next to hers. He set the sweatshirt on the floor in between the two seats, and propped his crutches on the other side of his chair. "Care to share your ottoman?"

She was so stunned it took her a moment to respond, but she finally nodded. He got out of his seat and, hopping and balancing, pulled his chair closer to hers so that he could put his leg up too. Her right foot, bandaged, sat next to his casted left one. That small movement seemed to exhaust him and he let out a large sigh, running his fingers through his hair, making it stand on end even more.

"When did this happen?" she asked. "Where did this happen?"

"At the Club."

So, he *had* gone back for Grace. For a fleeting moment she'd allowed herself to think that maybe he'd hurt himself leaving the hospital or something. That maybe he'd turned around so quickly on his way back to her that he'd run into something. That would be very Lewis-like.

"I was leaving."

"Oh." At the end of the night? After his kiss with Grace? Had she been with him? Helped him to the hospital? Had he tripped on the hem of Grace's gorgeous gown as they'd danced closely together?

"I mean, I never really stayed."

She looked over at him. "I don't understand."

"I got to the Club, but I didn't stay. I barely walked into the ballroom."

Something sparked inside Darcy. Hope. "Go on."

He ran his fingers through his hair again, pushed his glasses up his nose. He was adorable in the mornings, all bedheady and rumpled. She yanked at her ponytail. She didn't pull off rumpled very well. More like completely trashed.

"I realized that's not where I wanted to be," he said.

"It wasn't?"

He shook his head, and reached for her hand. "I wanted to be with you, Darce. You're all I could think about. I didn't know why you'd asked me to leave the hospital. I was trying to figure it out and I got a stupid idea to, well…But in the end, I just decided to screw the idea and get back to you. Make you tell me what happened. Why you kicked me out. But—"

"But…." she pointed at his leg.

"Yeah, I fell. It was crazy after that. It was right at midnight, so it took a while before I could get anyone's attention. I was going to text Brooks to see if he'd come back. He'd only left minutes before me. But I didn't have my phone."

"It was with me," she said.

"I figured that out,"

"Did you also figure out why I asked you to leave?"

A look of exasperation crossed his face. "No. I figured I'd just misread the situation. That you were pissed I climbed all over you."

"No. I wasn't pissed about that. I was very happy about that."

Relief crossed his face and Darcy realized she needed to walk him through this carefully. "I wanted what happened between us, Lewis. Badly, and for a long time."

"Really?" he seemed genuinely shocked, and maybe like he didn't quite believe her.

"Absolutely."

"So, then, why ask me to leave?"

"When you had your back to us, waiting for your...." she waved her hand in the general vicinity of his crotch.

"Yeah, yeah. Go on." His face grew red with embarrassment. Adorable!

"Your phone reverted to the full face picture on the game."

"Oh."

"Yes."

"But you knew I've had a thing for Grace. And obviously I designed that app way before last night, before I realized I..."

"You what?"

"That I—I mean...sort of...."

"Lewis, speak."

"Have feelings for you."

"And you know that now?"

"God, yes." And she believed him. The sincerity in his face, the hunger in his eyes, even when she looked like...well, like she'd spent the night in an ER.

"Wait, how did we not see each other in the ER? And how did my parents know to come and get me?"

He shrugged. "I told them. They brought me to the hospital. It was obvious my leg was broken, so they put me in a different area. I told Ellen and John not to say anything. To just bring you home."

"Why on earth not?"

"Well, at the Club it seemed like a great idea to come back and tell you how I felt. And then..."

"And then?" Dread crawled up her spine. Was he going to say his feelings changed?

"As usual I started overthinking why you sent me back to the party in the first place."

"Oh, Lewis. I sent you away because you needed to figure out for yourself who you wanted to kiss at midnight."

"Oh, I already had," he said, smiling at her. "But for much

more than just a New Year's kiss."

She smiled back, the dread gone. "Good."

He leaned across her chair to try to kiss her, but their bum legs knocked into each other and they both let out moans of pain. Sitting back in their respective chairs they smiled at each other and held hands.

He nodded toward the television. "You always did like the parades more than the bowl games."

"Yes, I did. Still do." Then a thought occurred to her. "How did you get home? Did my parents go back for you?"

"No. They offered, but I didn't want them to leave you alone here. When Brooks was able to, he came and got me."

"When was that?"

"Not for a long time. There was a weird ice storm and lots of accidents. Thankfully there were no fatalities. I've only been home a few hours."

"Did you get any sleep?"

"Not much." He motioned to her bottle of pills. "They gave me some of those, but I didn't want to take them yet. Not until…"

"Until?"

"We could talk." She squeezed his hand and smiled at him. He smiled back, and pushed up his glasses.

"Oh," he said, sitting up straighter, "I almost forgot." He looked at their legs, at himself, his head tilting. She knew he was trying to figure something out. Then he carefully got out of his chair, swung his body around to face her. "Can you lift your leg without too much pain?" She did and he stepped in front of her chair and sat on the ottoman, facing her, and placing her leg across his lap. Almost like he had at the hospital last night.

But much, much better.

He reached for his sweatshirt and started to unwind it and she realized it was wrapped around something. When he tossed the sweatshirt aside she let out a squeal. "My shoe! You found my shoe!"

"Well, actually, it found me."

"What do you mean?"

He ducked his head, chagrinned. "It's what I tripped on. How I fell."

"You're kidding me?"

"Nope." He looked at her. "That's why I went back in the first place. To look for your shoe. You didn't want me near you, and I didn't want to be with anyone else."

She gave him a look of disbelief. "Nobody else," he said firmly, with conviction. She could tell it was the truth. Lewis never lied. "I just thought if I found your shoe I'd at least have a good excuse to make you talk to me again."

He tried to place the glass slipper on her foot, but ended up balancing it on her toes due to the bandage wrapped around her foot and ankle. Thank God she hadn't left her other shoe in the hospital trashcan like she'd briefly considered last night. At one point after Lewis left, she'd almost thrown the shoe, and his phone, across the room, trying to erase the painful night.

"Just like Cinderella," she gushed, surprising herself. She wasn't much of a gusher by nature, but hey, when fairy tales were unfolding right in front of you…a gush or two was in order.

Lewis snorted. "I know I'm not anybody's idea of Prince Charming. King of Geeks, maybe, but—"

"You're my Prince Charming. You always have been." He looked up at her, giving her a 'Don't bullshit me' look. The same look he'd given her a moment ago. He still hadn't bought in to them being Destiny. She knew she had to pull out the big guns. She took a deep breath, let it out, and said what she'd wanted to say since she was five years old but didn't know the grown up words.

"Lewis Kampmueller, I've loved you my whole life. Nobody will ever love you the way I do. And I think it's time we take this beyond friendship."

The head tilt was instantaneous, and deeper than she'd ever seen. He was going to have some crick in his neck during their life together.

"Darcy. I…how…what…."

"Lewis, answer."

"Yes. Absolutely yes."

She smiled and touched his face. "You know, I never got a New Year's kiss."

"Me neither," he said, leaning toward her.

"What do you say we try to hit a new high score?"

And they did.

If you enjoyed "The Perfect Kiss," check out Mara Jacobs' other contemporary romances, The Worth Series:

Worth The Weight (Book 1: The Nice One)
Worth The Drive (Book 2: The Pretty One)
Worth The Fall (Book 3: The Smart One)

About the Authors...

Colleen Gleason is the international bestselling author of The Gardella Vampire Chronicles, a historical vampire hunter series set during the time of Jane Austen. She has written more than twenty novels in a variety of genres for HarperCollins, Penguin, Harlequin and Chronicle Books, and her books have been translated into seven languages.

To find out more about her books or to sign up for updates and sneak peeks, visit her website at: ColleenGleason.com or find her on Facebook at http://www.facebook.com/colleen.gleason.author.

Born and raised in Baltimore, MD, **Liz Kelly** read her first Kathleen E. Woodiwiss romance novel, *The Flame and the Flower,* when she was in tenth grade and has been hooked ever since. A graduate of Wake Forest University and a member of Romance Writers of America, she's thrilled to finally be writing everyday. Mother of two sons and a miniature Labradoodle, she and her husband reside in Naples, FL.

Visit Liz's website to keep up to date with her latest releases and share the title of your first romance novel: LizKellyBooks.com.

Holli Bertram is a Romance Writers of America Golden Heart winner in Romantic Suspense. For more information about Holli and her books, visit her website at hollibertram.com.

Mara Jacobs is the author of over six novels. She writes mysteries with romance, thrillers with romance, and romances with...well, you get it. Visit her at her website for information on her newest releases. MaraJacobs.com

CPSIA information can be obtained at www.ICGtesting.com
Printed in the USA
LVOW040600061212

310344LV00003B/373/P